BRONZE

BLACKWINGS
DEVIL SPRINGS

TEAGAN BROOKS

BRONZE

BLACKWINGS MC - DEVIL SPRINGS - BOOK FIVE

TEAGAN BROOKS

CONTENTS

This is a work of fiction. Names, characters, businesses, places, events, locales, and incidents are either the products of the author's imagination or used in a fictitious manner. Any resemblance to actual persons, living or dead, or actual events is purely coincidental.

Adult Content Warning: This book is intended for readers 18 years and older. It contains adult language, explicit sex, and violence.

I've been awake for something like thirty-six hours.
At this moment in time, I would like to dedicate this book to giant sticky notes, Hayley Faiman's pen, coffee, and vammies.
Love you, Mean it

1

SLOANE

"Please, Lorcan. My parents kicked me out. I barely have enough in savings to get by with a few nights in a hotel. I don't know what else to do," the woman cried as she rubbed her swollen belly.

My father said something I couldn't understand, but I knew by the tone of his voice that he was angry. He reached inside his suit jacket and pulled out his money clip. Placing the entire wad in her hand, he pulled her close. "Take this and go. If I ever see you or hear from you again, I'll kill you and the kid. Understand?"

She nodded her head rapidly as tears ran down her face. "Yes. Yes. I understand. I won't come back. I promise."

"Make sure you're the one who sees to that promise. Not me."

With that, my father slammed the front door closed, and I ran back to my room before he caught me spying.

I looked down at the journal in my hand and reread the words that triggered the memory.

I think Lorcan has gotten one of his floozies pregnant.

Words my mother wrote in her journal over twenty-two years ago.

Knowing I got my curious nature from my mother, I started digging through her filing cabinet to see if I could find any more information. Mom would have wanted to know for sure if my dad fathered another child. I knew she would have searched for some answers, but I didn't know if she found any. I wished I could pick up the phone and call her, just like I'd wanted to every day for the last four months since she died.

Shaking my head to clear my thoughts, I focused on sorting through her documents. Thankfully, she wasn't one to keep things that weren't necessary, so it didn't take me long to find the folder hidden underneath the hanging files. It wasn't labeled, but I found a note stuck to the first page inside.

My Dear Sloane,

I knew you would find this. I'm sorry there isn't more. It was difficult to find what little information I did. If you're going to proceed, do it with caution. If anyone tells you to leave, please heed their warning and leave. If word got back to the wrong person, you could put other people's lives in danger. Stop and think about that for a minute. I know you'll make the right choice.

I'm sorry I didn't tell you or your brothers that you might have another sibling out there. I wanted to be sure before I broke that news to you, and all of the information I found was circumstantial.

Be careful, my beautiful girl. I let this consume my life for a short period of time. I don't want you to do the same.

I love you, and I'll always be with you.

Mom

I lifted the note and continued looking through the contents of the folder.

Jackpot!

It appeared my dad fathered a child with a former intern, though her name wasn't listed anywhere in the documents. There wasn't a name for the child either, though Mom's note said it was a girl. Of the few addresses listed, all were crossed out except one. Continuing to flip through the papers, I found records where my mother had sent money to the addresses listed, but from what I could tell, it looked like she stopped doing that a few years after she started.

With the last known address right in front of me, I couldn't stop myself, even though I didn't have the first semblance of a plan. I packed my bags and headed to Devil Springs to meet my sister.

When I arrived in town, I found the closest four-star hotel and checked in. I was starving, and I wanted to soak my sore muscles in a hot bath before I worked on coming up with a plan on how to proceed. However, I fell asleep approximately two minutes after I got out of the tub.

When I woke the next morning, I ordered room service for breakfast before I pulled out my laptop and started looking for answers. First, I searched the last known address listed in my mother's notes. After digging around on Ritch County's website, I finally found the name listed on the deed to the property.

Adelaide Coleman.

Using social media, I learned that Adelaide was a divorced forty-three-year-old. It appeared she had two daughters and listed her hometown the same as mine. I couldn't tell if she was the pregnant woman from years ago. Her hair looked the same, but I didn't recognize anything about her face. However, it had been over twenty-one years since she came to our home, and my three-year-old self wasn't concerned with remembering what she looked like.

Most of her information was set to private, but I was able to view some of her pictures. However, the only ones I could see were of two girls I assumed to be her daughters —one of which was likely my sister. I was so excited I could barely contain myself.

Both girls were gorgeous, and surprisingly, they looked alike, which meant they also looked like me. Both had blonde hair, though each had a slightly different shade. It was hard to tell their exact height from pictures, but they both seemed to be on the petite side. The one with lighter blonde hair had a leaner frame, and her skin had cooler undertones, while the one with darker hair was the opposite with a curvier frame and warmer skin tone. Still, judging by looks, they could easily be related to each other, as well as related to me.

I saved a couple of the pictures in case I needed to do a reverse image search, but as luck would have it, I found a photo with both girls tagged in it. Unfortunately, the tags were in the corner of the picture instead of on the people in the photo.

Paige Coleman.

Heidi Coleman.

I clicked on Paige's name since it was the first one my mouse landed on. Her profile was locked down and only allowed me to view her profile picture, which was a cute shot of her and Heidi standing in front of a couple of motorcycles.

Clicking the back button, I clicked the tag to take me to Heidi's profile. A grin took over my face when her almost public profile filled the page. I decided to start by going through her pictures so I could put a face to a name, but it seemed like Paige and Heidi were joined at the hip. They were together in every single picture posted on Heidi's page, and there were hundreds of photos uploaded.

Switching gears, I scrolled through her "About" section

and reached for a notebook and pen when I saw she'd listed her current place of employment.

Precious Metals.

After clicking and opening the link in a new tab, I jotted down the phone number and address for the place described as a local family-owned sports bar and grill.

Then, I went back to her main page and started scrolling through her posts. She didn't generate her own content very often, but she did frequently share posts from others—particularly book-related posts. I squeaked and clapped my hands in excitement. Either my half sister or my half sister's sister was not only a book lover but a romance book lover.

After several more minutes of scrolling and not finding anything useful, I entered the address listed in my mother's files into the map app on my phone, surprised to learn that it was only a seven-minute drive. Grabbing my purse, I slipped on my shoes and dashed for my car.

Seven minutes later, I pulled into the driveway of a cozy, ranch-style house. My stomach fluttered with excitement. She could be in there.

My sister.

I had to force myself to walk to the door, instead of running, and to ring the doorbell one time, instead of pounding on the door until someone answered. I bounced on the balls of my feet while I waited. And waited.

I rang the doorbell again and knocked on the door a few times for good measure. Still, no one answered.

Frustrated and disappointed, I stabbed the doorbell several times with my finger and beat on the door. "Hello!" I called out. "Anyone home?"

Silence.

Sighing in defeat, I retreated to my car and started to head back to the hotel. However, I ended up driving around the town, looking for places to check out. But, I wanted to know more before I went out looking for answers again, so I spent the rest of the day in my hotel room searching for more information on the Colemans. Unfortunately, I didn't find much more than I already had.

I spent the first part of the next day working. I was just barely on schedule, and I wanted to hang on to that for as long as possible before falling behind yet again. It was a common occurrence for me, despite my numerous attempts to break the habit.

Finally, when six o'clock rolled around, I took a shower and got ready to head to the bar Heidi listed as her place of employment. Nervous didn't even begin to cover how I was feeling. I was so close to finding her that I could almost taste it.

After careful consideration, I chose to wear a pair of ripped, skinny jeans with what I referred to as a conversation starter T-shirt and a pair of strappy sandals. I was going for trendy yet approachable. With my hair and makeup finished, I grabbed my purse and keys before I could talk myself out of going.

As I drove to the bar, a part of me wished I had at least told Frankie where I was going. I could have really used one of her pep talks right before I walked into an unfamiliar bar in a strange town all by myself, hoping to find a sibling who didn't know I existed. Yeah, a pep talk and a handle of Vodka would have been stellar right then.

But I was nothing if not determined. So, I opened the door and walked inside, strutting to the bar in my big girl panties.

2

BRONZE

I looked up right as a hot blonde crossed the room and sat her firm ass on a bar stool, in my direct line of sight. For the first time in months, a woman caught my cock's attention, and I knew right then I wasn't going anywhere. I was considering heading back to the clubhouse, but my dick was straining for her promise land like his life depended on it.

My eyes stayed on her for several minutes after she ordered a drink to see if she was staying there or moving to a table. After a few sips, she stayed put, and I made my approach, silently hoping that Layla didn't embarrass the fuck out of me by trying to be helpful.

I loved Layla with my whole heart. I knew she meant well, but I was a grown-ass man with a solid game. I didn't need my older brother's Old Lady's help getting pussy. But, because I loved her and didn't want to hurt her feelings, I couldn't tell her that either. Or wouldn't. I knew it wasn't my fault, and she was very adamant that she didn't think anything of it anymore, but I still felt guilty about the awful things I said to Layla when we first met.

Glancing at Layla, I ordered myself a beer before I took a seat beside the beautiful blonde. I had to give credit where credit is due. Layla handed me a beer and went back to serving other customers without a word. To be honest, I was expecting her to tell me to get it my damn self, and I was glad she didn't. It's not that I was trying to hide who I was, but in my experience, women looked at bikers one of two ways—we were either criminals or the fuck of a lifetime. And while I wasn't ready to settle down like a number of my club brothers, I was getting tired of being overlooked as a person.

I took a sip of my beer and pulled myself out of my thoughts by glancing at her tits. Or that's what I was trying to do when I read the one word printed across her chest.

Moist.

Choosing my words carefully, I turned to her and grinned. "Nice shirt. Is that your way of weeding out the creeps?"

"Maybe," she replied and flicked her eyes to me.

Flashing her my best panty-dropping smile, I told her the truth. "Darlin', if you think there's a man in this room who hasn't associated the word stretched across your tits with your pussy, you're sadly mistaken. Granted, not all of them would say it, but every damn one of them's thinking it."

"Hmm," she replied and traced the rim of her glass with her index finger. "I don't know what to do with you. You're the first one to ask me about my moist pussy without actually asking me about it."

My cock twitched at her words. "Fuck me," I groaned and pressed the heel of my palm against my hard dick in a vain attempt to get some relief. "We can talk about your moist pussy later tonight." Talk about it. Play with it. Taste it. Fuck it. "Once we've gotten to know each other a little better," I added.

She smirked and finally turned to fully face me. And holy shit, she was gorgeous. Her hair wasn't overdone, and her skin wasn't caked with layers of makeup. It looked like I could actually touch her without getting girl shit all over my hands. Girl shit was sticky, and the smell lingered far too long. Girl shit was a hard no for me.

She snapped her fingers in front of my face. "Are you finished eye-fucking me?"

"Nah, baby. I've been building up my stamina for years. I can go all night," I said suggestively.

She rolled her eyes and reached for her drink. "I've heard that before."

I leaned in, slowly invading her space. "Not from me."

Inhaling sharply through her parted plump lips, she cleared her throat and tried to shake off my charm. "And you are?"

"Bronze Black," I said proudly and extended my hand.

"Sloane," she replied and shook my hand. "And I'm not telling you my last name because I just met you."

"Fair enough," I returned, reluctant to let go of her silky smooth skin. "Have you been to Precious Metals before?"

She shook her head. "Nope. It's my first time."

"Then you have to try our signature drink." I turned back to the bar and flagged Layla. "Bring her a couple of BWOLs."

"Coming right up," she chirped and disappeared behind the bar.

"Um, I'm not sure what you ordered for me, but if you think you're going to get me drunk and have your wicked way with me, you've got another thing coming, buddy."

I grinned devilishly and turned my head so she could see the dimple I knew was visible even through my beard. "My wicked way? How do you know my way is wicked?" I teased.

She laughed lightly. "Just a guess."

"My ways are wicked good," I clarified right as Layla returned with her drinks.

"Oh, vomit. Stop talking. Right now. Just let me drop these drinks off, and I'll be gone before I accidentally hear something I don't want to hear. There we go. La-la-la," she sang as she rushed away from the table.

"I take it you two know each other," she prompted.

"You could say that," I chuckled and immediately realized my mistake by the furrowing of Sloane's forehead. "She's my brother's Old Lady."

"Old Lady? Like an MC Old Lady?" she asked excitedly.

"Yeah," I replied slowly, trying to figure out why I was disappointed in her reaction. She wouldn't be the first bitch I fucked solely because she wanted to bang a biker, but she seemed different somehow.

She leaned back and glanced over me from head to toe. "You're not in your brother's club?"

"What makes you ask that?"

"Because you're not wearing a cut. Isn't that one of the rules? That you have to wear it unless you're out of town or in a car?"

"All right, Sweet Sloane, I think it's time for us to move this conversation to a table," I said and got to my feet. Leaning over the bar, I had to stretch for it, but I managed to snag my cut from where it was hanging under the bar and slid it over my shoulders. "Layla, have somebody bring our drinks and a couple of glasses of water over to our table," I called out as I took Sloane's hand and led her to a booth in the far corner of the bar.

I gestured for her to have a seat, snorting when she sat as close to the edge of the seat as possible. "That's not going to save you. It doesn't matter if you sit right beside me or stand across the room; if I want you, I'll get you."

3

SLOANE

A delicious shiver ran down my spine, and I struggled to keep my eyes from flicking up to his to see the sexy smirk I knew he was wearing. I needed to know about his club before I went further down the rabbit hole with him.

Trying to seem clueless, I focused on the patches on the front of his leather vest and asked, "Is your club like the one on that TV show?"

He grinned and leaned forward, bracing himself on his elbows. "Why? You want me to take you for a ride?" he asked suggestively.

"Bronze! Please work on your timing," Layla said desperately.

Extending her hand to me, she smiled, "Hi, I'm Layla, Bronze's sister-in-law."

"Also known as Queen Cock Blocker."

"That's not what your brother said," she retorted.

"Hi. I'm Sloane, Bronze's hostage for the evening."

She threw her head back and laughed. "Oh, that's great. Do you two need anything else?"

Bronze winked. "Bring her a couple more BWOLs, and I'll have my usual."

When she disappeared, I turned back to him and reminded him of my question. "So, about your club?"

He cocked his head to the side. "What about it?"

"I don't know anything about biker gangs," I lied and cringed at the term. I knew all motorcycle clubs weren't outlaws, just like all wealthy Irish businessmen weren't part of the mob. What I didn't know was if his club had any enemies, particularly Irish ones.

He shook his head. His devilish grin made me squirm in my seat. "We're a club, not a gang," he corrected, not surprising me in the least. I knew it was a touchy subject for members of that lifestyle.

"Okay," I said, pretending to be blissfully unaware of my faux pas. "Will you tell me about your club?"

He sat back in the corner and draped his porn-worthy arms along the back of the booth. "We're not outlaws, Sweet Sloane, if that's what you're asking."

"Oh, of course not," I said and waved my hand dismissively. "I was asking what kinds of things a motorcycle club does? Do you just ride around on your bikes together on the weekends?" Admittedly, I was genuinely interested in hearing his answer.

He threw his head back and laughed. "Oh shit. I haven't heard that one before."

"So that's a no?"

"That's a no. We're a club, but we operate as a business," he explained. "A business that owns and runs a group of businesses."

"So, like a corporation or an enterprise?"

"Yeah, you could say that."

I reached for a glass of water and, after digging through my purse, dropped a metal straw into it, taking a large gulp of ice-cold water. "Mmm," I groaned, not realizing how thirsty I was.

"That's kind of wicked," he mumbled and shifted in his seat.

I winked. "I know."

"Wait," he said and held up his hand. Pointing to my glass, he asked, "What is that?"

"This?" I asked and touched my straw. At his nod, I explained, "A metal straw." When he stared at me blankly, I continued, "You know, to reduce the amount of plastic ones that end up in the ocean killing important marine life."

"Wouldn't it be easier to just drink from the cup?" he asked.

"I prefer to wrap my lips around the tip and suck," I said in an overly seductive tone.

"I'd love to see that," he breathed.

Leaning forward, I closed my lips around the straw and slowly sipped my drink. "There. You're welcome."

He grinned again. Damn, the man was positively sinful. Sparkling blue eyes, dark blonde hair, muscles, tattoos, leather, and a few visible piercings. He ticked off every one of the boxes on my list, including a neatly trimmed beard.

"Bronze!" Layla shouted from behind the bar, where a large group of people had gathered.

"Fuck," he cursed. "She needs my help. I'll be back after we take care of that crowd. Enjoy your drinks while I'm gone," he said and scooted two BWOLs I hadn't noticed toward me.

I shook my head. "I'm not drinking any more on an empty stomach," I said vehemently. "I learned that lesson long before my twenty-first birthday."

"Good thing this is a bar and grill," he grinned and

stopped the waitress passing by.

"Hey, Bronze," she cooed and batted her eyelashes at him. "Do you need something?"

"Yeah, Table Seventeen needs a Triple Threat and bring two more BWOLs when it comes out."

"Got it. Should be about ten minutes," she said and almost skipped away.

He directed his attention back to me. "I shouldn't be long."

Damn it. I was just gearing up to ask him if Heidi was working. While he was gone, I made the best of it and used the time to scan the area looking for Heidi or Paige. Based on the pictures I'd seen, wherever one was, the other was there too. Unfortunately, I didn't see either one of them anywhere in Precious Metals.

Surprisingly, he returned to the booth moments before the young waitress returned with the order he placed.

"Is she even old enough to work here?" I asked, unsure of why her presence irritated me. Regardless, I failed to hide my annoyance, and Bronze picked up on it.

"Not that it's any of your business, but yes, she is."

I rolled my eyes. "Do I even want to know why you know her age?"

"Because I'm one of the owners of this bar."

"Oh," I said, genuinely surprised and popped a piece of fried goodness into my mouth, groaning obscenely when I bit into it. For a split second. Then, the scalding hot cheese made contact with my tongue. "Ah! Hahhht!" I shouted as I spit the wad of steaming goo into a napkin. Then, I promptly downed both BWOLs and half of my glass of water, trying to cool the burn and save my tongue.

"You okay?" he laughed.

"That shit is hot!" I stated unnecessarily.

"At least it wasn't one of the wings. Those were tossed in Judge's special hot sauce."

"Why's it special?" I asked between sips of water.

"He makes it with Carolina Reapers."

"Holy shit," I breathed. "Is it even legal to serve sauce that hot in a restaurant?"

He chuckled. "Sounds like you've had a run-in with a Reaper before."

"You could say that," I murmured.

"Don't leave me hanging, Sweet Sloane."

I sighed. "One of my brothers is a die-hard hot sauce fan. The hotter, the better. So, a few years ago when we all still lived at home, he bought a new sauce and put it in the fridge. As it turned out, the packaging was very similar to the packaging on the ketchup we used, and I was the one who made that discovery after mixing up the two. I swear, I thought I was going to die. For real, it felt like it was burning a hole through my stomach. And I only had one little bite."

"Did you try milk?"

I scoffed. "Did I try milk? Let me tell you something. Milk is great for jalapeños, but drinking milk after eating a Carolina Reaper is like dropping an ice cube into a pot of boiling water to cool it."

"Huh? Is that right?" he asked as he stabbed a boneless wing with his fork and nonchalantly popped it into his mouth. "Doesn't seem to bother me."

I leaned forward on my elbows and loudly whispered, "If your fingers touch that sauce, they won't touch me. Just putting that out there."

"Sydney!" he bellowed. "Bring us an order of loaded fries. We're finished with this," he said and pointed to the platter of food like it was going to jump up and attack him.

I couldn't control it and cracked up laughing. "Got big plans tonight?"

Before he could answer, twelve-year-old Sydney promptly cleared our table and returned to silently drop off more drinks.

"So, you said you were one of the owners of this bar?" I asked when she was gone, hoping to lead into a conversation about Heidi and Paige.

"Yeah," he nodded. "Why? You want to barter for free drinks?" he asked and waggled his brows.

I laughed and struggled to stay focused on the task at hand. I don't know if it was the alcohol or his undeniable charm, but I was getting lost in him far too easily. "No," I said and chewed on my lower lip. "I wanted to ask—"

"Here you go," Baby Sydney interrupted and placed a plate of loaded fries between us, followed by more drinks. "Anything else?"

"I think we're good for now, Syd. Thanks," he said while I sang happy songs in my head so I wouldn't wrinkle my nose in disgust at the way he called her Syd. Or maybe it was so I wouldn't scream at her for her shitty timing as I was once again interrupted right before asking about Heidi.

I reached for a fry and busied myself with eating while I tried to figure out how to bring the conversation back to him being the owner, so I could ask about Heidi's employment. And then an idea hit me. But first, I glanced around to see if any waitresses were on their way over to stop me.

"Do you have to fill in behind the bar often?"

He shrugged. "Only when we're short-staffed. We lost one of our best waitresses and bartenders a few months ago and haven't been able to find a replacement even close to her." He snorted. "We even tried hiring two girls at once, and they still couldn't keep up like she did."

"That sucks. Why'd she leave?" I asked and continued to stuff my face with food.

When I glanced up to see him staring into his drink, I knew I'd inadvertently brought up a sensitive subject. So, I did what I do best in those situations and called myself out for being rude or nosy to segue into a new topic.

"I'm sorry," I blurted and slapped my hand over my chest. "Don't answer that. I'm a curious soul and tend to ask questions that are none of my business," I laughed. "As you can imagine, I embarrassed my mother on more than one occasion when I was little."

His eyes flicked up, and I could see the interest on his face. So, for the sake of possibly banging the biker, I shared a hilarious story from my past. "One particular time, our next-door neighbor came over for her weekly coffee date with Mom. I was around five years old, so I was playing nearby while they were in the kitchen talking. I overheard Rebecca tell my mom that she caught her husband sleeping with another woman. Naturally, my mom asked who he was sleeping with. Before Rebecca could answer, my five-year-old self couldn't wait to ask my own question. 'You can get caught cheating while sleeping?' 'No, sweetie,' my mom answered, completely dismissing me. But I *needed* to know. Mainly because I didn't want to get in trouble for something I didn't know was possible. So, I continued. 'My teacher said people sometimes lie and cheat to win. Maybe she's a better sleeper than you are, and he wanted to win.'" I barely managed to get it out before I started hysterically laughing like I did each time I told that story.

Thankfully, he was laughing too. "Shit. You told that woman her husband cheated because she was bad in bed!"

"I didn't mean it like that! I was only five!" I insisted and playfully swatted at him.

The moment my palm made contact with his chest, his hand circled around my wrist and pulled, closing the space between us. When my body made contact with his, he wrapped one arm around my shoulders and buried his face in the crook of my neck. "Every time you laugh, your tits bounce beautifully, and I feel like it's only fair to warn you that I'm about four bounces away from putting my hands on them," he rumbled against my skin.

The combination of a sinful biker, a long dry spell, and a few glasses of liquid courage had the words coming out of my mouth without thinking. "I think it's only fair to warn you that I'm about to bounce four times."

He tightened his hold on me as I felt his teeth graze the skin of my neck. "I'm not playing, Sloane. I'll put you on my dick right here in this booth."

I tried to stifle the groan his words elicited from me, but he heard it. "You want my cock, baby?"

"Yes," I breathed. "But not here."

I felt him grin against my skin. "Where to, Sweet Sloane?"

"Uh, it'd be easier for you to follow me," I said, not wanting to admit I couldn't remember the name of the hotel. I knew where it was, though, and that's what really mattered.

He pulled back and shook his head. "Nope. We've both been drinking. Gimme a sec, and I'll get us a ride." After sending a text to someone, he placed his phone on the table. "He'll be here in about ten minutes."

"How many of these have I had?" I asked when I noticed two untouched BWOLs on the table.

"Why does it matter? It's just a number. Judge by how you feel," he advised.

"Drinking advice from a bar-owning biker. Now, if that's not a cliché, I don't know what is," I teased. Since I wasn't going to be driving, I saw no reason to let the two BWOLs on the table go to waste. Quickly downing both, I asked, "Any chance I can get two more before our ride gets here?"

"Why? You nervous?" he asked and studied me carefully.

"Oh," I laughed when realization dawned. "No, it's nothing like that. I just really like them."

He nodded knowingly and got to his feet. "Yeah, we hear that a lot. I'll be right back."

While he was gone, I dug through my purse and found some cash. When he returned with two drinks for me and one for him, I pushed the money to him. "If that's not enough to cover the tab, let me know."

He snorted and pushed it back to me. "Owners drink and eat for free. As do their guests."

"That's very generous of you. Thanks," I said sincerely. I really didn't expect him to comp my drinks, even though he'd joked about bartering for the tab earlier.

He shrugged. "It's something we've always done. Drink up," he said and pointed to his wrist even though he wasn't wearing a watch.

I opted not to point it out and helped myself to the last two drinks while we waited to be picked up.

When Bronze's phone lit up with a text, he grabbed my hand and pulled me out of the booth behind him. "Grant's here."

"Is that what you guys call Uber?" I laughed.

"Nah, Grant's a prospect for the club." He stopped beside a lifted truck and opened the back door for me. To my surprise, he climbed in the back seat with me instead of getting into the front with his friend.

"Where to?" the guy in the driver's seat asked.

"Oh," I giggled to cover my embarrassment. "Um, I'm staying at the hotel on Main Street. The one with resort and spa in the name. I can't remember the first part of it though. Do you know which one I'm talking about?"

"The Winchester?"

"That's it!" I shouted excitedly.

"Yeah, I know where it is," he laughed and put the truck into gear.

I was unaware of Bronze inching closer to me until he was practically plastered against my side. "Can I help you with something?" I asked and arched a brow.

"Yes, you can," he rasped and flicked his eyes to my mouth.

"We're here," the driver announced.

"Thanks, man," Bronze said and clapped him on the shoulder. "I'll catch you tomorrow."

"No problem, VP. Have a good night."

"I plan to," Bronze smirked and ushered me toward the hotel. "Thanks for the ride!" I shouted and gave a little wave before practically speed walking to the bay of elevators.

"No need to rush, Sweet Sloane," he said when he caught up with me. "I'm not going anywhere until I've fucked you hard enough that you'll feel me for days."

There was something hidden in his voice. Something hungry and full of need. Something barely restrained. Something that probably should have made me send him on his way. But it didn't.

Instead, I pulled him into the elevator when the doors opened. The moment they closed, he had me pinned against the wall with his unbelievably firm body deliciously pressed against mine.

"I can't wait to see how many times I can make you come," he rumbled.

"Fuck, yes," I groaned and fisted his shirt.

He bent closer, lowering his mouth to mine, and when he was only a hair's breadth away, the door opened with an obnoxious ding.

He growled. Growled. Then, he was the one pulling me into the hall. "Which way?"

"This way." I tugged on his hand and started down the long trek to my room. The hotel only had one set of elevators, and my room had to be the farthest one from them.

"Where in the hell are you staying? Out back in the janitor's closet?" he grumbled as we rounded the last corner.

Finally, we made it to my door, and I extended the key card toward the lock with my shaking hand. Pressing against me from behind, he smoothed his hands down my arms while resting his forehead on the top of my head. "Sloane," he said with a hint of warning in his tone. "I'm gonna fuck you the second you open that door. If you don't want that, now's the time to say it."

"Okay," I whispered, and his warmth immediately disappeared as he took a step back. I whirled around so fast I almost lost my balance. "No! Don't go," I said, much louder than I intended. "I meant, 'Okay, I understand, and I'm going to open the door as soon as my fucking hand stops shaking.'"

He watched me while I silently cursed my nerves and tried to steady my hand long enough to unlock the door. Finally, the green light flashed, and I shoved the door open with a little too much exuberance, causing it to slam into the wall. "Oops."

He placed one hand on my shoulder and stopped me

from entering. "You sure?" Was I? No, I wasn't. Not entirely. But there was something about him that drew me in and consumed me in a way no one ever had. I knew I would regret it for the rest of my life if I let go of the opportunity to experience *him*.

"Very," I managed to purr. What was in those drinks? I hoped sober me would remember that drunk me made a mental note to find out more about the BWOLs—mainly how I could convince Layla to give me the recipe.

Following me into my hotel suite, he whistled when I turned the lights on, causing me to blush. "Sweet Sloane doesn't skimp on the travel expenses."

For the most part, I tried to behave modestly and not let my affluent upbringing affect my lifestyle. In other words, I tried not to act like a rich bitch, even though technically, I was one. But, he was right; I didn't skimp on the travel expenses. After walking into a room crawling with roaches at a low budget hotel, I never made that mistake again.

Dropping my purse on the sofa, I kicked my shoes off. "Do you want something to drink?"

"No, but I do want something to eat."

4

BRONZE

I prowled toward her on a mission. "Is there anything else before I devour you?"

She quivered. Fucking quivered. And it was the sexiest thing I'd ever seen.

Or so I thought.

"Yes," she breathed, dropping to her knees in front of me and reaching for my zipper. She briefly fumbled with my belt and the button on my jeans, but once she got her hands on my cock, her movements were sure and steady.

With a devious grin, she looked up at me and licked her lips. "I want to devour you first."

With that, she wrapped her plump lips around the head of my cock and slowly took me into her mouth until the tip hit the back of her throat.

I groaned loudly and fisted one hand in her hair. "Suck."

She popped off my cock long enough to say, "Make me," before she engulfed me once again.

"Don't fuck with me, Sweet Sloane. You wanna play? I'll fucking play."

She pulled back again, and I hoped she said what I wanted to hear. "I want to play," she winked. "Now, make me suck your cock."

"Gladly," I told her right before I thrust my hips and shoved my dick down her throat. I kept a close watch on her reactions to make sure I wasn't hurting her, until I looked past my cock sliding in and out of her mouth. My eyes rolled back in my head when I saw that she'd pulled her shirt up to play with her nipples.

Her fucking tits were glorious. Perfect round globes that bordered on being too big for her petite frame—which meant they were perfect in my book.

I wanted to fuck her tits and come all over them. But that meant I had to pull my dick from her skillful mouth. Decisions. Decisions.

However, it was out of my hands when Sloane did something with her tongue that shot intense pleasure straight to my balls and had me coming down her throat before I could warn her.

And then my knees buckled when she sucked hard one last time and swallowed every drop of my release. Had I not braced my arms on the kitchenette counter, I would've hit the floor.

I took a few seconds to regain my bearings after blowing my load without the use of my hand for the first time in months. Then, I looked down at the little vixen on her knees in front of me, licking her lips like the cat who got the cream. "My turn," I rumbled and extended my hand to help her to her feet.

"Get naked, and get on the bed. Back to the headboard, legs spread wide," I instructed and punctuated it with a slap to her firm ass.

She did as I said without hesitation. And I knew why the moment she was in position. Her pussy was glistening with her arousal, and I couldn't wait to bury my face between her legs. But I wanted to taste her cunt for the first time when it was covered in her come. And that's exactly what I was going to do.

Running the tip of my finger down her slick slit, she arched her back and groaned before reaching for me. I quickly pulled back out of her reach. "Keep your hands behind your back," I clipped.

She did as I said and looked up at me through her lashes, attempting to appear shy, but I saw the desire filling her eyes. I knew she was as into it as I was.

"Good." I situated myself between her splayed thighs and lightly traced one nipple, then the other. Alternating between the two, I enjoyed watching her struggle to stay in position.

With both hands caressing her breasts, I moved my fingers up to resume toying with her nipples. "I can't wait to see how good your cunt tastes."

"Please," she groaned.

I leaned in until my lips were almost touching hers. "But I want it to be covered in your come the first time I run my tongue through your sweet snatch."

A beautiful flush washed over her face while her tits heaved with each panting breath she took. "Since I'm getting what I want, I'll let you tell me how you want me to make you come before I bury my face in your pussy."

Before she could answer me, I kissed her, pushing my tongue into her mouth. She returned the kiss with so much passion that things quickly escalated. I was seconds from baring my cock and thrusting into her when she pulled away and answered my question. "With your fingers. Make me come with your fingers," she blurted, followed by a groan. "Please, Bronze, please."

Trailing my lips down her neck, I lavished one breast

for a few moments before moving to the other, slipping two fingers inside her at the same time. She moaned loudly and bucked at the intrusion, but quickly returned to her position.

I looked up to see her watching me suck her tit while her mouth hung open. My cock twitched at the sight. And that was my cue to move on to the next round.

Setting a steady rhythm with my fingers, I used my thumb to massage her clit. Then, I increased the pace until she was screaming my name and pulsing around my fingers.

Leaving them in place, I slid down and devoured her pussy until she was pulling on my hair and begging me to fuck her—after she'd had another climax.

I sat back on my heels and studied the beauty before me, thinking of all the different ways I wanted to fuck her as I reached for the condom I'd placed on the bed.

With my cock sheathed, I hooked my arms under her knees and pulled her down the bed, not stopping until she was impaled on my cock.

"Oh, shit, Bronze! I'm going to come. Go! Go! Go!" she yelled frantically and reached down to circle her clit.

As much as I wanted to tease her, I could feel her pussy rippling and knew she was too far gone to stop. Being the gentleman I was, I granted her wish and hammered into her, thankful I'd already had one release. Because there was no way I would have lasted more than a few minutes if I hadn't. She felt so good massaging my dick with the walls of her cunt, even through the latex barrier.

When she finally stopped spasming, I pulled out and flipped her to her knees, thrusting my cock into her the moment she was braced on her hands.

After a few pumps of my hips, I slapped her ass and

told her, "I want in deeper. Press those tits to the bed, baby."

"Oh fuck. Just like that," I groaned when she dropped down, and my cock slid even further inside.

I pulled back and slammed forward, over and over. Soon, she was shoving her hips back to meet my thrusts, causing the slapping of our sweaty skin to echo around the hotel room.

"Fuck, Sloane. I'm close, but you're gonna give me one more."

She shook her head. "I can't."

The fuck she couldn't. I pulled out again and flipped her onto her back. Remaining on my knees, I pushed my dick back inside of her and started rubbing her clit with both thumbs.

"Cup your tits and rub your fingers over your nipples for me," I told her.

She circled the taut buds before moving on to pulling and tugging on them. I felt her walls begin to tighten and knew she was close.

"I don't know if I want to come in your tight cunt, or if I'd rather yank it off and come all over your tits." I paused for half a dozen thrusts or so before I made a decision. "I'm gonna come on your tits now, fuck with you in the shower while we rinse off, and then I'm going to fuck you into the mattress when we're finished. And that's when I'm going to blow my load deep inside your tight cunt."

My dirty words and filthy promises had her exploding into another orgasm. I barely held out for her to ride out the final waves of pleasure before I pulled out and tossed the condom somewhere.

With my fist wrapped around my shaft, it only took a few tugs before thick ropes of come shot from dick and splattered across her beautiful breasts. I braced my hand on the wall and looked down at her flushed face.

"Ready for that shower?"

"As long as you're ready to do everything you promised," she returned with a shy smile.

"I'm more than ready."

GLANCING AT THE CLOCK, I REALIZED I'D SLEPT MUCH later than I usually did and was about to be late. I didn't want to leave. Not in the slightest, but I was scheduled to work at the bookstore, and I knew Tatum wouldn't be there for the first part of the day, meaning I was the guns and muscle if anything went wrong. "Do you have any plans for today?" I asked, rushing to gather my shit and get dressed.

"Yes, I'm looking forward to an exciting afternoon filled with staying in my hotel room and catching up on work."

"Well, if I have to work, it's only fair that you do too."

"How is that fair?" she asked, pretending to be offended.

"Because I said it was," I teased.

She rolled her eyes and wrapped the sheet around her naked body as she got up and walked to the bathroom, emerging a few moments later dressed in the undershirt I was looking for. I damn near went to my knees when my eyes landed on the visible outline of her nipples through the well-worn cotton.

"Fuck it," I cursed and dropped everything in my hands to the floor.

"What?" Sloane gasped.

"Fuck it. I'm gonna be late because seeing you in my

shirt made my dick hard as a rock. And after being inside that sweet pussy all night, my hand isn't gonna cut it," I said and pulled her to me.

When her body collided with mine, she was all over me, trying to climb me like a tree. I lifted her by her bare ass cheeks and quickly moved us to the couch. She worked on my pants while I pulled a condom from my wallet and ripped it open. Once it was in place, she took my cock in her hand, positioned it at her entrance, and slammed herself down.

"Yes," she groaned. "Fuck, yes."

Gripping her hips firmly, I guided her movements so she was fucking me how I liked it—hard and fast.

"Fuck, Sloane," I breathed. I needed her to hurry up and come. For a number of reasons. But the main one was because I wasn't going to last much longer. She felt too good. "Damn it. Fucking come!" I demanded and smacked her plump ass.

"Bronze!" she shrieked, though I had no idea if it was from the slap to her ass or from the orgasm she had seconds later. Regardless, I stopped fighting my release the second her cunt clamped down on my cock, and we found our climaxes together.

"Shit, Sloane," I panted, sweaty and out of breath.

"I know, I know. You're going to be late," she said and disentangled herself from me.

"Yeah, but it was fucking worth it."

5

SLOANE

After Bronze left, I climbed into bed and went back to sleep until my cell phone ringing from back to back calls woke me up. When I glanced at the name flashing on the screen, I bolted upright in the bed. It was my personal assistant, my partner in crime, my handler, and I was going to be in trouble if she figured out I was sleeping instead of writing. It wouldn't take much for me to go from being barely behind to holy-shit-I'll-never-catch-up.

I cleared my throat, drank a couple of sips of water, and blurted some random words to warm up my voice. That was as good as it was going to get, so I tapped the screen and answered the call. "Hello," I said, pleased with how awake I sounded.

"Where in the hell have you been, you crazy demon?" she yelled. "I've been worried sick about you! I'm over here trying to figure out how I'm going to finish writing the rest of your book if you're dead. Because there will be a riot of mass proportions if that book isn't released; doesn't matter if it's because you died. They. Will. Riot. And I can't write the thrusting, throbbing cocks like you can. They'd know my cocks were imposter cocks. Now, don't keep me waiting. Where in the hell are you? It looks swanky from what I can see."

I cringed throughout her entire tirade until she said the two words that had me erupting in a fit of laughter. "Wait. Did you just say 'imposter cocks'?"

"Yes, I did. And you don't even get to laugh until you've apologized and explained and made me like you again."

I chuckled, knowing she wasn't seriously angry, but I understood where she was coming from. "I'm sorry I haven't checked in. I was working on cleaning out my mom's office, and I found something that needed my personal attention."

"Don't leave me hanging! What is it?" I hesitated, unsure of what to say, and she caught it. "It's me. Say what you gotta say."

"It's better if I don't say what it is just yet," I confessed. My mother's written warning had me concerned about sharing my newfound knowledge with anyone. Besides, Frankie knew more than most about my family, so I knew she would understand.

"Uh-huh. That's fine. Keep your secrets. Can you at least tell me where you are that requires your personal attention? And why are you holding out on me? Let me see the room, bitch!"

And just like a best friend, she heard the uncertainty in my voice and changed the subject.

"Have you heard of Devil Springs?"

"Maybe. It's in Tennessee, right?"

"Yeah, in Ritch County, right at the base of the mountains," I explained. "Anyway, that's where I am."

"Looks like you found a good place to stay."

"Girl, let me show you," I said excitedly and carried

my phone around the suite and into the bathroom to show her the luxurious amenities.

"Look at that tub! I'm surprised you found a place like that in such a small town."

"I thought so too, but it's actually a lot bigger than I thought. It's a three-McDonald's size town."

She choked on a laugh. "That's how you judge the size of towns? By the number of McDonald's it has?"

"Think about it for a minute. How many did the town you grew up in have?"

"One when I was growing up, but there's two now."

"Okay, and what about where you live now?"

"Five," she said.

"Yeah, and Cherryfield has fifteen."

She gasped. "I can't believe you're right! You can judge a town's size based on the number of McDonald's it has."

"I'm glad I could share some useless knowledge with you. You'd be surprised what kind of little gems I've got stored in my brain just waiting for their day to shine."

"Oh, now I have to know. Tell me another useless fact."

"A pig's orgasm usually lasts for thirty minutes."

Her mouth dropped open in shock. "Do pigs masturbate? Stop laughing and Google that shit. I have to be prepared for this if it happens. What am I going to say if that happens in front of children?" she asked while I laughed my ass off at the thought of her sassy pet pig having a thirty-minute orgasm at an inopportune time.

"I am not asking the internet if pigs masturbate. That's a question no one needs to know the answer to," I managed to say through my amusement.

"Okay, okay, we have to get our game plan together for the week, so I can do some research and prevent my nieces and nephews from being scarred for life by a porcine porn show."

Thankfully, I didn't have anything on my schedule for the following week that required special attention. I was in the middle of writing the first story in a collection of short stories for an upcoming release. As long as I had my laptop—or at least a notebook and pen—I could do my job from anywhere.

With our few loose ends tied up, we ended our chat, and I spent the rest of the day working on the first half of a short story about best friends who go through with an arranged marriage in order to gain access to their trust funds only to find out they must produce an heir—the old-fashioned way.

When I heard a knock on the door, I saved my progress and called it a day before checking to see if I reached my daily word count, which should have been a red flag since it was something I never did. But I was excited to see if Bronze was at the door. Part of me didn't want to let myself believe he was coming back while the other part had my fingers figuratively crossed from the moment he left.

Pausing to take a deep breath and calm myself, I peeked through the peephole, did a celebration dance, and calmly opened the door. "Hey," I greeted and widened the door in invitation. "You hungry?"

He entered my room and nodded. "Yeah, I could eat."

"Good," I smiled. "I was thinking about going back to Precious Metals. The cheese fries were delicious." As far as I was concerned, cheese fries were cheese fries. The only thing special about the ones at Precious Metals were that they were from the place I thought I might find my sibling.

He snorted. "They're good, but not good enough to have me hanging out there when I'm not working."

"Oh, I didn't think about it like that. You've been there all day. Of course, you don't want to go back."

He shook his head. "I wasn't at the bar today. My job is being the VP of the club, which means I work wherever I'm needed."

"Hmm," I mused. "I don't know if I would like that. While it wouldn't get boring, I think I'd want to know what I was getting into each day."

He laughed. "It's not like that. The club owns a couple of businesses, which means the president and VP sometimes have to fill in to cover a shift. That's why I was working at the bar last night."

"That's right. You mentioned being short-staffed," I recalled.

"Yep. We've got a few interviews set up for this week. If we could get one or two halfway competent people in there, things would be fine, at least during the week when it's not as busy."

"Gotcha. But we still need to eat. Do you have any other suggestions?" I asked and placed my hand over my empty stomach, hoping it wouldn't growl like the beast it was.

He smirked. "After last night and working all day, I'm beat. How about we order room service? Maybe watch a movie, while soaking in that bougie ass bathtub."

Dinner, a movie, and a bath with Bronze. Yes, please. "Sounds like a good plan to me. Let me know what you want, and I'll call it in," I said and passed the menu to him.

After we made our choices and placed our order, he asked a question I should have been prepared for. "I didn't get a chance to ask what brought you to Devil Springs last night."

Just like the giant dork that I was, I started to gasp and promptly choked when I inhaled a tiny bit of saliva. Then, I proceeded to cough and cough until I was red-faced with mascara smeared under my eyes, all the while thanking the stars above that I didn't pee in my pants.

"You okay?" he asked.

"Fine," I choked out and ran to the bathroom to get a drink of water and attempt to fix my face. I didn't wear makeup often, and when I did, I didn't wear a lot of it. But, I had put on the basics in case he came back.

"Sorry about that. I guess I swallowed wrong. I hate when that happens."

"Yeah," he agreed. "Because there's not shit you can do about it." Thankfully, he gave me a few more minutes to compose myself before he asked again, "So, what brought you to Devil Springs? Are you here on business?"

"Yes!" I almost shouted. I hadn't planned on meeting anyone other than my sister, and her family if she had any, which meant I hadn't bothered to make up a cover story. However, he inadvertently gave me an excuse for being in town as well as a way to ask about Heidi and Paige. "I am here for work, and you might be able to help me."

Spreading his arms along the back of the sofa, he leaned back and grinned. That damn dimple of his popped up, and I swear it winked at me. "Whatever you need, I'm at your service."

"Behave," I laughed and playfully swatted his chest.

"Only for a little while. Because where's the fun in that?" he returned. "Now, how can I help you?"

I sat back and picked at the stray lint, so I didn't have to look him in the eye while I lied to his face. "I'm here looking for someone, but I haven't been able to find her. That's actually why I was at the bar last night. She listed Precious Metals as her place of employment."

"Who're you looking for?"

"Heidi Coleman."

Recognition and something I couldn't put my finger on

washed over his face for a flash before he masked it. "I hate to be the bearer of bad news, but Heidi's no longer an employee at Precious Metals."

"Oh," I gasped in disappointment, but I refused to let it deter me. "Do you know where I can find her? Or Paige?"

He shook his head while his brow furrowed in confusion. "No, they haven't been around for months."

"What?" I almost shrieked. "Where did they go?"

He shrugged. "I don't know. They didn't leave a forwarding address when they moved."

6

BRONZE

"They moved?" she asked.

I shrugged. "Yeah, Paige moved first," I paused and tried to think back. "I guess it was around five months ago. Then, Heidi left about a month later."

Her shoulders slumped while disappointment filled her beautiful eyes. "What am I going to do now?"

"Why are you looking for them again?" I asked. I thought she'd said she was here for work, but her reactions seemed to be of a personal nature.

Before she could answer, there was a knock on the door, followed by, "Room Service."

Even though it was her room, I got up to answer the door. "I've got it from here," I said and wheeled the cart inside before closing the door.

"It's his job to bring the food in and see if we need anything else," Sloane pointed out and made her way to the cart.

"Then he should be grateful for the break," I chuckled and almost groaned when the smell of a perfectly seasoned hamburger hit my nose.

"This one's yours," she murmured and attempted to move the plates around like they were on a merry-go-round.

"Oh, for fuck's sake, Sloane. I had my face buried in your pussy several times last night and once this morning. You can touch my damn hamburger," I blurted.

"I can't believe you said that," she gasped with mock indignation. Then, she took a huge bite of her burger and groaned, calling my cock to attention once again.

"You're gonna have to cut that shit out," I grumbled.

"Cut what out?" she asked innocently.

"Oh, I don't know," I said exaggeratedly. "Could it possibly be the sex noises you're making while you eat?"

I watched her while she brought the burger to her mouth for another bite. "I think that bun is bigger than your face. Or it was before you started eating it."

She looked down at her hamburger and cocked her head to the side. Then, the little shit grabbed the top of my bun and would have shoved it in my face if I hadn't caught her hand before she could. "The fuck?"

With her wrist still enclosed in my hand, she smirked. "I figured if it was bigger than your face, it would definitely be bigger than mine."

I laughed and repeated the words she'd said to me the night before. "I don't know what to do with you."

"Treating me like a princess is always a safe bet."

"Oh no, I've learned my lesson about making bets with girls," I muttered and silently cursed Tatum. "Now, back to Heidi and Paige. You said you were here for work?"

She swallowed her food and slowly wiped her mouth before answering, which made me think she was either choosing her words carefully, or she was coming up with a lie. "Yes, that's right. I'm here to interview them, or at least one of them."

"What for?" I asked bluntly.

"To help me accurately portray the characters in my upcoming novel."

"You're writing a book?" I asked in surprise.

"Yes, I am," she said with a proud smile.

"What's it about?" I was genuinely intrigued, and since I was never much of a reader, I fully blamed the bookstore for my sudden interest.

She grinned and shook her finger at me. "You'll have to wait until it's released like everyone else."

"Hmm, let me think. If you're here to talk to Heidi, and maybe Paige, for a character, I'm going to guess it has something to do with their relationship," I said and paused when something else occurred to me. "When did you set up this interview? Because like I said, they've been gone for a while now."

She sighed. "It didn't work out with the first two applicants I chose. Heidi is my third attempt," she explained and held her crossed fingers.

"If Heidi applied for the interview, wouldn't the application have her contact information?"

"It did," Sloane sighed and rubbed her forehead. "But it's been well over a year since she submitted the form, and clearly at least her address has changed since then."

"That seems like a long time between the application and the actual interview," I prompted.

"Like I said, it didn't work out with the first two. Admittedly, I didn't do the prep work I usually do before traveling for an interview, which is why I'm scrambling to find her. I really don't have time for this to end up being a wasted trip."

Fuck. It dawned on me that she had no idea about what happened between Paige and Heidi, and I was going to have to be the one to tell her.

7

SLOANE

"It was a stupid move on my part. I made an impulsive decision because I was frustrated as hell at having to start again. So, now I'm here, and I can't find Heidi or Paige. And, yes, it would be easier to move on, but I really feel like Heidi is the one," I shared, solidifying my explanation by ending with a true statement.

"Well then, I wish you the best of luck."

"Oh!" I gasped excitedly. "Maybe you can help me! Do you have her phone number?"

"What?" he asked and suddenly leaned forward.

"You were her employer. You should have her number or have access to it. Will you please share it with me?"

"Why don't you have it?" he returned.

"Do you answer every question with a question?"

"Do you?"

I sighed in exasperation. "Whatever. I don't have it because I forgot to include a spot for phone numbers on the application." The excuse came to me easily since I'd once forgotten to include a spot for city, state, and zip code on a paperback order form.

He exhaled slowly and leaned back in his seat, though he was far from relaxed. "I'll give it to you if you want it, but it was disconnected last month."

"I want it," I told him pointedly. He seemed like he was telling the truth, but admittedly, I wasn't always the best judge of character, and I was going to have to remember that if I was going to keep him from pulling the wool over my eyes. After he pulled the clothes from my body.

He wrote the phone number on the back of a business card from his wallet and handed it to me. "Here you go."

"Thanks," I chirped and snatched it from his fingers. Then, I promptly dialed the number and pressed send.

Bronze doubled over laughing. "I knew you were going to do that."

I ended the call and rolled my eyes. "Of course I was. Who wouldn't check?"

"Most people would've waited until after I was gone."

"I don't have time for that shit," I blurted.

"Am I keeping you from something? Besides your interview, that is?"

I shook my head. "I meant in general. I don't have time for people's pity petty bullshit."

"Pity petty?" he chuckled.

"Shut it. I needed a P."

"I can give you a P. And a D. And a C."

I clapped my hands together. "Focus. What else can you tell me about them? Do you know why Paige moved? What do you think happened to Heidi?"

"You obviously have some serious interviewing skills," he teased and took a long, slow sip of his drink before his next words threw me for a loop. "Let's start with the easiest one. Paige moved away because she broke up with Heidi."

Of all the things he could have said, that was not even a remote possibility in my mind. "What?" I shouted, far louder than I intended, but seriously. What? "That can't be!" They were sisters, weren't they? I started to ask but realized that was something I would have known from the application—if it was real.

But I had to know, even if I blew my cover story because of it. "I'm sorry, would you repeat that?"

"Paige broke up with Heidi and moved away," he repeated and chuckled. "You thought they were sisters, didn't you?"

"Yes," I nodded rapidly. "That's exactly what I thought. They're not?"

"I thought the same thing when I first met them," he laughed and shook his head. "No, they're definitely not sisters," he said in a way that told me he knew from experience.

I wanted to wrinkle my nose in disgust. Hearing about my current partner's previous conquests was not on the list of things I liked to do.

"Listen, I normally don't discuss things like this with other people, particularly women, but I think it's pertinent in this case."

"Oh this sounds like it's gonna be great," I drawled and didn't bother to hide my lack of enthusiasm. Because I already knew what he was going to say. Or at least I thought I did.

"Heidi and Paige were already a couple when I met them. I don't know for how long, but they said they started dating when they were teenagers." He paused and cleared his throat. "Heidi worked at Precious Metals, but both Paige and Heidi helped out at the clubhouse bar. One night, it came up that Paige enjoyed watching Heidi have sex with a man, and Heidi enjoyed doing it. There was some discussion about how they went about finding a man to participate, and long story short, I ended up being, um, there for them like that."

"Why do I need to know this?"

"You asked about their relationship, so I'm telling you about it."

"Their relationship to each other," I clarified.

He held his hands up with his palms out. "I was just trying to help. I thought telling you about them might help with your story since they're not here for you to interview."

And that's why I tried to avoid outright lying if I could help it. Because it always came back to bite you in the ass in ways you never imagined—like listening to the man who rocked your world the night before tell you about having sex with a woman who might be your sister.

I inhaled deeply and told myself I needed to hear him out—in case he shared something that would eventually lead me to my sister.

"So, you had sex with Heidi but not Paige?" I asked and crossed everything I had while I waited for his answer.

"Right. I never touched Paige, and she never touched me. I was about to tell you that when you interrupted me, again."

"My apologies. I'll hold all questions until the end," I said in an overly sweet voice while I thought of a few different ways to torture him in one of my books.

"Before you go thinking it was one big orgy, night after night, it wasn't like that. It was more of a 'you scratch my back, I'll scratch yours' kind of thing. Friends with benefits or whatever you want to call it. And, it only happened a handful of times."

When he continued to stare at me in silence, I tossed my hands in the air. "What? You told me not to interrupt with questions." And I really wanted to tell him to shut up right after the word orgy left his mouth. "Get on with it," I insisted.

He shook his head and snorted. "As you wish. So, the first time we made plans to get together, there was an explosion at the clubhouse before things happened. Since the explosion was near my room, we were all hurt—me worse than them—but I think it scared Paige. They both had concussions, and Paige's arm was broken. Heidi was back to work in a few days, but Paige was off for six weeks while it healed. Skipping forward, it was a few months before they brought it up again. Not long after that, two of the club members were attacked one night when leaving work and almost died. Right after that, Paige stopped showing up for her scheduled shifts at the club. Then, Heidi came home from a shift at Precious Metals to an empty house. She said Paige left a note breaking up with her but didn't give any explanation for it. When Heidi tried to call, her number had been disconnected. About a month later, Heidi called in sick to work. Later that night, she sent me a text saying she was having a hard time with the breakup and thought moving out of the house they shared together might help. I agreed with her and told her the club would help her move when she found a place."

He paused and pinched the bridge of his nose. "I told her to take some time off—as much as she needed. She asked if she could have two, maybe three, weeks off to find a new place, get herself moved, take time to process her new life, and come back to work with a fresh start." He shrugged. "I've never been through a breakup like that, but her request sounded reasonable to me. She never took time off, rarely called in sick, and always came in to help out whenever we asked. I was happy she was finally taking some time for herself. After her two weeks off, she'd found a new place and started moving in but said she needed more time and asked for another week. That was the last time I heard from her."

I waited a few beats to make sure he was finished before I tapped my phone to stop the voice recording, which he noticed immediately. "Were you recording me?"

"Yes," I admitted and slapped my hand over my face. "I'm sorry. It's a habit. I always record interviews." While that part was true, I was also so blown away by what he was telling me that I was afraid I would miss something important. "I'll delete it when we're finished."

"Before we continue, you got anything to drink in here?"

I gestured toward the not-so-mini-fridge. "Help yourself."

He walked over to the small kitchen area and set about making himself a drink. "Do you want one?"

"No, thanks," I replied and got up to retrieve the complimentary bottle of wine the hotel sent up the day after I checked in.

"You're not going to share?" he teased.

"I would've until you said that," I retorted and stuck out my tongue.

When we settled back into our seats, he gestured for me to get on with it. However, there was only one thing I wanted to ask about. "Where are their mothers?"

"Heidi's mother lives in town, but they haven't been on speaking terms for years. And Paige's mom died years ago."

"Damn it. I was hoping Paige's mom might be a possible lead."

"I hate to break it to you, but unless you know something I don't, I doubt you're going to find any new leads."

Oh, like the part about one of the girls being my half

sister. Nope, I was honoring my mother's request and keeping her suspicions to myself until I had proof. Even without that piece of information, there had to be something new to learn, at least for me. "You're probably right, but will you write down the names and addresses you have? I'm not going to do it tonight, but I want to do a few more searches. I get that you've already done it, but all of this is new for me, and I want to see the search results for myself."

"No need to explain. I'd be the same way," he assured. "You got a piece of paper or something I can write on?"

I gestured to the multiple notebooks scattered around the room. "Pick one. Any one. Don't judge me. I'm an author. This is totally normal behavior."

"I'm sure it is." With that, he wrote down the information he had and handed the notebook to me. I quickly glanced at the paper and recognized one address as Adelaide's, but the other was a new one for me to check out.

"Whose address is this?" I asked.

"That's the rental house where Heidi and Paige used to live. You wanted what information I had, but I can tell you not to waste your time. The house is basically empty."

"Basically?"

He shrugged. "There were still a few boxes in one of the rooms the last time I went over there."

"Did you go through them?"

"Not really. I looked inside one or two. They were full of books, so I assumed the others were too. I can't think of anything in them that would be helpful to you."

"Oh, well, I'll just have to look elsewhere," I said and refused to let his words discourage me.

8

BRONZE

I finished my drink and placed my glass down with a notable clink. "Help yourself to another if you'd like," Sloane offered.

"You sure?" I asked. Normally, I wouldn't have even considered it, solely because the price of mini-fridge liquor was outrageous, but after the conversation we'd just had, I wanted another.

"Of course. You comped how many of my drinks at the bar last night? Plus food. I'm sure those two drinks cost far less than all that."

I knew there was no point in arguing with her. Instead, I made my drink, knowing I would stop by the front desk on my way out and put some cash toward her bill. With any luck, she wouldn't notice until after she was long gone.

Disappointment unexpectedly washed over me at the thought of her leaving. "How long are you planning on being in town?"

She shrugged. "I don't know. It depends on how long it takes me to find Heidi. I'll figure out the rest from there."

"Sloane," I said slowly. "Don't get your hopes up. I've

been trying to find Heidi for months with no luck." She was clearly excited to have new information at her fingertips and chomping at the bit to start sorting through it. I started to tell her Spazz already searched every avenue I had, but just like with the phone number, I knew she would want to see it for herself. And who knew? The chances were slim, but maybe she'd get lucky and find something we hadn't.

I sat back and enjoyed watching her squirm in her seat for several minutes before she finally came to a decision. "I'm sorry. I know this is incredibly rude of me, but she's the reason I'm here. I can't wait until tomorrow to start on this."

I chuckled. "I knew that was coming." Picking up my glass, I emptied the contents and got to my feet. "I'll leave you to it."

Her head shot up. "What? No. You don't need to leave. I'll only be a few minutes, but I have to at least peek at a few things. Plus, you'll be here if I have any questions."

I snorted. "I've been down that road. Trust me; you'll be more than a few minutes."

She waved her hand dismissively. "I won't, but help yourself to another drink while you're waiting."

After spending my day at a bookstore in an itchy pink dress on a few hours of sleep, I decided I was going to make myself comfortable. I started by making another drink and kicking off my boots. "Will it bother you if I turn the TV on?"

"No, as long as it's not a show with excessive violence, obnoxious screaming, music with lyrics, or basketball."

"That's specific," I laughed.

"To be successful, it's beneficial to know what things are distracting and remove them," she said. "Those are my things."

"I've never heard that before."

She looked up from her computer screen and grinned. "That's because I just made it up."

"You should put it in a book."

I left her to her searching and found a survival reality show marathon to watch. Because I was sure enough to bet my bike that she wouldn't come up for air for at least two hours.

RING. RING. RING.

I reached over to smack my phone but hit empty air. After a few more blind attempts, I grumbled as I sat up and opened my eyes. For a brief moment, I didn't know where I was. Then, it all came back to me. I was in Sloane's hotel room and must've fallen asleep.

Ring. Ring. Ring.

My phone. Quickly getting up, I stumbled around the room and finally found it on the coffee table next to Sloane's computer.

"Yeah," I answered, not bothering to look to see who was calling.

"Hey, man. You coming to spar today?" Savior asked.

"Fuck," I groaned as I realized how late it was. "Yeah. I'll be there in a few," I said and ended the call.

"Did I make you late for something again?" Sloane asked sleepily from the bed.

"Yes, but I preferred the way you did it yesterday," I teased.

"Sorry," she yawned. "I must've fallen asleep while searching. I guess you were right."

I laughed. "I wish I had time to gloat about that, but I gotta run meet Savior at the gym."

"What time is it?" she asked and rubbed her face.

"A little before one."

"In the afternoon?" she shrieked and jumped out of bed.

"Yes. Got somewhere to be?" I teased while putting my boots on.

"How little is little? I have a video conference at one, and I don't even have a bra on!"

"You don't have pants on either," I pointed out.

"The navel up is all that's important for video meetings," she stated like it was common knowledge.

"As long as you stay seated."

"Touché," she replied from inside the bathroom. I hoped she wouldn't be long, because I didn't have the time to wait for her. Surprisingly, she emerged less than a minute later and launched herself into my arms. With her legs wrapped around my waist, she captured my lips and kissed me with an intensity I wasn't expecting.

Breaking the kiss, she jumped out of my arms before I was ready to release her. "Chop. Chop. We both have places to be and things to do."

"Speaking of, I have to work until nine tonight."

"Okay, what're you doing when you get off?"

"I better be doing y—fuck!" I cursed. "It's my weekend at the clubhouse; I've gotta be there from eleven to seven tonight and tomorrow night." I paused and looked to ceiling while I tried to remember what I had scheduled after that. "Pretty sure I work the morning shift the next day, but after three o'clock, I'll have a few days off," I said suggestively.

She stopped running around long enough to face me and ask, "Is that so?"

"It is what it is, Sweet Sloane."

"Okay, so come by when you get off work."

"You're still going to be in town two days from now?"

She shrugged. "I should be. Even if I found Heidi an hour from now, I'd still have several days of work to do before I can head out."

"Well then, I'll see you soon, Sweet Sloane." With that, I pulled her to me and devoured her mouth one more time before I left.

9

BRONZE

Rolling over, I stretched and yawned before I opened my eyes. Judging by the lack of light filling my room, I knew it was far too early to be awake, but I didn't want to look at my phone and know for sure.

Closing my eyes again, I settled back into the bed to go back to sleep until my alarm went off for work when the sound of someone lightly knocking on my door filled my ears. "What?" I barked and started to get pissed when no one answered me.

Throwing off the covers, I stormed toward the door and yanked it open, ready to lay into whoever was determined to keep me from sleeping. But no one was there. Then, I heard it again.

Realizing the sound was coming from the front door, I pulled on a pair of jeans and grabbed my gun from the nightstand. No one should've been knocking on the front door to the clubhouse because they shouldn't have made it past the gate.

I didn't bother checking the security feed to see who it

was. Trouble didn't usually knock. To my surprise, I pulled the door open to find a furious middle-aged woman I didn't recognize. She glanced at what looked like a picture in her hand and back to me. Before I could open my mouth, she nodded and shoved something into my arms.

"Your demon spawn killed my daughter and ruined everything! You keep that thing away from me!" With that, she turned and quickly walked toward her car, which obviously plowed through the gate we recently had repaired.

I looked down at the squirming, and now screaming, baby in my arms.

"Hey!" I yelled and started after her. "Hey! Crazy lady, wait! What the fuck?"

She whirled around and aimed a pistol directly at me. In the most eerily calm voice, she said, "I have just lost my child. I will kill you and yours if you take one more step."

"I won't. Just go," I vowed and prayed she would leave as I cradled the screaming infant against my bare chest.

She waited for several long seconds with her gun trained on me before she finally got into her vehicle and drove away. All the while, I stood stock-still with absolutely no idea what to do. I was a grown-ass man and had been in plenty of unthinkable situations—ones that many men wouldn't have been able to face. But the possibility of being the father of the child in my arms was the breaking point where my brain and body no longer functioned properly.

And that's how my older brother found me. Standing in the forecourt holding a crying baby with a look of utter shock mixed with complete panic on my face.

"The fuck is going on?" Copper barked, though I could hear the worry in his voice. "Whose baby is that?"

"I-I don't know," I stammered. "She said it's mine! I opened the door, and she shoved the baby into my arms. I tried to stop her, but she pointed a gun at me. What the fuck am I supposed to do, Copper?" I asked, hoping my older brother would know how to handle the situation.

"Wait. She who?"

"I don't know. Some woman I didn't recognize," I said shakily.

Copper's hand landed on my shoulder. "Let's go inside and get this shit sorted."

I dazedly followed him into the clubhouse with the crying baby still in my arms, unsure of where to go or what to do. "Sit down and tell me exactly what happened."

I relayed the events of the morning the best I could with the baby wailing the entire time. Just as I finished, Layla came running through the front door with a phone pressed to her ear. Her eyes landed on the baby, and she gasped. "Oh, it's a fresh one," she almost whispered. "Like newborn *newborn*."

"Who the fuck are you talking to?" I demanded.

Copper tagged the side of my head with his fist. "Don't disrespect my woman, especially when she's trying to help you. She's talking to Leigh, who's at the store getting baby shit."

I blinked at my brother. "How? When?"

"Fuck," Copper swore. "You can go into shock later, but I need you to function right now," he demanded and met my eyes. "Who's the baby's mother?"

"I don't know," I confessed and tried to think back. "I've never seen the woman who brought the baby."

"Well, start thinking, bonehead. Who were you fucking eight to ten months ago?" Copper asked.

Layla took that as her opportunity. "Can I?" she asked

and held out her hands. I didn't miss the way her fingers lightly danced with delight, but something happened in that moment. Some deep-seated natural desire to protect the innocent child in my arms from any potential harm sparked to life inside me. I hesitated. Layla smiled knowingly. "I won't leave your sight."

"I'm sorry. I-I don't—I didn't—"

"It's okay," she soothed. "You don't have to explain anything to me."

Reluctantly, I handed the baby over to her. She immediately began gently rocking the bundle while she softly cooed. Soon, the cries quieted to little whimpers. "Is it a boy or a girl?"

My eyes widened, and I jumped to my feet. "I don't even know what kind of kid I have! What kind of parent does that make me?"

"The kind that just found out," Leigh said as she entered the common room with bags and bags of baby stuff. She pulled out a pack of diapers first. "Bring the baby over here. We'll find out while I teach you how to properly change a diaper."

Layla handed the baby back to me, and I approached Leigh as if she were holding a ticking time bomb instead of a tiny diaper. Leigh shook out a folded pad and placed it on top of one of the tables. Then, she carefully put the baby on the pad and unwrapped the blankets.

"What in the hell is that?" I shouted. "Its insides are coming out of its stomach! We need to go to the hospital!"

Leigh started chuckling. "That's the umbilical cord," she explained. "It turns black and falls off within a week or two."

"You ever seen this shit before?" I asked my brother.

He shook his head. "Nope. Knew what it was though."

"Sure you did," I grumbled.

Leigh was still studying the umbilical cord with a look of concern etched on her face. "Something wrong?" I asked and wanted to laugh because I should have asked if something *else* was wrong.

Leigh silently reached for the tiny hat covering the baby's head and gently lifted it, gasping when the baby's clearly unwashed head came into view. "Bronze," she said slowly, cautiously. "You were right. We need to go to the hospital." She paused. "Right now."

"What? Why?" I shouted, failing to quell the internal panic building inside of me.

"Because this baby is very, *very* new. Maybe only a few hours old."

"Okay, okay. I'm following your lead. How do we get it there?"

Leigh turned to Copper. "There's a baby carrier and car seat base in my trunk. Will you get it and install it in whichever vehicle y'all are going to take while I help Bronze get the baby ready to go?"

"Why do you have that?" I asked.

She huffed. "I bought it on sale a few months ago because I liked that pattern, and I knew one of you were bound to need it sooner or later."

"Or you were saving it for when Judge and River have one," Copper said knowingly as he picked up her keys from the pool table where she dropped them with the bags she was carrying.

"All right, let's see what we've got here," Leigh announced and started to unfasten the diaper. My world froze. Because a part of me already believed that the baby squirming on the pool table was mine. And I wasn't ready. I wasn't ready to know if I had a son or daughter. I wasn't ready for any of it.

Closing my eyes, I heard her gasp and waited for the words I knew would forever change my life.

"It's a girl."

When I opened my eyes, blue-gray ones that mirrored my own were staring back at me. With one look, she stole my heart and replaced it with her soul. Reaching out, I ran my fingers over her tiny cheek. "You sure are a beautiful little girl," I murmured.

She closed her eyes and clenched her hands into fists as she let out a hellacious wail and proceeded to pee all over me, Leigh, and the pool table.

"How is she doing that?" I blurted as I watched the tiny little baby continue to anoint the common room with an impressive arc of piss.

"Where is it coming from?" I asked and genuinely wanted to know because there was no way a baby her size could piss that much. Nope. Wasn't possible.

"Quit gawking and get some damn towels!" Leigh snapped.

"On it." I turned and rushed down the hall to whichever bathroom I came to first.

When I returned, Leigh wrapped the baby in a towel and held her out to me. "What? No," I said and waved my hands in front of me.

"You can take the baby in the clean towel or wipe up all the piss. What's it going to be?" Leigh demanded.

I nodded and reached for the squirming bundle. Her cries had tapered down to little whimpers, and I briefly wondered if she might be cold. Before I could say or do anything about it, Leigh was reaching for her again.

"Did you wash your hands?"

"Of course, I did," she huffed.

I laughed and handed her the baby. "I know, but after

all the times you've said it to us, I've always wanted to have a chance to say it back to you."

"I don't even want to know what else you've been waiting for a chance to say."

"Good, because I won't tell you and ruin the surprise."

"All finished," she declared and handed me a fully dressed baby. "I'll show you how to do everything next time. We really do need to go."

Right on cue, Copper came back inside to tell us the car seat was installed and ready when we were. "The truck's running. I just need to grab my ph—What the fuck happened to my phone?"

I looked over and saw his phone lying in a puddle of piss. "Sorry, Uncle Copper. I got too excited and made a little wee on your phone," I said in the best baby girl voice I could manage.

"For fuck's sake," he cursed and curled his lip in disgust. His eyes flicked to another spot on the table, and a smile suddenly appeared on his face. "She got yours too, Baby Brother."

"Fucking hell," I grumbled.

Changing his tone, he added, "Should probably hold off on the Uncle Copper shit until a paternity test proves that's your child. Just because some crazy-ass woman showed up at the clubhouse and put a baby in your arms saying she's yours doesn't mean she is. You feel me?"

I nodded in agreement. He was right, very much so. I was getting way ahead of myself. But, it was hard not to because I could see my features in her tiny face.

However, Copper's words triggered the logical side of my brain, and I realized something else might be going on. For all we knew, someone could be using the baby as a distraction or as a way to pin something on the club. "Shit! We can't leave the clubhouse unattended."

"I've already called Grant and Coal to come in. Leigh's going to wait for them and meet us at the hospital once they arrive," Copper explained.

"I don't think that's a good idea. If this is some kind of setup, I'd rather the clubhouse be completely empty than have Leigh here alone like a sitting duck."

"It's a moot point now," Copper said at the sound of two motorcycles pulling into the forecourt. "They're here. Let's go."

When I got to the truck, Layla showed me how to fasten the car seat straps and told me I had to ride in the back with the baby. At my look of panic, Layla climbed into the seat on the other side and rode in the back with us.

"Where are we supposed to take her?" I asked.

"We're meeting River at the hospital, and we'll go from there," Copper said.

River was waiting for us just inside the sliding glass doors that led to the ER. "Come on back. I've already got you registered and checked in."

I carried the little bundle, who had been screaming since the moment Copper turned off the truck's ignition, to the exam room and placed her in the plastic baby bed as River instructed.

River reached for the baby and started to undress her as she continued to wail. "Aw, it sounds like somebody's hungry," River cooed and pulled something out of a drawer with one hand while she continued to examine the unhappy infant. After placing a few items on the small table attached to the baby bed, she looked up at me. "Go wash your hands."

I heard Leigh stifle a laugh as I did what River said and returned to her side when I was finished. River handed me a tiny baby bottle. It was so small I would've thought it belonged to a doll. "It's time to eat, hungry girl."

"River," I said low enough for only her to hear. "The only thing I know about babies is how to make them. And that this one right here can soak a pool table in piss in less than a minute."

"Sorry," she mouthed, then spoke louder. "Bronze, let's have you sit in this chair right here, and I'll hand you—uh, does she have a name yet?"

"No, but let's call her Blue for the time being. I don't want to keep referring to her as the baby, and since she hasn't been confirmed as my biological child, I don't think I should call her my daughter just yet. So, Blue it is."

"Cute," River smiled. "Did you choose that because of her eyes?"

I snorted. "No, she's wrapped in a blue blanket, and it was the first thing that came to me. But I'm going to say it was because of her eyes if anyone else asks."

"Okay, so I'm going to hand you Blue like this, and once you're both comfortable, you're going to touch her lip with the nipple of the bottle to let her know it's there."

"Then what?" I asked, hoping I hid the trepidation in my voice.

River laughed. "Chances are she'll do the rest of the work. If not, I'll be here to help."

With those vague words of reassurance, I touched the tip of the bottle to Blue's lip and watched in amazement as her head turned toward the nipple, and her lips started moving as if she was trying to find what touched her with her mouth.

"That's called rooting. It means she's looking for her food source, because she's ready to eat. Go ahead and put the nipple in her mouth. She's probably so pissed off right now she'll latch on like a champ."

That's exactly what she did, emptying the small bottle

of formula in what had to be record time. "How do I know if she's still hungry?"

"You'll know because she'll continue to look for a food source, and she'll start to cry when she doesn't find one. I've got a handout that goes over what each type of cry sounds like and means. I can't stress to you how much easier your life will be if you take twenty or thirty minutes to commit everything on that piece of paper to memory. Also, I have a magnet you can stick on your refrigerator that tells you how much to feed her and how often." River cleared her throat and shifted her weight. "You're aware that the hospital is obligated to notify the police about this situation, right?"

"I've already notified them," Copper interjected. I glanced at him in surprise, and he answered my question before I could ask it. "Right after Blue pissed all over my phone. I had to use Layla's. You owe me a new cell phone, by the way."

"Knock, knock," a woman called out as she entered the room.

"Oh, Dr. Daniels, we're so glad to see you," Leigh said sincerely.

"I certainly wish it was under better circumstances," she said while washing her hands. "Now, let's have a look here." With gentle movements, she carefully examined Blue, taking a close look at her umbilical cord. She put a tiny stethoscope to her chest and listened, then did the same to her back.

"I'm probably about to make her mad. I'd like to apologize for that now," Dr. Daniels said and did something with Blue's legs that caused her to let out an angry wail. "Just checking to make sure her lower joints are intact and stable. Some babies are born with their hips dislocated or very loosely in place."

She continued to examine Blue, who was still fussing but not exactly crying. My eyes remained trained on Dr. Daniels, watching every move she made. It didn't matter if Blue was or was not my daughter; I silently declared myself her guardian and protector until that position was proven to be mine or the person it rightfully belonged to was found.

When she was finished, she carefully wrapped Blue in a blanket the same way Leigh had. Seeing how it seemed to instantly comfort Blue, I said, "I'm going to need one of y'all to show me how to do that magic blanket thing."

Every woman in the room laughed. "That's called swaddling, and I'll show you how to do it when things settle down unless an opportunity presents itself before then," Leigh said.

Dr. Daniels cleared her throat to get everyone's attention. "First, Baby Black appears to be a healthy baby girl. After examining her, I estimate her age to be between six and twelve hours old. It does appear that she was cared for by someone with at least a little bit of medical knowledge and access to medical supplies, judging by the way her umbilical cord was cut and clamped. However, due to her age alone, she'll be admitted to the hospital for at least twenty-four hours, if not longer. Under the circumstances, we're going to assign Baby Black a bed in the newborn nursery, but we're also going to reserve a room on the Mom and Baby unit for you—and the mother should she be located. That way, Blue can stay in the room with you as much as you want. If you need to take a shower or get a few hours of sleep, you can ask your nurse to take her to the nursery," she explained.

"My nurse?" I asked.

She chuckled. "The nurse assigned to Blue. Typically, mom and baby have the same nurse, unless the baby goes to the nursery. I'm going to go put in her admission orders now, and then it'll probably take fifteen or twenty minutes before you can be moved to your new room. In the meantime, there are some officers here who would like to speak with you."

With that, she exited the room, and two familiar faces stepped inside. "Hello, everyone. I'm going to skip the formalities and get right to it," Officer Dunk said. "Copper gave us a brief explanation over the phone, but we'd like to hear it from you."

Blue looked like she was trying to squirm around even though she was securely swaddled in a blanket. Instinctively, I scooped her into my arms and held her against my chest, successfully settling her for the first time. Then, I cleared my throat and relayed the events of the morning to the officers.

"And you don't know who the mother is?" Officer Underwood clarified.

"The only person it could be is Heidi Coleman, but her mother isn't the woman who brought the baby to the clubhouse."

"Heidi Coleman? Why does that name sound familiar?"

"She was a waitress at Precious Metals, but she was also injured when the clubhouse was bombed."

Dunk snapped her fingers. "I bet that's it. I probably recognize the name from the police reports."

"Did you know she was pregnant?" Underwood asked in a way that didn't sound like an accusation.

But I exploded anyway. "No, I didn't fucking know!" I roared, causing Blue to stir in my arms and let out a quiet whimper.

Placing his hand on my shoulder, Copper squeezed, silently telling me to get a handle on myself.

"I apologize," Underwood said. "I should've worded that differently. I just wanted to confirm that you did not know about the pregnancy at the time she disappeared."

"Not one fucking clue until this morning," I said honestly.

"Might be the reason both of them took off in the first place," Copper pointed out.

"No," I said vehemently. "There has to be another reason. Heidi would've told me if she was pregnant with my baby."

"You sure about that?"

"All right, we have a few more questions, and then we'll call this into the chief and get the ball rolling. We'll likely need to obtain a copy of the surveillance footage from this morning, but this isn't the official request," Dunk said and shot Copper a pointed look.

He reached for his phone, cursed, and took Layla's phone from her outstretched hand. "I'll call Judge right now and have him email the footage to you."

"Thanks," Underwood said and rattled off a few more questions, followed by a promise to be in contact soon.

Before they left, I stopped them to make one request. "I would like to keep this out of the media if possible." I nodded in Blue's direction. "Whatever her story turns out to be, she doesn't need to find out about it from news articles and reports."

Both officers nodded and smiled kindly. "We'll do everything we can to keep this as quiet as possible."

I had barely taken a full breath after they left when the door opened again, and River entered the room. "Let's get you two moved upstairs and settled into your new home for the next day or two."

From the moment we arrived in our hospital room on the Mom and Baby unit, there was a seemingly endless stream of people coming and going—starting with Phoenix and Uncle Tommy walking into the room.

"Of all the calls I expected to get, *this* was not one of them," Phoenix said as he crossed the room and engulfed me in a hug. "You hanging in there?"

"Don't really have much of a choice. It's the only thing I can do," I said honestly. "I can't say I'm surprised to see you, but I didn't know you were coming. Did Shaker bring you?"

"He did," Phoenix nodded and smiled warmly. "He had to get back to Keegan, but he wanted me to let you know that he's there if you need him; the whole club is. You know I'll always be here for my family. And since Pop and Gram happened to be in Croftridge visiting, Pop wanted to come with me in case he could be of any help."

"I can give you all the legal advice you'll ever need over the phone, but trust me on this, you get much better results when you call in favors in person. And there are quite a few people in this town who owe me a favor or two," Uncle Tommy added as he shook my hand and pulled me in for a hug. It didn't matter if the entirety of both clubs called him Pop, he would always be Uncle Tommy to me.

"Appreciate it. Means the world to me that you two are here," I said.

"We're happy to help. Though your Aunt Dolores wasn't too thrilled about not being able to come meet the alleged newest addition to the Black family with us," Uncle Tommy said with a chuckle. "I wouldn't be expecting any special Christmas cookies from her this year."

I grinned. "Oh, I'm already planning on using all of Blue's cuteness to get cookies every chance I can."

Uncle Tommy laughed, "Based on those cute little cheeks alone, I'd say that's a good plan."

"What do you think I should do first?" I asked.

"You need to get a court-ordered paternity test as soon as possible. A friend of mine, Judge Hinkley, will be in his chambers in about an hour. If you'd like, I can stop by and get that order for you. Also, I think we should talk to him about granting you emergency guardianship until the paternity results come back or the mother is located. On that note, have a couple of the Old Ladies on standby to get the clubhouse ready to bring a baby home if Hinkley gives you custody. There's no doubt that social services will be involved in this case."

He paused for a moment and held my gaze. "Now, I personally don't give a shit, but it's not my opinion that matters. The state considers recreational marijuana use illegal, and it's better that I know now if passing a drug test is going to be an issue for you."

I snorted. "You could've just asked me if I smoked weed."

"I don't care if you smoke it, eat it, or vape it. What I want to know is if you can pass a drug test," he snapped.

"Yes, I can. Piss, blood, or hair," I said proudly.

Uncle Tommy grinned and clapped his hands together. "That's what I wanted to hear! All right, you stay here and keep doing what you're doing while Phoenix and I go see Judge Hinkley. You want us to pick you up some lunch while we're out?"

"Yeah, that probably wouldn't be a bad idea," I said. "Any kind of sandwich or burger from wherever you go will be fine. And a cookie." I typically wasn't a picky eater, but I wasn't concerned with what they brought me back for lunch because I wasn't sure I could eat anything. The knots that had been in my stomach since Blue was placed in my arms continued to tighten as the hours passed.

Hundreds of various outcomes played through my mind, from Heidi and I sharing custody of our daughter, to Blue being given to her real set of parents—which was neither me nor Heidi. But the one that I kept going back to was me raising Blue as a single father. What was Sloane going to think?

Fuck! I needed to call Sloane and tell her what was going on. Reaching for my phone, I stifled a curse when I remembered it didn't work. Copper said he'd bring me one of the burners from the clubhouse to use when he came back by the hospital, so it'd have to wait until later.

My thoughts were interrupted when two nurses entered the room to collect cheek swabs from me and Blue for the paternity test. I didn't doubt that Uncle Tommy would be able to get the order for the test, but I was surprised at how fast it was executed. And I hoped he was having as much luck with the order for guardianship.

By the time Phoenix and Uncle Tommy returned, my hopes for good news had significantly dwindled, but I tried to stay positive. With a somewhat forced smile on my face, I said, "I already know you got the order for the paternity test. They came by to collect our samples over two hours ago. Thank you, Uncle Tommy."

"You're welcome. Sorry it took us so long to get back with your food. You're probably starving by now," he said and handed me a paper bag and a drink.

"I appreciate it," I said and placed the bag to the side. "But I don't feel like I could eat anything right now."

Phoenix snorted. "Yeah, I know exactly what you're talking about. The part that's making you want to puke will go away once you get the results. Well, it did for me. But then again, I got the results I was hoping for."

I shrugged. "I can honestly say I don't know what result I'm hoping for. I haven't really had much time to think about that part." Not expecting a response, I turned my attention to Uncle Tommy. "What about the order for guardianship?"

When he took a seat and clasped his hands together in his lap, I knew he was not going to deliver the news I wanted to hear. "It's not what we were hoping for, but hear me out before assuming it's bad news. Judge Hinkley didn't grant you emergency guardianship because the baby will still be in the hospital when the test results are received, which will be tomorrow morning. He said it would be much easier to ensure you had custody if the test is a positive match than it would be to revoke any custody you were granted if the test isn't a match, and I have to agree with him on that. In the meantime, he didn't put any restrictions on her visitation. In other words, we're going to keep this quiet, and you can continue to stay in the room with Blue and interact with her as you have been."

I nodded. "Yeah, I guess that makes sense. Will the test results really be back tomorrow morning?" I asked. I wasn't aware they could be done that fast.

"Yes, they will. The testing process is much faster than it used to be, and now results can be delivered electronically, which is helpful in emergent situations like this one." Uncle Tommy studied me for a few moments and smiled. "It'd make things a whole lot easier if gut feelings were admissible in court, wouldn't it?"

I rubbed my hand over my face and let out a combination of a laugh and an exasperated sigh. "Is it that obvious?"

"It is to me, but I've seen the look on a man's face after he loses his heart to his daughter many different times in my life, and this is exactly what it looks like."

"She looks like both of us," I murmured. "She has my eyes and mouth, but her nose, chin, and ears definitely belong to her mother." Blue's features were the perfect combination of mine and Heidi's. And it wasn't wishful thinking. I had no doubt she was mine. And I also knew she would break hearts when she got older—specifically mine.

"I hope like hell she is yours," Copper grumbled. "Because you're already in way too deep to simply let her go if she's not."

"There's nothing wrong with caring about someone," I argued. But I knew my feelings for Blue had rapidly developed and sailed past caring within the first hour of her being in my life.

"If it hurts you more than it helps them, it's wrong," he said, using a phrase our mother used to say when we were younger, and some of the older boys we played with were too rough. Instead of telling us how to respond or handle it for us, she let us make our own decisions with only that bit of wisdom as guidance.

"It won't," I vowed and silently hoped I wasn't wrong.

Before I knew it, night had fallen and the steady stream of people in and out of our room had dwindled down to only me, Blue, and Copper after we said our goodbyes to Uncle Tommy and Phoenix.

"I'm going to head out too," he started. "Unless you want me to stay."

"There's no reason for you to stay. I'm not good company right now, and I'm probably going to just sleep anyway."

Copper shook his head. "You haven't been around many babies, have you?"

"A couple. Why?"

He chuckled. "No reason."

Ignoring whatever he was trying to rag me about, I snapped my fingers when I remembered to ask, "Did you bring one of the burners?"

"Shit. Yeah, it's right here." Reaching into his cut, he pulled out two and handed one to me. "Check the missed calls. The last one should be the number to this phone, which I'll be using until our new phones arrive, which should be by nine o'clock tomorrow night."

"Damn it. I need a phone number that's saved in my phone."

"Whose is it? I'll ask Spazz to get it for you."

"Sloane," I started and realized I didn't have a clue what her last name was. "Fuck, I don't know her last name. I met her at the bar a couple of nights ago."

"Why in the hell are you worried about some bitch you just met? You really think she's gonna want to play second fiddle to a newborn baby, especially one you don't know for sure that's yours?"

"Well, no probably not, now that you mention it, but that's not the only reason I need her number. She's in Devil Springs looking for Heidi, and I wanted to let her know we may have found her."

"Bronze," Copper said slowly, placatingly. "I know you've been put through hell today, and there's more waiting for you tomorrow, but have you lost your damn mind? Some girl shows up looking for Heidi, who's been gone for months, two days before her alleged daughter was shoved into your arms. Fuck, no, you're not telling her shit."

"What? No, she wasn't like that. She's writing a book and wanted to interview Heidi to help her write the character correctly."

The more I tried to explain Sloane's innocence, the more I saw it from his point of view. "Okay, I get it. It does seem a bit too coincidental when you lay it all out like that. But on the off chance that she's telling the truth, can you swing by The Winchester and let her know I'll be tied up with something for a few days?" It was obvious he didn't want to, so I took it a step further to ensure he would. "And if it turns out she was lying and had something to do with all of this, telling her I'll be busy might keep her in town for a little longer."

"Glad to see a maybe baby hasn't affected your self-esteem." With that, he tagged me on the shoulder. "Get some rest, Bro. Tomorrow's gonna be a big day."

10

BRONZE

I was sitting in the recliner with Blue, who was sound asleep in my arms after finishing her bottle, when there was a knock at the door. Before I could get to my feet, Copper entered the room, followed by Judge and Batta.

"What're y'all doing here?" I whispered and got up to place Blue in the tiny plastic box the hospital staff referred to as an open crib.

"You're getting the paternity test results this morning," Copper murmured simply, as if no further explanation was needed. And it wasn't. Honestly, I was expecting Copper to be there when I received the results, and I should've been expecting Judge and Batta. The four of us had been by each other's sides since we were able to stand on two feet, literally.

Judge handed me a coffee as he entered the room. "Thanks, man," I said quietly and clapped him on the shoulder.

"If you don't give him the other thing, I'm telling," Batta whisper-yelled across the room from beside Blue's crib—where he was smiling down at her like the big teddy bear he was.

Judge huffed and held out the brown paper bag he was attempting to hide behind his back. "Mom sent these."

I snatched the bag from him, and damn near burned my hand when I spilled my coffee trying to tear into the bag. The sweet smell of my favorite cookies filled my nose as soon as the bag opened, and I groaned loudly in delight, completely forgetting about the sleeping baby a few feet away.

"Shit," I hissed and shoved an entire cookie into my mouth. "Mmm! Oh, sweet mother of all that is holy. They're warm!" I groaned once again.

Blue made a noise that could only be described as a cross between a snort and a snore before she let out a mighty wail, letting our room and everyone around us know she was pissed the hell off about being woken up.

Batta jumped back with his hands in the air. "I didn't touch it!"

I glared at him and held a finger over my lips. "Shh! It's your voice, not your hands," I explained, keeping my tone low as I scooped Blue into my arms and tried to soothe her back to sleep.

Batta's forehead wrinkled as he quietly pretended to be confused. "But chicks love my voice."

"Not this one," I murmured flatly.

"We'll see about that," he muttered and crossed his arms over his chest—just like he did when he pouted as a child.

The sound of a knock had the four of us turning toward the door. A man dressed in scrubs and a white coat stepped inside. "Good morning," he said, thankfully keeping his voice low. "I'm Dr. Long, and I have some test results to go over with you. Would you like to step into the hallway for some privacy?"

"No," I said and slowly got to my feet, careful not to jostle Blue and wake her again. Placing her in the bassinet, I held my breath for a few seconds after I laid her down and hoped she stayed asleep. After a few beats of silence, I turned around and faced the doctor. "They're my family. It's fine for them to hear the results."

He nodded curtly and looked at the tablet in his hand. "Bronze Black's sample and Blue Black's sample resulted in a 99.99% probability of paternity. Here is a sealed and certified copy for you to keep. I've already arranged for a courier to deliver a sealed and certified copy to your lawyer's office, as well as the copy responding to the judge's order, first thing this morning."

I wasn't hit with a flood of emotions like I expected. I remained calm and thanked him, extending my hand by muscle memory. Once he was gone, I inhaled deeply and turned around to face my brothers. I was fine. I smiled at Copper reassuringly, and everything went black.

"If you don't stop shining that damn light in my eyes, I'm going to call Judge to come whoop your ass," I grumbled.

"He's awake!" River shouted.

"Shut the fuck up!" I groaned and slapped my hands over my head, immediately stiffening when they didn't land on my hair. "Why does it feel like there are bandages on my head?" I asked, failing to hide the rising panic in my voice. Because the last time I had bandages on my head, I'd had brain surgery after someone tried to blow up our clubhouse with me and several others inside.

"Because you passed out, and the studs on Batta's bracelet split your head open when he caught you," River explained.

I glanced around the room. "Why isn't anyone here?"

"Copper and Judge stayed upstairs with Blue, and Batta went to the bathroom to wash your blood off his arms."

I cocked my head to the side. "Who's Blue?"

River blinked at me before her face paled, and she kicked the door open. "Dr. Alvarez! Room Four. Stat!" she shouted into the hallway.

"Damn it, River. I was just fucking with you," I chuckled and held up a pillow to defend myself from her swats.

She glared at me for a brief moment before she went back to the door. "Cancel that, Dr. Alvarez. False alarm," she called out, not bothering to hide the displeasure in her voice.

I cleared my throat. "So how bad is it?"

"Three staples about two inches above your left ear," she snapped.

"Oh come on, River. I deserved to have a little bit of fun, didn't I?" I said, putting on my best "forgive me" face.

She looked at me pointedly. "You will not succeed in manipulating me with your big, blue eyes or that fake little lip quiver you pull when you're trying to get cookies. But you just wait, it won't be long before you'll know what it feels like to think something is seriously wrong with someone you care about."

Fuck. She made me feel like an ass. "River, I didn't mean to upset you."

She smiled, but something was off about it. "It's okay. Let me check your wound. If everything looks good, we'll see about getting you back upstairs to your girl."

A few minutes later, a man came to the door with a wheelchair. "Mr. Black, I'm here to take you down to ultrasound."

"Why?" I asked and sat up to face the man.

He shrugged. "You'd have to ask your nurse or doctor. I just respond to the transport requests they send me."

"Then that's what I'll do," I said and pressed the call button.

River appeared moments later with a bright smile on her face. "Did you need something?"

"Why is he here?" I pointed to the transport guy.

"When Copper checked you in, he signed the consent form allowing us to order any tests deemed medically necessary. After reviewing your chart, I noticed you were behind on your preventative healthcare, so I took the liberty of ordering a prostate ultrasound for you."

"No one is sticking anything in my ass today or ever!" I roared and clutched the side of my head with one hand. "Now, my head's starting to hurt again, but I'll forgive you for five cookies."

WHEN I RETURNED TO BLUE'S ROOM OVER AN HOUR LATER —while being pushed in a wheelchair against my will—I found her sound asleep in her plastic box while Copper sat stationed by her side. He got to his feet and let me take his seat. "That didn't take as long as I thought. You doing okay?" he asked quietly.

"My head fucking hurts," I grumbled and pointed to Judge. "And your woman tried to make me have a prostate ultrasound. Do you know how those are done? They stick a condom-covered wand up your ass to have a little look-see," I whisper-shouted and stabbed my finger in her direction. "She needs to be punished!"

Judge slapped a hand over his mouth and doubled over laughing like I knew he would. He loved that woman more than the air he breathed, and there was nothing she could do to dim the light that shone for her in his eyes.

"Gotta go. Take care, Mr. Black," River blurted and ran away like her ass was on fire. Judge darted for the hallway, barely making it a few doors down before he erupted into guffaws that echoed off the bare walls.

When he finished laughing, Judge returned long enough to stick his head in the door to tell me he was heading to work. "Unless you need me to stay. Just say the word."

"Thanks, man. I'm good. Appreciate you being here this morning," I whispered and got up to shake his hand.

"I'm going to head out too. There's no way I can be this quiet all fucking day. But I'm here if you need me," Batta added.

"How come women can speak normally, but men have to whisper?" Copper asked.

I shrugged and dropped into the recliner that'd been my home for a few hours shy of twenty-four. "Don't know, and we're not going to try to find out right now. The doctor said to let her sleep when she wants to sleep. Besides, we need to get the brothers together and start looking for Heidi. We've given the police enough time without intervening. She can't be too far away if she gave birth to our daughter yesterday morning."

Copper opened his mouth to respond when there were three sharp knocks on the door, letting everyone in the room know at least one police officer was on the other side.

"Come in," I called out, happy to see Dunk and

Underwood enter the room. I wasn't anticipating good news, and I preferred to hear it from them rather than someone I didn't know.

"Morning," Dunk said quietly.

I stood from my seat after glancing at Blue in her baby bed to make sure she was still sound asleep. "You don't have to lower your voice," I whispered. "Apparently, male voices above a whisper disturb my slumbering princess, but female voices at any volume don't disturb her one bit."

As expected, both officers erupted into a fit of giggles. "I've got to drop by when your brothers are visiting to see all of you big burly bikers whispering like little schoolgirls," Dunk giggled.

"Clearly, I'm being repaid for one of the hells I put my mother through." Before I could ask why they stopped by, the door opened again, revealing a solemn-looking Layla. I knew instantly whatever news they were about to deliver was going to be far worse than anything I could have imagined.

"There's a conference room down the hall that's available for you to use," Layla said. "I can stay with the baby while you go speak with the officers."

I wordlessly nodded and placed a kiss on Blue's forehead, letting my lips linger while I prayed that whatever they were about to tell me would not devastate her innocent new life.

But as I walked down the hall toward the conference room, I knew that wasn't going to be the case.

"She's gone, isn't she?" I asked after taking my seat. I didn't want to drag it out any longer than it already had been.

"Yes, she is," Dunk said solemnly.

It occurred to me at that very moment that my life had

irrevocably changed. I was facing a life ahead of me raising a little girl as a single father. The only thing I knew about babies was what I learned in the hospital, and there was plenty of help available. What was I going to do once I was completely on my own? She would need things I wouldn't know how to do or handle—like putting her hair up in a ponytail. Oh fuck, what was I going to do when she started wearing bras or got her period? I couldn't even begin to respond; I could barely breathe as it was.

Copper placed his hand on my shoulder and squeezed—the same thing he had been doing to calm me down and show his silent support for as long as I could remember. And it was the only thing holding me together.

Keeping my eyes focused on the table, I asked a question I wasn't sure I wanted to know the answer to. "What happened?"

Dunk cleared her throat and flicked her eyes to Copper. Assuming he already knew what happened, I started to get pissed. I opened my mouth to ask what the fuck was going on when Dunk swallowed thickly and started to speak. "We found the bodies of Heidi Coleman and Paige Coleman in the basement of their home in Reedy Fork."

Underwood shook her head and dropped her gaze to the floor. The knots that had been steadily tightening in my gut twisted as I struggled to breathe through the crushing pain exploding in my chest. Heidi was gone. The mother of my child.

Mother.

Of my child.

My child.

"What else?" Copper asked for me since I was in no state to formulate words.

Underwood touched the tablet she was holding and looked at the screen. "The medical examiner's preliminary findings indicate that Heidi died from blood loss when she hemorrhaged after giving birth."

I closed my eyes at her words and fought to erase the images that flashed in my mind—images of Blue screaming in a cold, dark corner while her mother bled to death. Subconsciously, I pressed my hand against my chest in a futile attempt to ease the pain I knew all too well would never go away completely—the pain of losing someone you cared about.

And yes, I did care about Heidi. I wasn't *in love* with her, nor was she with me. We were casual friends who had sex a handful of times. I certainly didn't want anything bad to happen to her, but finding out she gave birth to my child changed things for me. Without Blue's existence, I would have mourned her loss just like the loss of any other friend or acquaintance, but Blue amplified the pain immeasurably, because I felt her loss deep in my soul. I knew what it was like to live without your mother, and I was much older than her when I lost mine.

"What happened to Paige?" I asked, sounding harsher than I intended to. Because I had no idea what she was going to tell me that would send another flood of unspeakable thoughts and images to fill my head.

"Paige died from a self-inflicted gunshot wound," Dunk said sadly.

"There's more," Underwood continued. "They found evidence at the scene that suggests Heidi was there against her will. From what we have so far, it looks like Paige lured Heidi to the house and held her hostage in the basement after finding out Heidi was pregnant. We don't know Paige's plan for after the baby was born, but they're still going through all the evidence collected at the scene. We don't know when things went wrong, but Paige called Adelaide Coleman at six thirty-two yesterday morning and spoke to her for seventeen minutes. We believe Adelaide may have been at the scene for a brief period of time, though keep that to yourself for the time being."

"Paige killed herself because she killed Heidi," I said, my tone so dark even I got chills.

"Listen to the rest before you make any judgments," Dunk advised.

"The medical examiner, Dr. Trinh, said he didn't find anything obvious in his initial exam that would explain why she hemorrhaged, but there were several other tests he was going to perform that might provide an answer for the final report, which should be available in approximately six to ten weeks, possibly longer."

"How did you find them?" I asked. We briefly looked for Heidi so we could mail her last paycheck but never found an address for her.

"Sorry, we were getting to that and got off track," Dunk said, looking up from her tablet. "We identified the woman who dropped off the baby from the surveillance footage Copper sent us as Paige's biological mother, Phyllis Banner."

"What? That's not possible. Paige's mother is dead."

Officer Dunk handed a photo to me. "Is this the woman who brought the baby to the clubhouse?"

I took the photo and glanced at it. There was no question in my mind. "Yes, that's her."

"That's Phyllis Banner, Paige's biological mother. Why'd you think she was dead?"

"Because Paige said she was," I grumbled. "And I fucking believed them!" I could feel the anger building inside of me, and it was all I could do to hold it down. "They obviously lied to me!"

"Have you found her? Or Adelaide?" Copper asked, stepping in to give me a moment to collect myself.

Underwood shook her head. "No, not yet. We're still looking. We've got an APB out for Adelaide as well as a warrant for Phyllis Banner's arrest. We're keeping a watch on both houses, but so far, neither one of them has returned to their place of residence. Do you know of anywhere else they may have gone?"

"No, none that I can think of."

"If you see or hear from Phyllis or Adelaide, be sure to give us a call before you take things into your own hands," Dunk said seriously.

"I'll try, but I can't promise more than that."

"Is there anything else?" Copper asked, clearly trying to hurry the conversation along.

"Yes," Dunk said excitedly. "We want to know if we can hold the baby. Neither one of us has even gotten a good look at her yet."

Thankfully, they only stayed for a few minutes, each briefly holding Blue before returning her to me. The moment they were gone, I turned to my brother. "What in the actual fuck?" I asked, miraculously remembering to whisper.

"Should I leave?" Layla interrupted.

Copper shook his head. "That's up to Bronze. As far as I'm concerned, this is family business, not club business."

I turned to Layla. "You're welcome to stay, but you might not like what you hear."

"You don't need to leave, Locks," Copper said and directed his attention to me. "Ain't no use in wasting time speculating. You'd be better off waiting until the police finish investigating and focus on other important matters in the meantime."

"Such as?"

"Such as securing your parental rights now that paternity's been proven. E*specially* since the mother's been found dead."

11

SLOANE

After Bronze left, I turned off all notifications and spent the rest of the day alternating between searching online and completing my daily word count. By the time I decided to call it a day, it was well after dark, and I was mentally exhausted, which is why I once again fell asleep on the sofa holding my laptop. At some point during the night, I managed to sleepwalk to the bed, which saved me from waking up with a sore back.

Since I didn't have any plans until the following afternoon when Bronze said he would come back, I treated myself to several in-room spa services, which took up most of the morning. Feeling like a new woman, I got in my car and set out to explore Devil Springs.

After eating lunch at a locally owned diner, I parked along Main Street and started checking out the downtown area on foot. As I got closer to what appeared to be the central area, the sound of rushing water became louder and clearer.

I wanted to squeal in delight when a bridge and waterfall came into view. Pulling out my phone, I snapped a few pictures and saved the location as a potential site for a photo shoot in the future. The bridge had suspension cables only on one side, allowing for a multitude of unencumbered views as it curved in front of the falls.

Surveying the area, I was pleased to find a park filled with numerous places to sit and enjoy being outdoors—or sit and write some dirty stories as it was in my case.

Far too many hours later, my phone whistled at me and scared the shit out of me since I'd never heard it make that noise before. Looking down to see Frankie's name on a notification from an app that I didn't know I had, I closed my laptop and planned to respond once I got back to my car. However, I changed my mind once I realized it was very close to being dark, and there weren't many people out and about.

"When did you install this on my phone?" I asked.

"Well, hello to you too," Frankie answered. "Wait, what are you doing?"

"I'm walking back to my car. What are you doing?"

"Don't try to deflect. We have more important things to discuss once we've established where you are or that you're safe. I'll accept either at this point."

"I spent the day in a park downtown working on one of my stories," I explained. "The day got away from me, and now I'm walking back to my car with you as my security guard."

"Tell me, my dear demon, why are you lollygagging around this town? You're there for some reason I'm not privy to, yet you spent the day outside writing. Don't get me wrong; I'm always happy when you produce words, but you don't need to be there to write. So, that leads me to believe there's another reason you want to stay in town, besides the one you aren't telling me about."

"What?" I shrieked.

"I knew it! It's a man!" she shouted excitedly. "Tell me all about him." I gasped at her correct guess and promptly choked. "That's not gonna work. Go get you some water. I'll wait."

Shit. Fuck. Damn. I had been doing a great job of ignoring any feelings I maybe, possibly, kind of, not really had for a certain charismatic biker. There was no sense in denying it to her any longer. Plus, if she knew what was going on, she could be prepared for the pep talks I would likely need.

"Stop justifying telling me, and fucking tell me," Frankie insisted.

"I will if you'll get out of my head," I huffed. "Give me one second to get situated in the car."

"You don't situate yourself with your mouth."

I growled like a wild animal before I huffed and started telling her about Bronze. When I was finished, I added, "Some of the things I need to do can only be done during regular business hours Monday through Friday. As such, I think it's only fair that I'm allowed to have fun after hours. Enjoying myself doesn't equate waiting around for him."

"No, but getting all defensive over a simple question sure as shit equates feelings." She paused and inhaled deeply. "I don't know how to respond here. While I'm happy someone's caught your attention, I get the gist this isn't an ideal situation for feelings to be involved."

"I have we-had-great-sex feelings, not we're-going-to-get-married-and-have-babies feelings," I reassured, even though just the thought of marrying Bronze and having his babies caused a delicious chill to shoot through my body.

"Own it, Sloane. You like the biker."

"Fine," I huffed. "I like the biker."

"My work here is done," she chirped and ended the call.

I shook my head and focused on driving back to the hotel. I didn't realize how tired I was until after I ate dinner and took a shower. Clad in only a thin T-shirt and a pair of underwear, I climbed into the bed and fell asleep with my soaking wet hair saturating my pillow.

The next morning, I woke to my computer ringing with a picture of Frankie's smiling face on the screen. There was nothing I could do to fix the hot mess I knew I was, so I bit the bullet and answered. "Good morning," I rasped.

"Good morning? How about good afternoon?" she quipped. "Are you just waking up?"

I sat up and stretched with a yawn. "Yeah. What time is it?"

"Eleven," she said flatly.

"What?" I gasped. What the hell? I was the girl who didn't need an alarm clock because I never slept late. Yet, I'd done it two days in a row.

"Pro tip: If you didn't stay up to all hours of the night doing who knows what, you wouldn't sleep all day."

"Thank you for that helpful piece of advice. Watching the back of my eyelids for over twelve hours is what I was doing."

"Don't get snippy with me because you overslept. Go get your coffee and call me back."

She knew me so well. A mug of coffee needed to be in my hand within ten minutes of opening my eyes or everyone in my general vicinity was going to have a bad day, including myself.

"On it," I said and ended the call.

While drinking my coffee, I thought about what I wanted to do with my day until Bronze got off work. I really wanted to have something new to give him, but I hadn't been able to find anything, which meant it was time to ask Frankie for help. But first, I needed to put in a few hours of work before the day got away from me—more than it already had.

When my phone rang several hours later, I remembered I never called Frankie back. "Hello," I answered quickly.

"If the reason you forgot about me is anything other than a huge cock, I'm going to be hurt," Frankie teased.

"Do fictional cocks count?"

"Only if they're thrusting and throbbing."

I laughed while I made my way down to my car. I was probably being overly cautious, but I didn't want to take a chance of anyone overhearing our conversation. And I knew my car was the best place to ensure my privacy because my dad had it overhauled to make it as safe and secure as possible. The man even made sure it was bulletproof for crying out loud.

"I need your help," I said, bypassing any formalities once I was safely inside.

"Confess your sins, Demon," she replied without missing a beat.

I snorted. "You better sit down because this one's a doozy."

"Tell me what you did so I can start fixing it." She was always there, ready to fix whatever problems arose, no matter what time of day or night.

"It's doesn't have anything to do with the book world. It's personal."

"Your problems are my problems. Spill."

So, I did. I started telling her everything else that happened from the moment I found the letter at my mom's house. I didn't feel the need to repeat the parts about Bronze unless it was pertinent to the new information I was telling her, like him being my possible sister's employer.

Just as I finished, I heard the rumble of an engine approaching.

"Holy shit! A biker wearing the same cut as Bronze just pulled into the hotel parking lot. And he's walking inside. I'm gonna go see what he's doing."

"No!!" Frankie shouted. "Have you learned nothing from the books you read?! You don't fuck around with bikers. Especially you."

"Too late. I already fucked one, and I'm following the other one. It might be his brother."

"Sloane, they all call each other brother."

I scoffed. "No, he said his biological brother is the president. And this dude kinda looks like Bronze."

"Did you say 'president'? Oh, I think I'm having chest pains. What in the hell is wrong with you?" she continued shouting at me while I stealthily crept into the hotel and tried to spy on the biker.

"Where did he go?" I whispered.

"He's probably sneaking up behind you right this second to kidnap you and hold you prisoner in a cell underneath their clubhouse. I bet it's where your long-lost sister is! Run away. Now!"

At her words, I whirled around to check behind me. "Shit, Frankie! That's not funny."

"It wasn't supposed to be."

I pinched the bridge of my nose and exhaled slowly. "Stop trying to scare me. If he's here to see me, I want to know why."

"I'm trying to save you, not scare you. Stop making my job harder and listen to the woman who is thinking clearly right now." Her words fell on deaf ears. I couldn't let it go, and deep down, she knew that as well as I did.

Thanks to Frankie freaking me out, I was hiding by the

ice machine down the hall and peeking out every few seconds to see if I could spot him anywhere.

My heart started pounding in my chest when I saw him stepping out of the elevators. "Shit, Frankie! He's walking toward the front desk."

"Abort mission! Get out of there!"

"Fuck! Fuck! Fuck!" I whisper-shouted into the phone. "The man at the front desk just pointed me out. What do I do?"

"Listen to me! Run!"

"That'll make me look guilty. I haven't done anything wrong," I argued.

"Excuse me," a deep voice rumbled behind me.

Everything froze for a split second when I realized running away was no longer an option. I slowly turned around to face him. "Oh, I'm sorry. I must be in your way," I said and stepped away from the ice machine.

"I'm actually looking for you."

"Me?" I squeaked and cleared my throat.

"Act like you don't know who he is. Pretend like you think he wants an autograph," Frankie quietly insisted.

I plastered a fake smile on my face. "If you have a pen, I'll be happy to sign something for you, but I don't have any books or swag on hand to give you."

"Too much. Stop talking," Frankie coached in my ear.

"That's not why I'm here," he said and gave me a pointed look. "I'm here about Bronze."

"I'm muting myself. Tell me you'll call me back and put the phone in your pocket so I can still hear. Make it quick and get out of there."

"Uh, let me call you back in a few minutes," I said and slipped my phone into my back pocket. Turning to face the biker, I asked, "What about Bronze?"

He didn't beat around the bush or sugarcoat anything. "I don't know what it is you're doing in Devil Springs, and I sure as shit don't know what you've been doing with my brother, but you need to leave. Now. And don't come back."

"What?" I snapped and started getting angry. "Are you threatening me?"

He smirked. "No, sweetheart. I don't have time to go around threatening every whore my brother fucks."

Oh hell no! I was not a whore and refused to tolerate being called one. President or not, he received the same response as the handful of other people who used that word to refer to me. "I prefer bitch," I told him and raised my open palm as if I were going to slap him right across his handsome face. "Nah, you're not worth it," I sneered.

He maintained his mask of indifference, though I could sense his growing anger. "I'll be back in a few hours, and you better be long gone."

"What if I'm not?" I prodded.

He glared into my eyes with gorgeous blue ones, just like Bronze's. "One way or another, you're leaving Devil Springs today." With that, he turned on his heel and left me standing there speechless without a backward glance.

A strange noise caught my attention. It took me a few seconds to realize it was Frankie pressing buttons on the phone. Pulling it from my pocket, I held it to my ear and ran for the stairs. "Holy shit! Holy shit! Holy shit!"

"Is he gone?" she demanded.

"I don't know. I ran when he walked away from me," I panted.

"Ran where? Where're you going? What's happening?"

"To my room!"

"Sloane!"

"I just need a minute to think."

"No, you don't. You need to pack your shit and get out of there."

"I can't! Not until I find my sister!" I screamed and felt my eyes filling with tears. "I want to meet her!"

"For fuck's sake. You can go back another time, but right now, you need to leave. Put me on speakerphone and start packing while I see what I can dig up."

"Okay," I breathed and tapped the speaker button. "I'm in my room, and all the locks are locked."

Proper packing went out the window. I stuffed and crammed everything I brought into the closest bag or suitcase. Frankie shouted something I couldn't make out while I was gathering my toiletries. "What was that?" I asked. "I was in the bathroom and couldn't hear you."

Frankie's next words paired with her calm and even tone sent chills through my body. "Sloane, you need to leave. Get your purse, laptop, and whatever can't be left behind. I'll arrange to have what's left delivered to my PO box. Stay on the phone with me until you're safely in your car. If anything, and I mean anything, happens between now and you leaving, I'm calling your father."

She didn't have to say anything else. Frankie would never call my dad unless it was a dire situation. "I'm walking out the door right now."

"Good. Stay calm, at least on the outside. You're okay, and we want to keep you that way," she encouraged.

When I reached my car, I threw everything into the backseat and locked the doors the second I was inside. "Okay, I made it to my car. Now, tell me what the fuck is going on!"

"Are you driving?"

"Tell me!"

"Keep the source in mind, but I'm looking at a comment posted on the local news's social media page that says the bodies of an apparent murder-suicide have been identified as Heidi and Paige Coleman."

"What?" I practically screamed.

"Heidi and Paige are dead."

I WAS STILL ON THE PHONE WITH FRANKIE BUT LOST IN MY thoughts while she was searching for more information when I remembered something. The other address Bronze wrote down was where Paige and Heidi used to live, or that's what he'd said. I wasn't sure what to believe anymore, but figured it wouldn't hurt anything to drive by the house so I could see for myself. Taking a deep breath, I pulled onto the street, hoping I wasn't making a foolish mistake.

I slowly rolled by the house and surveyed the area. There was a For Rent sign in the front yard, and it looked like the house was still unoccupied.

"What are you doing?" Frankie blurted out of nowhere, scaring the crap out of me.

"Driving."

"What else?"

"How do you do that?" I asked and honestly wanted to know.

"I know you too well. You're probably doing something I would be doing, which is always something we shouldn't be doing."

"Okay, so I told you one of the addresses Bronze wrote down was for their old house," I started. "And he mentioned something about a few boxes still being there."

"Have you lost your damn mind?"

"It might be the only chance I ever have of knowing

the truth! Especially if they're really dead. I can't live the rest of my life not knowing!"

"Just ask your dad!"

I scoffed. "If I thought he'd tell me the truth, I would."

"You can't just walk into some random house."

While approaching the front door, I kept a close watch on my surroundings and tried to play it cool. I could be a potential tenant for all anyone knew. Crossing my fingers, I twisted the knob and wanted to shout with glee when it turned, and the door eased open. "I can if the door's unlocked," I whispered. "And what do you know? It is."

"Don't go inside. Don't go inside. Don't go inside."

"Shh!" I hissed. "You're echoing off the empty walls."

"You're already inside?"

"Yes, and you're going in my pocket again."

"No! Don't pocket me!"

I hurried toward the back of the house, freezing when my eyes landed on several boxes in one of the bedrooms. They were lined up beside each other on the floor with a single box haphazardly closed sitting in the middle of the room.

"I have to. I need both hands." Then, I kicked it into high gear and started opening the four boxes along the wall. The first three were full of books. The last one had books too, but it also had three photo albums on top. Grabbing the albums, I peeked into the box in the middle of the room. Since it was filled with random items and wasn't very heavy, I put the photo albums in the box, picked up my load, and hauled ass back to my car.

Falling into the driver's seat, I pulled my phone from my back pocket and started to get the hell out of there. "Shit," I cursed. "I forgot to close the front door."

"Fuck the front door, you batshit crazy demon. You just committed a felony. Go!"

"But there're books in there," I argued.

"Sloane!"

"Fine," I huffed and drove away.

"I'm going to need you to turn your location services on. My anxiety can't handle any more of your shenanigans right now."

"My anxiety can't handle any more either," I admitted and gasped when it finally hit me. "I just broke into a house!"

"And stole things! What were you thinking?"

"I don't know!" I shouted.

"Okay, we can figure out what to do about that part later. Right now, we need to get you home safely. Everything else can wait."

"You're right. I should probably get off the phone and concentrate on driving."

"I'll let you go if you promise to call me *before* you stop anywhere."

"I'm only stopping if I have to get gas, and I shouldn't need to because I have a full tank. But I promise to call if I do."

With that, we ended the call, and I used the long drive to process the newest turn of events. By the time I pulled through the gates of my mother's estate and the locks clinked closed behind me, I was mentally, physically, and emotionally exhausted.

After parking in the garage and turning off the ignition, I realized I wouldn't be able to take a nap or do anything else until I at least looked through the box and flipped through the photo albums, even after the epic adrenaline rush wore off.

With my purse, my bag of essentials, and my stolen goods, I went straight to my bedroom after relocking the garage door and setting the alarm. The only thing I didn't like about my mother's estate was how sprawled out it was. If someone broke into the house, there were a million places for them to hide.

The house was luxurious, to say the least. It was exactly what one would expect a wealthy, pissed off wife to get. My mother did not have any issues spending my father's money, and because she opted to quietly live somewhere else and let him conduct his life however he saw fit, he let her spend however much she wanted to—within reason, though their "reason" was much different from most people's.

"I thought you were out of town for work," Tiernan said from the doorway to my bedroom, causing me to let out a startled scream, which opened the floodgates. I burst into tears from the weight of the events from the last few days.

I was wrapped in my older brother's arms before I could get one good choking sob out. "Whose ass do I need to kick?" he rumbled like the overprotective older sibling he was.

I sniffled and inhaled deeply, trying to get my emotions under control. I hadn't told him or my other brothers about the possibility of us having a sister out there. I thought it would be better to meet her and tell her about our existence before I shared the news of her with them. However, fate intervened, and the best I would ever be able to do was tell them that we *had* a sister. But, I decided to keep everything to myself until I had more information to share—preferably a DNA test confirming her relationship to us, though I had no idea how I was going to get one of those.

"No one's," I mumbled against his chest. "I came home as soon as I realized the research I was doing turned out to be a waste of time. I'm just tired and frustrated," I told him—none of which was completely a lie, or the truth for that matter.

"You wouldn't be lying to me, would you, Sloaney Bologna?"

I pulled back and slapped his chest, lightly giggling through my tears. "I hate when you call me that."

"Judging by that laugh, it doesn't sound like you hate it all that much," he laughed.

"What're you doing here anyway?" I asked. Even though it was technically half Tiernan's, he wasn't there most of the time. However, he usually let me know when he was coming since I was the only one living there full time. My oldest two brothers, Kian and Declan, never lived with us at Mom's house. They were both adults and living on their own when Mom moved into her own place.

I had a closer relationship with Tiernan than I did my other two brothers—partially because he was only two years older than me and partially because our personalities meshed well together. He usually spent his time traveling, though I wasn't one-hundred-percent sure exactly what he did. Growing up as an O'Shea, I knew not to ask questions about information that wasn't readily offered. In other words, if Tiernan hadn't told me what he was doing on his frequent travels, it was none of my business, and I was better off not knowing anything about his activities.

"Sorry about not giving you a call this time. I had an unexpected business meeting pop up," he said and paused as an excited smile appeared upon his face. "If the meeting goes well, I'll be in town a lot more over the next few months. Is it going to be a problem for you if I stay here?"

I rolled my eyes at my brother's ridiculous question. "You own half of the property and have your own wing, Tiernan. As long as you don't have a massive party or diddle your dates in the main dining room, I doubt I'll even know you're here, especially when I'm deep in the throes of writing another masterpiece," I returned with a wink.

He reached out and ruffled the hair on top of my head. "Have I told you how damn proud I am of you lately? Saying fuck you to the world and going after your dreams. Not only going after them but achieving your dreams like a boss."

I felt my cheeks heat in embarrassment. I was nothing if not modest about my career. "Oh, stop. You act like writing a couple of stories is a big deal."

"It is a big deal, Sloane," he said in exasperation, gearing up for the same argument we'd had on more than one occasion. "You didn't just write a couple of stories. You wrote a book. *A book*. Published it all by yourself—without telling anyone—and made it onto a best-seller list."

"I'm not doing this again with you," I said firmly. "We're going to have to agree to disagree and leave it at that."

He huffed and shook his head. "For now," he replied and turned to leave the room. "You sure you're okay?" At my nod, he added, "You know you can talk to me about anything, right?"

I smiled softly. "I do, Turnip," I replied, using the nickname I gave him when I first started talking and couldn't pronounce Tiernan correctly. "Love you."

He grinned. "Mean it."

With that, he left the room, leaving me alone to finally look through the contents of the box and photo albums. I was so excited I could barely contain myself. Hopping onto my bed and crossing my legs underneath me, I opened the flaps to the box and looked inside.

The box was filled with a variety of random items,

perhaps ones that were collected during a final walk-through of the house—hair accessories, makeup, a set of keys, a small wooden jewelry box, a few pieces of mail, and a number of other things that were irrelevant as best I could tell.

I immediately reached for the jewelry box and opened it, gasping at what I saw. While the few bracelets, earrings, and rings stored inside were breathtaking, it was the contents of a small velvet bag that had me shouting with glee and promptly slapping my hand over my mouth, hoping Tiernan didn't hear me.

Inside the dark green, drawstring pouch was a tooth. A whole, intact molar. It was creepy as fuck but also incredibly lucky because it was filled with testable DNA. Or so I hoped. I needed to do a little research to be sure. But that wouldn't be a problem. What concerned me was figuring out who the tooth belonged to.

When I finished with the box, I turned to the photo albums to see what treasures they held inside. Once again, I was amazed as I turned page after page of nothing but photos of Heidi and Paige spanning what had to be at least five years, if not more, of their lives.

"Hot damn!" I breathed when my eyes landed on a picture of Paige in bed with a compress held to her cheek and gauze hanging out of her mouth. Finally! I had something to go on.

12

BRONZE

After we were discharged from the hospital, I planned on taking Blue to the clubhouse and figuring things out from there. However, Leigh had other plans. When my parents died, Copper inherited our grandparents' house, and I inherited our parents' house, which was less than a mile from Leigh's home. "What are you doing?" I asked suspiciously.

"Hush, and don't ruin the surprise," she playfully scolded from the front seat.

When she pulled into the driveway, she didn't say a word until she was opening the car door to help me with Blue. "I know you're planning on taking her home to the clubhouse, but the Old Ladies and I have a surprise to show you first."

With that, I followed her inside to find my parents' house—my home—partially redecorated.

"Anything we replaced or removed from the house is in storage at the clubhouse. I didn't want to accidentally do away with something you wanted to keep. Same thing with the paint. We have colors picked out, but I wanted to get your approval on that." She held up one finger to hold my response at Bay. "But first, the big surprise."

She led me down the hallway to what used to be the office. "Copper said we should use this room. If that's not okay, everything can be put back the way it was." She nervously opened the door to reveal a perfect nursery for a newborn baby girl.

"It's perfect," I managed to say, struggling with the emotions clogging my throat. "Thank you."

"You're welcome," she said and wrapped her arm around my waist. "I'm not overly emotional, and neither are you. Let's leave it at that, okay?"

I squeezed her shoulder and took a few moments before I cleared my throat and agreed with her. "Deal."

She spent the next few hours showing me where everything was and helping us get settled. Of course, Copper and Layla arrived less than half an hour after we did, and the rest of the club and Old Ladies trickled in to visit throughout the day.

Leigh stayed until Blue went down for the night. Before she left, I turned to her and admitted the truth. "I'm terrified for you to leave. I don't know what I'm doing, Leigh. What if I mess up?"

She pulled me into her arms just like a mother would, even though I'd outgrown her years ago. "You'll be just fine. I'm right down the road, and you can call me if you need me. Don't forget, you were raised by a wonderful mother. If you're ever unsure of what to do, think about Goldie and how she would've handled the situation. We all make mistakes. All you can do is love your child and do what you think's best for them. The rest will work itself out. Now, go get some sleep while she's sleeping, because that's the only sleep you're gonna get for a few months."

"You're supposed to leave on a positive note," I grumbled.

"Your mother would be more than proud of the man you've become. Now go in there and keep making her proud."

"That's what I needed to hear," I confessed and dropped a kiss on the top of her head before reluctantly letting her go.

Fuck me. I was completely alone with my daughter for the first time, and I wanted to run out the front door screaming into the night. Instead, I opened the door because there was yet another knock on it.

Thinking Leigh forgot something, I yanked it open, surprised to see Lana Dunk standing there. "Hey, Lana. I wasn't expecting you. Come on in," I said and held the door open for her.

Officer Dunk cleared her throat. "Thanks, but I just came by to drop these off. I meant to get by here earlier, but I got held up at the station," she explained and held out a sealed envelope to me. "These are unofficial, off-the-record copies of some papers that were found folded under the pillowcase on what we presume to be Heidi's bed. I thought it was something you should read. And I trust those copies will disappear when you're finished with them."

"Of course," I agreed and took the envelope from her. "Thank you."

"Take care, Bronze. Kiss that cute baby girl for me."

With that, she left, and I returned to my bedroom with the envelope practically burning my hands. I couldn't begin to imagine what was inside, but I hoped the words I was about to read would be the words Blue and I would need to get through the tough road ahead of us.

To The Person Reading This,

Sorry. Dear Diary seemed silly, but I felt like it needed some kind of salutation even though you're probably a stranger. Sorry again. I'm stalling because I don't want to write what I'm about to write. I'm going to do it anyway because it needs to be done, but I don't want to. Okay, enough of that. Here we go.

I have a bad feeling about the delivery. I don't know if it's because of the situation Paige has put us in or if my feelings about something bad happening are valid. If something happens and I die during childbirth, I hope Bronze finds out about the baby. It was never my intention to keep my pregnancy from him. I hope he doesn't hold anything against Paige. I know it was the news of my pregnancy that sent her over the edge, and I highly suspect she hasn't been taking any of her medications for a while. Unfortunately, I don't have access to her bottles and can't count the pills like I used to when this happened. She refuses to talk to me about anything related to her mental health.

Anyway, if something happens to me, I want Bronze to raise the baby. I don't know if it's a boy or girl. If it's a boy, I want to name him after his father. If it's a girl, I want her to have her father's middle name, Talon. Other than that, I hope the baby has his beautiful blue eyes.

I can't believe Paige did this. It's killing me that he doesn't know he's about to become a father. I was on my way to tell him when she did all this.

Every time I try to talk some sense into Paige, she flies off the handle. She insists I'm going to leave her for Bronze once the baby is born because "he can give you something I can't." I guess she means children. I have no plans to leave her for Bronze or anyone else, but I also plan to allow Bronze to participate in the baby's life if he wants to. And I know he would want to if he knew.

If I'm being honest, I'm really pissed at Paige about her jealousy over Bronze. She is the one who wanted to invite him into our bed because she wanted to watch me have sex with him. Don't get me wrong, I thoroughly enjoyed myself, but it was all her idea. So how in the hell can she be pissed at me for something that happened because of what she wanted? She knew pregnancy was a risk. We talked about it in depth before our first adventure with bringing a man into our bed. I was already on birth control, and we agreed that the man would have to wear a condom. The chances of me getting pregnant were next to zero, and she agreed to proceed with the caveat that we would sit down and discuss what to do if a pregnancy occurred. But when it came down to it, she went back on her word. There was no discussion about our future. I told her as soon as I found out I was pregnant. I was scared and completely freaked out. And what did she do? She told me she needed time to process the news and that we would discuss it when I got off work. But when I got home, she was gone. As in, she packed up all of her belongings and moved out while I was working a double shift at Precious Metals.

The only thing she left was a note on the coffee table breaking up with me. I couldn't believe that's how she'd end it after seven years together. I wish I'd seen that for the red flag it was. She wasn't really breaking up with me. Not in her mind. She simply created a reason for her to be away for however long she needed to be ready to put her plan into motion.

I still don't completely know what her plan is. She hasn't let me see a doctor since I've been here, but she's been taking some classes online and ordering whatever she needs to make sure me and the baby are healthy. She even learned how to draw blood so she could send mine in for testing. I don't have a clue how she's managed to arrange the tests or order the medical equipment she's ordered, but she has. So far, everything is okay with me and the baby. I didn't believe her at first, but she showed me the results mailed from the lab and let me open the sealed envelope each time they arrived thereafter.

Even though I know the pregnancy is going smoothly, I still can't shake the feeling that something bad is going to happen. And I don't care what Paige says, it's not because I'm scared of having a baby without an epidural. Not that she ever asked me, but I wanted to deliver any children I had naturally, maybe even at home or at one of those birthing centers with the huge bathtubs. So, I don't think that's the reason for my anxiety.

Whatever it is, I've felt it from the day Paige tricked me into coming over to her new house to talk and subsequently locked me in the basement. The feeling never goes away, and it gradually grows stronger as time passes. I hope I'm wrong, and Paige is right that it's about the pain of childbirth. I'm too scared to think of what it might mean if she's wrong and I'm right.

Whatever happens, I hope my baby is safe, healthy, and knows how much I love him or her. And if he or she can't be with me, I hope they're with Bronze. He's going to make a great father.

Heidi

Motherfucker.

I jumped to my feet and inhaled deeply, ready to roar in pain and anger, when a soft snore from the baby monitor caused me to pause. I glanced at the screen to see Blue sleeping soundly in her baby carrier and forced myself to rein it in long enough to think about what I was doing.

Picking up the portable monitor and hurrying to the garage, I used the last bit of restraint I had to quietly close the door before I laid into the punching bag that had seen me through several deaths—my grandfather, my parents, and now my friend.

I don't know how long I was out there, but I was covered in sweat and well beyond out of breath when I dropped to my knees and let the pain consume me.

I cried for the loss of my friend and the mother of my child, which bled into the loss of my parents and my grandfather. How was I going to raise my daughter without them? Before I knew it, I had spiraled into a dark place with no light in sight, until I felt a familiar presence at my side moments before my brother's arms surrounded me.

He waited silently for me to get my shit together. When I finally did, he sat back on his heels and said, "Now that you got that out of your system, you're going to get your ass up and go raise your daughter like the motherfucking boss you are."

"I'm scared to death," I confessed.

"From what I hear, every father is. Congratulations, you're normal. Now, get the fuck up. This floor is bruising my tender ass."

And that's what I did.

I got the fuck up and raised my daughter.

13

BRONZE

I'm not going to lie; the first few weeks at home with Blue were hard, but not as hard as everyone made it out to be. I knew my take on things was different because every single member of my club family was more than willing to step in and lend a helping hand, especially the women in the club.

Leigh took it upon herself to teach me everything she knew about babies. And just when I thought we'd finished with the lessons, Blue entered a new stage that came with a completely different set of things to learn, which usually rendered my new skills useless. It was a never-ending cycle, but I was beyond grateful for Leigh's guidance. I also had a newfound appreciation for my own parents and wished there was some way I could tell them how grateful I was for everything they did for me and Copper.

Then there was River. She had been permanently elevated to angel status in my book. First of all, she was not kidding about the different kinds of baby cries. I did what she said—read the information and took the time to memorize it. Once I was finished, I anxiously waited for

Blue to cry so I could test the theory as well as myself. I felt like a bit of an asshole when I cheered for getting the "I'm hungry" cry correct while she was screaming her head off for her bottle.

As a father, I didn't have the ingrained maternal instinct that most women did. I hadn't even had time to adjust to becoming a father before I suddenly was one. Giving me the ability to identify my daughter's needs by the sound of her cries was enough to angelize River in my eyes forever, but then she went and saved Blue's life, and mine by default.

* * *

We'd been home from the hospital for almost four days, and things were going fairly well. Or so I thought. The only issue we were having was getting Blue to go back to sleep after her middle of the night feeding. For some reason, she fought sleep the hardest after that feeding. One night, in particular, it was so bad that I put her in my truck and drove around until she fell asleep, which happened to be when we were near the clubhouse. Since I had a portable crib and all her essentials there, I pulled into the forecourt and carried her inside as if I were handling a live bomb.

After sleeping for a few hours, Blue woke up right on time for her six o'clock feeding. I made her a bottle and changed her diaper while letting the warm formula cool for a few minutes. I knew it wasn't too hot for her, but I felt like you could never be too careful when it came to heat or fire. Being severely burned was one of my biggest fears, which naturally extended to my daughter.

We were developing a bit of a routine, and I was becoming more comfortable and confident in my role as a father. Dropping into the rocking chair Leigh had delivered to the clubhouse, I placed the bottle in Blue's mouth after making sure we were both comfortable.

"Good morning," River said from where she was perched at the bar drinking a cup of coffee before she left for work.

"Morning," I replied and focused my attention on Blue.

At first, everything went the same way it always did. She immediately hoovered the nipple into her mouth and started drinking with fervor. Then, she coughed. It was so tiny I almost ignored it, but thankfully, I didn't. Instead, I yanked it from her mouth and examined her face. It was hard to tell at first. I wasn't sure and thought my eyes were playing tricks on me. But after a few more seconds, I knew what I was seeing was real.

Throwing the bottle across the room and getting to my feet, I yelled, "She's turning blue!"

"Give her to me and get the bulb suction!" she demanded.

I handed Blue to her and grabbed the hospital-green bulb that just happened to be laying on top of the bar, holding it out to River. "I want you to thump the bottom of her foot," she said and started suctioning Blue's mouth and throat. I did as she instructed and flicked the tender skin on the bottom of my baby's tiny foot.

"No!" River yelled. "Harder! You need to make her cry!"

The urgency in River's voice had me thumping the bottom of my newborn's foot as if she were a grown man. Her entire body tensed right before she let out a ferocious cry. River pulled the bulb from her mouth again and squeezed it, shooting a stream of formula across the room.

Meanwhile, Blue continued to scream at the top of her lungs while her face turned as red as a tomato.

"Holy shit!" I breathed, bracing myself on the rocking chair when I felt my knees weaken. "What the fuck just happened?"

River turned from where she was hovering over Blue, where I presumed she was examining her, and said, "She choked, and we need to know why. Call her doctor's office and have them page whoever is on call. Tell them exactly what happened. Then, ask them if they want you to bring her to the office or the hospital because we are taking her to one of those two places. I can watch her while you're on the phone, but I'll gladly talk to the physician on call if you need me to."

I made the call and relayed the information as River instructed.

The doctor wanted us to be at the office when they opened in less than an hour. All the while, Blue was crying because she was still hungry, but we were given specific instructions not to feed her anything until she'd been examined. Thankfully, while I was scrambling to get us ready to go, River got someone to cover her shift so she could go with me to the pediatrician's office.

The few hours that followed were a whirlwind of activity blurred by a cloud of fear. We went from the pediatrician's office to a specialist's office and ended up at the hospital for a test that allowed them to look at her stomach using x-rays instead of having to stick a tube down her throat. I couldn't remember what it was called, but it involved them giving Blue something in her bottle that would make her insides show up on the screen. I made a mental note to ask River what the test was called so I could be better prepared for the aftermath if Blue ever had to have that test again.

Because no one prepared me for the epic chalky white shit my tiny girl would take afterward. A shit so epic it covered both me and her literally from chest to feet in poop that looked like wet cement while having the consistency of paint.

I tried to yell for River but started to vomit halfway through her name. "Rivvurrrlllggghhh!"

She appeared seconds later, as did my brother, Layla, Leigh, Batta, Tatum, and Judge—all watching me throw up to the side so I wouldn't get vomit on my shit-covered daughter or my shit-covered self, as if it mattered at that point. I started to chuckle at the thought, and promptly choked on the puke spewing out of my mouth, redirecting the flow to my nose. While every fucking one of them stood there and watched, refusing to touch me or my shit-coated spawn.

It was one of the longest days I could recall—waiting to find out what was wrong with my daughter, and more importantly, what could be done to fix it. As it turned out, Blue had acid reflux, which the doctor assured me was very common in infants. He suggested she may have actually gagged instead of choked, but in any event, her body responded by protecting her airway; thus, Blue turned the color of her name.

Ultimately, we were sent home with a prescription for me to add to her bottle before putting her down for the night, and that was that. No more turning blue for Blue and no more near heart attacks for me.

However, there were times it seemed like she was struggling to drink her bottle. I mentioned it to Leigh, and she suggested trying a different bottle or a different nipple.

"Jonah had a little bit of trouble eating when he first started bottle-feeding. I went through probably twenty different brands before I found one that worked well for him, and it's still a popular brand today. I'll run to the baby store and grab the kind I used, plus a few others for you to try. Do you need anything while I'm there?" Leigh asked, already hooking her purse over her shoulder.

"Yeah, can you get me a tube of nipple cream?" Her eyes grew comically wide, causing me to burst into laughter. "I'm being serious," I managed to say between laughs. "I had to start wearing my jewelry again, and my shirts are making my nipples chafe."

Leigh doubled over laughing, dropping her purse to the floor. "Oh!" Leigh guffawed. "This is because she tried to nurse you! I'm dying!!" She continued to laugh until another thought hit her that she had to share. "You're not even capable of breastfeeding her, yet you still have sore nipples!" She slapped her thigh and looked toward the sky. "Oh, thank you, Goldie! I needed that!"

"You're not welcome," I grumbled. I wouldn't be ready to laugh about it until my nipples didn't feel like they'd been rubbed with sandpaper.

Leigh returned later that afternoon with more than "a few others" for us to try. "Did you get every bottle they had on the shelves?"

"Technically, no. I got one of each kind on the

shelves," she smirked. "Before you say anything, I can take back whatever we don't use, and maybe even some of the ones we do try if they guarantee satisfaction."

"Fair enough," I agreed. "Let's start with the kind you used with Judge."

And that's what we did. At first, I thought we were going to be facing a long period of trial and error, but Leigh changed the nipple to one made of a different material and told me to try again. My jaw dropped in delightful surprise as Blue emptied the contents of her bottle without one single problem. "Holy shit," I breathed.

"Watch your mouth around the baby," Leigh scolded.

"That is physically and physiologically impossible, even if I had a mirror," I retorted proudly.

"You're the essence of 'being too smart for your own good,'" she said and gave me a pointed look, complete with an arched eyebrow.

"Is there a Guinness World Record for the person who can arch their eyebrow the highest? Because we should really check into that. I think you could win."

"Just wait until you're not holding that baby," Leigh said in a low tone.

Luckily, that was the last major hiccup we had while adjusting to our new world. That's not to say that things went smoothly. Far from it. But it was the usual stuff that happened to new parents and nothing that affected her health or well-being. I still experienced my fair share of having outfits ruined by a shitty diaper that overflowed up the back—which usually happened within ten minutes of me putting the outfit on Blue—or her wanting to eat or be changed the moment I sat down to take a bite of whatever meal I'd just prepared. Parenthood was exactly what everyone who had kids said it was, and nothing like what most people without kids believed it to be.

After the initial shock, I handled things well for the first couple of weeks. But as time passed, my pent-up emotions festered inside of me. I needed to find an outlet before they exploded into a mess of hurt feelings and damaged relationships. I was angry about so many things—Heidi's death, raising Blue without her mother, raising Blue without my own mother, and if I was being honest, I was still mad about almost losing my life when Dez's punk ass little brother stabbed me.

I could feel Copper watching me like the hawk he and our father were named after. Thinking it was best if I brought it up before he felt the need to, I stopped by his office to talk to him.

"I need to fight," I told him without preamble.

"So fight," he said, as if it were that simple.

I sighed and pinched the bridge of my nose. "I don't mean sparring at the gym, Copper. I mean real matches," I explained, and paused for a moment before I dropped the detail I knew he would have a problem with. "Underground matches."

"No fucking way!" he roared and rose to his feet.

"I'm doing this with or without your permission. The only reason I'm telling you now is because I don't keep secrets from my club brothers, and I don't want there to be any blowback on the club. Meaning you and the guys can't come to my matches."

He released a string of curse words under his breath and started to pace the short length of his office. "Fuck, Bronze. I get it. I really do, but this isn't the way to go about dealing with your shit."

"It might not be the way you'd choose, but it's the right way for me. Fighting in the Marines is what got me through losing Mom and Dad. I'd be dead or in prison if I hadn't enlisted and started boxing. It's what I know, and it works for me."

He glared at me, but I knew I would need to make some sort of concession before he would let it go. "Would it make you feel better if I touched base with Luca Peccati first?"

Copper stopped pacing and faced me, cocking his head to the side. "The fuck does Luca have to do with this?"

"His nephew got the idea to get into underground fighting from somewhere," I suggested. When he continued to stare at me waiting for more, I admitted, "I checked out one of the fights in Cherryfield last week."

His head shot up. "Is that why Blue spent the night with us?"

I snorted and shook my head. "No, Blue spent the night with you because Layla asked if she could. I said yes and didn't waste the opportunity I was given."

"Make a connection or a point," Copper grumbled.

"I ran into Luca at the fight. I'm not sure if he has a team of fighters, takes bets, or both. He does have a shit ton of bodyguards, and it's clear that he's a big fucking deal. Hell, maybe he owns the place—"

"Get on with it."

I rolled my eyes but made my point. "Luca said he would get my foot in the door if I was interested in fighting."

"And what does he want in return for that favor?"

I smirked. "Your reassurance that he won't anger our club by allowing me into his."

"You serious?" Copper asked skeptically.

I nodded. "Yep. He said all he'd be doing was vouching that I wasn't a fed, cop, scam artist, or someone who would share information about the fights with the media, particularly social media. After that, getting on the card's up to me."

Copper rubbed his chin in the same way most of the males in our family did when they were considering their next words. Many thought the gesture meant they were thinking, but I knew they were actually choosing how to break the decision they'd already made. "I appreciate you not wanting the club to have any affiliation with the fights, but I can't let you go to matches alone," he said and held up his hand to keep me from interrupting. "Grant isn't patched in yet, so he can go with you. Neither one of you'll wear your cuts. Also, Coal's been talking about a guy that's been coming to the gym. He says he's been asking about the club and might be interested in prospecting. You know who he's talking about?"

"It'd have to be Drew. I haven't been back at the gym that long, but Drew has been in there working out every day that I've been back. He's young. I'm talking between eighteen and twenty."

Copper resumed pacing, though his pace was much slower, and most of the tension had left his shoulders. "I'll stop by the gym tomorrow and have a chat with Drew. If he wants to prospect for the club, he can earn that chance by making up the second part of your entourage."

"What about Coal? He's gonna feel left out if both of his buddies get to go to the big city while he has to stay home," I pointed out.

"That's a price he pays for wearing the cut," Copper clipped.

"Relax, bro. I was kidding. You need to get laid before your blood pressure goes up so high it makes you have a stroke. And I love you, but I will not wipe your ass."

"What if I broke both arms?"

"Depends on how you broke them. But that's not what

I'm talking about. I'm saying I won't wipe your ass if it needs to be wiped because you had a stroke from too much pent-up tension. Go fuck your wife. Wait. Are you two married?" I asked. I knew they weren't, even though they'd been together for a couple of years, lived together, and he'd claimed her as his Old Lady.

I also knew I'd look up to see Copper staring at me with worry all over his face. He'd been doing that every time I couldn't remember something since I had to have emergency brain surgery after the clubhouse was bombed. I was a bit of an ass for fucking with him like that, but that's what little brothers were supposed to do. "Again with all the worry. I'm just giving you shit because you haven't married her yet. Have you even asked her? Seriously, man, what the fuck are you waiting for?"

Before I could turn away, Copper flicked my nipple with his fingers. "You motherfucker!" I roared.

"Is Blue still trying to get milk out of your tender teats?" he laughed.

I eyed him knowingly. "Just wait. It'll happen to you one day." And I was going to make damn sure it did. Even if I had to spill some sugar water on his shirt while he was holding his own child.

"I don't know why in the hell you're staring at my chest like that, but if you think you're going to pierce my nipples while I'm asleep or some shit, you better think again, Little Brother."

I shook my head with a small smile on my face. "Nah, nothing like that."

He pivoted on his heel and returned to his seat behind his desk. "Is there anything else?"

"Yes, as a matter of fact there is. Blue would like to know when her white unicorn will be delivered. She said Uncle Copper promised to get her one she could keep at

Grammy Leigh's house," I said, moving out the door as I spoke. Once I hit the hallway, I picked up my pace.

"If you've had a fucking horse delivered to Leigh's barn and said it was from me, you're going to come home to find a front yard full of fucking sheep!" Copper yelled, following after me.

"How are you going to get them to fuck?" I laughed.

"What did you do, fucker?" he demanded as he continued to chase me.

"Nothing to worry about. It's not a horse; it's a pony!" I shouted just as my bike roared to life. "Peace!" I called out and held up two fingers while I rode away, smiling when I glanced in my mirror and saw him standing in the forecourt fuming. I had to leave him pissed off at me about something so that I didn't leave him worried about me. Because I knew he was going to worry. Knowing how moody Copper could be when something was bothering him, I decided to call Layla and give her a heads up.

She giggled into the phone. "I know how your brother is too, and I can assure you that I know how to help Copper work through his moods."

"Stop! Stop! Stop!" I shouted into the phone.

"What? Are you afraid I'm going to tell you your brother fucks me like he hates me when he's upset?" she asked with faux innocence.

"Fuck this shit. I'm coming to get my baby. I think you might be a bad influence on her," I playfully scolded.

"Pssh. You forget who you're talking to. I've heard plenty of stories and seen enough with my own eyes to know that I'm most certainly not even one of the top ten worst influences around her," Layla said confidently. "You're welcome to come pick her up, but she just went down for her afternoon nap. You want me to call you when she wakes up?"

"That'd be great. Thanks, Layla." With that, we ended the call, and I headed in the direction of the baby supply store. If I busted my ass, I might be able to buy everything I needed before Blue woke up from her nap.

Layla called just as I arrived at the gym to unload my purchases. When I told her I'd be there as soon as I finished unloading at the gym, she offered to bring Blue to me since she had plans to meet Josie at the bookstore next door.

"What in the world are you doing?" Layla asked when she found me in the basement putting together various pieces of baby equipment.

"Setting up duplicates of the essentials we have at home so Blue can comfortably spend more time here with me," I explained.

"You know I don't mind watching her," Layla said for the umpteenth time.

"I know, and that means the world to me, but I don't like being away from her more than I have to."

"How am I going to keep spoiling her if you're cutting my hours?" Layla asked playfully, though I could tell a part of her was truly disappointed at the thought of losing time with Blue.

"Actually, I wanted to talk to you about something. I'm going to need a babysitter for a Friday or Saturday night here and there over the next few months. Would you be interested in letting Blue spend the night with you on those nights?" I asked, laying the groundwork perfectly.

"Of course I would!" she answered excitedly before pinning me with a look and arching an eyebrow. "Wait a minute. Are you asking me to babysit so you can let her potential siblings go for a swim in the rubber pool?"

I looked up from the portable crib I was assembling

and blinked at Layla. "What in the actual fuck did you just say?"

Layla's cheeks turned an adorable shade of pink. "You know," she mumbled and cleared her throat. "Have safe sex."

I laughed so hard I choked on my own spit. "You just referred to a condom as a rubber pool. No wait. It was 'the' rubber pool."

My raucous laughter caused Blue to stir, a little whimper filling the air. Layla gently placed the baby carrier on the floor beside me. "She either has a bad case of gas, or she pooped on the drive over. Either way, have fun with that," she said and strolled away.

I turned the carrier to see my daughter stretching and yawning. I could already tell by the way she wrinkled her face and squirmed that she was sitting in squashed shit.

Glancing around, I was happy to find the diaper bag within arm's reach. I pulled it to me and set about changing Blue before she could get going with her little fit. After I fed and burped her, I placed her in the swing I'd already assembled and continued working while she alternated between playing and napping. It took longer than I thought, but when I was finished, I had several safe places for Blue to play and sleep, all of which could easily be moved to different locations. If the gym was anything like my house, I'd be moving the swing from room to room. It was her favorite; therefore, it was my favorite.

For the next two months, Blue spent almost every day at the gym with me. I, however, did spend every single day at the gym training. Because I had a fight to prepare for. And it wasn't just any fight. It was the fight that would get me on the card. From there, the matches would build in difficulty until I bested one of the top-level fighters. Then, I would be given the chance to leave with my winnings or join the best of the best and continue to earn the same exorbitant amount for each fight I won. But the first one could be some punk off the street who didn't know what the fuck he was doing, or it could be an experienced fighter trying to join the league, like me.

14

SLOANE

It'd been three months since I drove away from Devil Springs like my ass was on fire, and I was finally about to have my hands on the answers to so many of my questions about my sister. Bouncing on the balls of my feet, it was all I could do to stay put and not get in my car to meet him halfway. Because that would have made me look like a crazy lady. Okay, a crazier lady.

My heart rate accelerated when I heard him turn the corner. Ready to burst with glee, I ran to the gate the moment his wheels stopped in front of my house. "Judging from the size of that smile, I must have something you want," he drawled.

"You do, and you know it," I teased and then clapped my hands together. "Please don't make me wait any longer."

He laughed, extending his hand in a grand gesture. "I hope it's everything you wished for," he joked.

"I know it will be," I replied, taking my prize from his hand. "Yes! Yes! Yes!" I cheered and, in a moment of overexcitement, I pulled him in for a hug. "This is it! Thank you!"

He patted my shoulder. "You're welcome, Ms. O'Shea. You have a good day now, you hear?"

"You too! See you tomorrow!" I called out and waved goodbye to my mailman. Then, I turned and sprinted back inside, not caring one bit how ridiculous I may have looked.

Skidding to a halt in the kitchen, I leaned on the counter and tore into the envelope. After weeks of back and forth with the various county offices involved, I finally had my hands on everything related to my sister's case.

First, to get any of the reports, I had to prove I was the next of kin of the deceased. In order to do that, I needed to know which girl was my biological sister. So, I stopped there and turned my attention to the tooth.

Frankie had a friend who worked in a lab and agreed to help us out in exchange for a set of signed books. I sent the tooth, some of my father's things she said would have testable DNA on them, and my own cheek swab. She promised to run the samples, print official results, and delete the records from their system. But, because there was a different process for extracting DNA from a tooth, it was going to take much longer than usual to get the results. I didn't care how long it took, as long as I got them.

I was just as excited to see my mailman on the day I received those results too. It took weeks, but I finally had undeniable proof that Paige Coleman was my half sister.

Next, I began the process of requesting any and all public records I could get my hands on—particularly any documents related to her death, as well as Heidi's. Unfortunately, I learned that I would only be receiving Paige's records—anything related to any other parties involved would be blacked out or hidden with a notation.

Taking a deep breath to steady my shaking hands, I started going over the first of many reports. After reading through each report twice, several of my questions were answered, but I had a number of new ones as well. First, what happened to Heidi? Second, how was their story kept out of the news?

And what about Phyllis Banner? Paige killed herself in her mother's basement. The mother that Bronze told me was dead. I felt my blood start to heat, just like it did every time I thought about him.

Frankie was right. I should've known better than to fuck around with bikers. I didn't really think he had anything to do with their deaths, particularly Paige's. But I did think he was giving me the runaround so he could get in my pants. Then, in the biggest douchebag move ever, he sent his brother to scare me away. Well, the joke was on them, because I got what I came for anyway.

My thoughts were interrupted when my phone started ringing. I groaned when I saw the name on the screen, suddenly remembering the plans I'd made. "Hey! I was just about to call you," I lied. "I'm running a little late. You guys go ahead with dinner, and I'll meet you for drinks."

"You better," Maura playfully chided. "Or we're coming over there and dragging you out of that house, iron gates or not."

"I know," I laughed. "I'm coming. I promise."

"Good. See you soon," she chirped and disconnected.

Sighing, I slid the papers back into the envelope and pushed them to the side. Even if I did manage to find a new clue or avenue to investigate, there wasn't anything I could do until Monday morning. In the meantime, I was long overdue for a girls' night out.

Pulling on a sleeveless shirt that sparkled, I paired it with a short and stretchy black skirt and a pair of heels so spiked they should've come with a permit. After going heavy on the eyeshadow and light on the lips, I grabbed the essentials and headed out to meet my cousins. Unfortunately, with both of them being in grad school, I didn't get to spend as much time with them as I once did.

When my mom moved back to Cherryfield, where she grew up and where her family still lived, the three of us were always together. Well, we were until we got caught sneaking back in after being out at a party. That was also when my mother dubbed Jessica "a bad influence" because she gave me the alcohol that got me drunk for the first time.

Jessica saw me first and squealed, coming toward me with her arms wide open. "Sloane! Girl, you're looking sexy as hell in that outfit. Bet you won't be going home alone tonight."

"Oh hush," I laughed, returning her embrace. "It's so good to see you! Where's Maura?" I asked when I glanced around and didn't see her anywhere.

"Right here, you blind bitch," Maura said from my side, scaring the shit out of me.

"You changed your hair!" I gasped. "I didn't even recognize you, but damn, I love it!" Maura had gone from a gorgeous red to a platinum blonde, and it looked stunning on her.

"Thank you! I'm still not used to it. I keep forgetting that it's blonde and scare myself every time I pass a mirror."

We made our way to a bar that wasn't terribly crowded and managed to find a high-top table available. "Hurry! Go grab that one before someone else does! I'll go get our drinks," Jessica blurted and shoved me in the direction of the empty table.

When Jessica returned carrying a tray—yes, a tray—of

drinks, Maura turned to me excitedly. "Are you really going to make us ask?"

I cocked my head to the side in confusion. "Ask what?"

"Did it come today?" they asked in unison.

"Did what come today?" I asked and felt panic start to rise within me. I hadn't said a word to them about the results or reports. There was no way they could know about Paige.

"Your books," they said in unison.

"Oh!" I almost shouted. I'd completely forgotten they'd each requested a copy of my newest release. "No, they didn't. The shipment got delayed, so I'll have to mail them to you when I get them."

"Damn, I was looking forward to reading it on my return flight," Jessica said.

"Me too," Maura commiserated.

"You can read it through the app on almost any electronic device."

"It's not the same," they said in unison.

"So, bring me up to speed. What's been going on? What did I miss?" I asked, hoping to take the focus off of me.

They talked and talked. I tried to pay attention, but I couldn't stop thinking about what I read—and didn't read—in the reports. I don't know why, but suicide never crossed my mind as a possibility. I didn't think it was a dual suicide since Paige left a brief note saying she couldn't go on living without the love of her life.

I had a feeling finding out what happened to Heidi would put all the pieces together. I understood the need to protect the privacy of others, but damn it, I needed to know what happened, if for no other reason than my own personal sanity. I also wanted to know how two young women in their mid-twenties were found dead—one of which was reported missing—and the story was never mentioned on any news outlet after the initial article about the discovery. Furthermore, the only information about their deaths other than it being suspected as a murder-suicide was the basic information found in public records—name, date of birth, date of death, and town of residence.

I briefly considered asking my father for the truth, but I wasn't sure I'd believe anything he said. On the other hand, he couldn't deny threatening the pregnant woman at our door all those years ago, because I saw her with my own eyes and heard him threaten her with my own ears.

I inhaled slowly as a horrible thought suddenly occurred to me, and then I immediately dismissed it. I was well aware of who my father was and the powerful reach he had. But even Lorcan O'Shea wouldn't have had his own offspring killed. Would he?

"You okay?" Maura asked.

"Uh, yeah," I stammered and reached for my drink.

"We're pretty beat from traveling all day. If you want to call it a night, that's fine with us," Jessica added.

"I hate to go home early because I hardly ever get to see you. But it's been a long day, and I could use some rest."

With that, I closed out our tab while Maura called a cab for them, and Jessica called one for me. I'd have to take one back to the garage to get my car the next morning, but I'd rather do that than attempt to drive home after having a few drinks.

Outside of the bar, we exchanged hugs. I waved goodbye while I stood on the sidewalk waiting for my cab and watched theirs pull away. As their driver turned at the intersection, a car passing by caught my eye. It wasn't the thumping bass or the exorbitant flashy sports car that made me do a double take. No, it was because that car belonged to my brother, Tiernan, who most certainly had not let me know he was in town like he always did. As his little sister, I had an obligation to follow him and see if I could find a way to annoy the piss out of him for his payback.

Forgetting about my cab, I quickly walked down the street and turned the corner, headed in the direction of the parking garage I assumed was Tiernan's destination. My assumption was correct. Tiernan parked his car, somehow scoring a space on the first level right beside the exit. My jaw dropped when the passenger door opened, and Declan got out carrying a large duffel bag.

Standing in the shadows, I waited for them to pass before I stepped out and followed them, easily blending in with the Saturday night crowd. They weaved their way through the city streets, obviously with a specific destination in mind. I started to get nervous when the crowd between us began to thin, but then they turned down an alley and stopped in front of the second door on the right.

Plastering myself against the wall, I strained to listen. "You on the list?" a man asked.

"O'Shea," Declan clipped. He always got annoyed when he wasn't immediately recognized. Secretly, it tickled me to no end because it was preposterous to expect every person you came in contact with to know who you were. For fuck's sake, we were the spawn of an organized crime boss, not descendants from the royal family.

"Any guests?"

"Do you see any?" I rolled my eyes. He could be such an asshole sometimes.

The man at the door deserved credit. He didn't flinch or seem to give much of a shit that two of those O'Sheas were standing in front of him. With a nonchalant nod, he took a step back. "Go on down."

I risked a glance around the corner to see Declan and Tiernan entering the building. After waiting for the longest ten minutes in history to pass, I walked down the alley and knocked on the same door. In the seconds it took for the man to answer, I contemplated turning and running for the hills but figured I didn't have much to lose. If he wouldn't let me in, I'd just call Tiernan and get in anyway. But where was the fun in that?

"You on the list?"

"I'm a guest of Declan O'Shea," I said confidently and stuck my boobs out for good measure.

"He expecting you?"

I grinned seductively. "No, I'm here to surprise him." I didn't like the thought of him thinking I was my brother's whore for the night, but I was willing to deal with it if it got me inside the club.

"You know where you're going?"

"Sure do," I giggled.

His eyes raked over me from head to toe. "Go on down," he said, repeating the same words to me and stepping to the side. "Lucky bastard," I heard him mutter when I was halfway down the stairs, causing me to shiver in revulsion.

That was also when my excitement at getting past the doorman was replaced by a rush of nervous energy mixed with a touch of fear. I had no idea what kind of place I was walking into. What if it was one of those BDSM clubs, and I'd just become my brother's slave by declaring myself his guest?

And that's the thought that should've had me running for the stairs, but it didn't. I knew both of my brothers would keep me safe, once I found them. Even if I didn't find them, there was a good chance dropping my father's name would get me out of almost any situation that could arise.

With that in mind, I pressed forward and moved deeper into the club, the sound of a crowd getting louder with each step I took. I finally came to a foyer with three doors where several people were milling about, thankfully not clad in latex and chains. Since I had no idea what was behind the doors, I leaned against the far wall and waited for someone to open at least one of them. Five minutes later, I had my answer. Each door led to a room filled with small bleachers surrounding a fighting ring in the center.

Since there weren't any active fights, I wandered around from room to room looking for Declan and Tiernan. I did find a bar along the way and got myself a drink to help ease my nerves before continuing to explore.

I was in the first room on the left when the lights overhead flickered, and someone came over the speaker to tell us to take our seats. Based on how quickly the crowd collectively followed the instructions, I followed suit and planted my ass in the first seat I found.

From the moment I sat down, I could feel the man sitting beside me was staring at me. I glanced around the room to see if there was a vacant seat anywhere, but I didn't think I was allowed to move after the way everyone dove for a seat.

He leaned closer, halting at the edge of invading my personal space. "Does your father know you're here?"

My head snapped up, and I glared into the eyes of a man I'd never met in person but instantly recognized—Luca Peccati. "I'm an adult, Mr. Peccati."

"Yes," he agreed. "You're also an O'Shea."

"Does that mean I'm not welcome here?" I asked,

preparing to find my brothers and get us the hell out of there if necessary.

"It means, as with any event of this nature, friend or foe may be in attendance." My brows wrinkled in confusion. "For starters, you're an O'Shea sitting beside a Peccati. Look around, Sloane. Who else do you see?"

Reluctantly, I raised my head and let my eyes slowly sweep over the faces filling the bleachers. The first thing I noticed was an abundance of men who were obviously working as security, though I didn't know if they worked for the club or were personal guards for some of the people attending the fight. Unless they all belonged to Luca. I stiffened at the thought and forced myself to focus on the task at hand.

"Is that Nikolai Volkov?" I whispered.

"Indeed, it is," he confirmed.

"In the next section to the right, that's Gabriel DeLuca and Pietro," I breathed.

He cleared his throat. "Do you understand now?"

It finally hit me. I was in an underground fight club, and judging by the crowd in attendance, it was a high-dollar one. "Oh," I said. "Well, thank you for bringing that to my attention."

"Why are you here?"

"I was supposed to be meeting a friend, but I think I'm in the wrong place," I lied and pointed to the door. "Is it okay for me to leave?"

He shook his head. "No. Once the door closes and locks, it remains locked until the end of the fight."

"Why?"

"There's a number of reasons, but one is to prevent people from trying to sneak out and cheat the system by placing a large bet on the winning fighter halfway through the match. Everyone in here placed a bet on one of the fighters before they entered this room," he explained.

"I didn't," I blurted, causing his eyes to widen before they narrowed sharply.

"Then, you shouldn't be in here. How did you get in?" he asked in a way I knew it was best to answer with the truth.

"I told the doorman I was here to surprise Declan," I admitted. "And I told him I knew where I was going."

Luca sharply nodded his head once. "I see. Well, Ms. O'Shea, it would be in your best interest to secure a bet with me right now before the match begins."

There was no doubt in my mind that he was dead serious, literally. "Fine," I relented. "I want to place the lowest bet you'll take on the fighter you think will win."

He chuckled. "You're lucky that I won't take advantage of such a vague bet because I know your father. Others would not be so thoughtful."

"Dad has always spoken highly of you," I said offhandedly before my curiosity got the best of me. "Why is a bet required?"

"That's not information you're privy to," he said sharply, then softened his tone. "Even Maxim and Pietro placed bets in order to enter with Nikolai and Gabriel." He paused when the lights flickered. "Ah, it's about to begin."

I turned to the ring and watched quietly as the two fighters squared up in the center. There was very little fanfare before the two large men started pummeling each other in a barbaric fashion. The sounds of their taped fists slamming into each other's flesh almost had me throwing up. It seemed like it went on forever before one of them finally fell to the floor in a bloody heap.

As people got up and began to circulate, Luca stayed

planted in his seat. "Am I allowed to leave now?" I whispered.

He shook his head, but the corners of his lips tipped up in a small grin. "No, dear, there's one more match scheduled for this room tonight."

I felt my face turn green. "I'm not sure I can sit through another one of those," I confessed, causing him to chuckle.

"I can assure you this match will not be as long as the first one." He snapped his fingers in the air, and a man suddenly appeared at his side. "I would like a drink. And bring Ms. O'Shea a fresh one as well."

The attendant returned several minutes later, magically refilling my drink correctly without asking what it was. The crowd had thinned out, and the room started to fill with new people. Luca turned to me. "Now, tell me why you're really here."

I decided to see if part of the truth would satisfy him. "I saw someone I recognized come in here, and I wanted to say hello."

He nodded slowly. "Nice try, Ms. O'Shea. Now tell me the rest."

I opened my mouth even though I had no idea what to say when the lights flickered. Glancing around, I noticed everyone was already in their seats. Had I missed the announcement? Before I could give it much thought, the fighters appeared in the ring, and my jaw dropped open in absolute disbelief.

Because I recognized both fighters.

In the left corner, wearing green trunks like the proud Irish fighter he was, Declan bounced on the balls of his feet and tossed a few punches in the air.

In the right corner, wearing black shorts with bronze

stripes down the side, Bronze Black was leaning casually on the corner post waiting for the fight to begin.

Bronze Fucking Black.

That motherfucker! Fiery rage began to fill my veins at the sight of his deceptive face. I started to rise to my feet when Luca's hand shot out and pulled me back down. "Where do you think you're going, Ms. O'Shea?" Luca asked.

"But that's—" I started.

"Your brother. You said you knew he was here. Have you been lying to me, Ms. O'Shea?"

I don't know if it was the initial shock of seeing him again or the surge of anger that washed over me, but I was on the verge of snapping his head off regardless of who he was. Instead, I managed to regain my wits enough to respond accordingly. "Please, call me Sloane. And yes, I knew Declan was here, but I didn't know he was fighting."

"Interesting," he mused.

"How so?" I asked and managed to pull my eyes away from the ring to face Luca.

"Because he fights here regularly."

Well, shit. My eyes darted around the room once again looking for three familiar faces—my father's, Kian's, and Tiernan's. "Of course, the Irish mob family would have a mini-reunion at an underground fight club."

Luca covered his mouth with his hand, but I heard the light chuckle that escaped him. "Oops. I didn't mean to say that out loud. But since I did, is my father here?"

It occurred to me that if my father knew Declan was fighting, he would attend his fights; therefore, Luca would have handed me off to my dad. I knew the answer but asked anyway to hopefully ease my nerves. "Does my father know Declan is here?"

Luca cleared his throat and straightened his tie. "Pay

attention, Ms. O'Shea. The show is about to begin." It didn't occur to me until much later that Luca never answered my question.

I think I held my breath from the moment the fight started to the moment it ended, which was thirty-eight seconds later.

Holy.

Shit.

Declan had been fighting for well over fifteen years and was what I considered to be a good fighter. I could only recall him losing one match, and nothing even close to a knockout happened. And Bronze knocked him out in thirty-eight seconds.

Rising from my seat, I started to move toward the ring to make sure Declan was okay when a firm but gentle hand pulled me back. "Your brother will be fine. You, however, might not be if you leave my side. Am I understood?" His tone brooked no argument.

"Yes, Mr. Peccati," I agreed, unsure of why his words unnerved me the way they did.

He stood and extended his hand to help me to my feet. When we stepped into the aisle, he looped my arm through his elbow and held it tightly against his side. We didn't make it more than two steps before we were surrounded by people.

Suddenly several larger men shoved their way to the front, turned, and started forcing the crowd back. "Thank you, Vincenzo. Please see that Nikolai Volkov and Maxim, as well as Gabriel DeLuca and Pietro, are escorted to the lounge immediately. Give me ten minutes. Then, I'll start seeing the others one at a time in my office."

With that, Luca and I exited into the foyer, leaving the crowd of spectators locked in the room. He turned to me with very stern eyes. "I'm going to escort you to the stairs.

From there, Piero will escort you to your vehicle. You will then get into your car and drive straight to your house."

"But Declan—"

"I will check on him and call you myself. Now, off you go," he said and shooed me toward the man waiting at the top of the stairs. The next second, he reached out and placed his hand on my shoulder to stop me. "We need to settle your bet first."

"Oh, right," I said. Any other time, I would have been much more concerned with the outcome of placing a bet in the manner I did, but all I cared about was getting out of there as fast as possible before I ran into Bronze and did something I would regret. Like tell my dad what he did, because clearly he could handle my big brothers with no problem whatsoever. "Did I win or lose?" I asked and placed my hands on my hips.

Luca grinned and reached into his jacket. "You won, Ms. O'Shea," he said and held out a stack of bills for me.

I looked at his outstretched hand like he was holding a pit viper instead of a wad of cash. "Did I win betting against Declan?" Because I didn't want to take it if I did.

"You won. We'll leave it at that," he said and reached for my hand, placing the stack of money in my palm.

My eyes widened in shock. From one glance, I guessed I was holding at least five thousand dollars. I floundered for what to do with the money. It wouldn't fit in the tiny purse I was carrying. As a last resort, I stepped closer to Luca so we were almost touching and made quick work of stuffing half of the bills in each bra cup.

When I stepped back, I almost laughed at the look on his face. Instead, I said what I was thinking. "I shudder to think how much I could've lost."

"Let that be a lesson to you, Ms. O'Shea."

"Oh, it has been. And it was well-received. Good night,

Mr. Peccati," I said and jogged up the stairs to meet my next escort.

The man Luca called Piero didn't utter one word in my presence, but he kept his eyes trained on me. When we arrived at my car, he simply nodded and disappeared into the night once I locked the doors. Leaning back against the headrest, I closed my eyes and tried to process the events of the evening.

Bronze Black knocked out my brother.

Bronze Black was in Cherryfield.

Bronze Black was fighting in an underground fighting ring.

And Bronze Black lied to me, used me, and toyed with my emotions. A familiar anger bubbled in my chest. So much so that I considered going back inside to look for him until I remembered Luca's warning.

Cranking my car, I yelped when someone knocked on the window. I turned to see who was knocking and was met with a pair of familiar stormy blue eyes. "What the fuck are you doing here?" he roared.

"What the fuck am I doing here?" I returned and got out to face him. That's when I noticed the other two men standing beside three motorcycles, one I assumed belonged to Bronze. "What the fuck are you doing here?" I demanded and made a show of looking around the area. "What? You didn't bring your brother to do your dirty work for you this time?"

"What?" he asked and seemed genuinely confused, but I knew how good of an actor he was.

I snorted in derision. "I fell for your act one time, but it won't happen again."

"The fuck are you—"

Bronze's words were silenced by the audible chambering of a gun nearby.

"Is there a problem here?"

Quickly glancing toward the voice, I exhaled in relief when I saw Piero and Vincenzo, each holding a gun, though neither were pointed at anyone. "You need to leave. Right now. Luca will not be happy about this."

"That's what I was trying to do!" I shouted and threw my hands in the air.

"Why?" Bronze demanded at the same time.

Piero turned to Bronze and pinned him with a glare so harsh it made me shiver. Bronze held his hands out in a placating manner. "Look, man, her and I have some shit to sort out, and I'm not going anywhere until that happens."

A throat cleared in the shadows, and Luca Peccati stepped into the light. "I'm not going to ask why you approached your opponent's sister in the parking lot. I'm not going to point out what a poor decision you made. However, I am going to stand here while Ms. O'Shea drives away, and then the rest of us are going to my office to talk."

"Works for me. Ta-ta!" I shouted and peeled out of the lot before my door was completely closed.

I hadn't fully processed everything that happened by the time I got home, but I did know one thing for sure—there was no way in hell I wasn't going back.

15

BRONZE

"Motherfucker!" I bellowed seconds after jumping out of the direct path of Sloane's car. What the fuck? Apparently, whoever was writing the story of my life loved almost killing me.

I stood there in complete and total shock with my hand over my heart as I tried to keep it from beating out of my chest and catch my breath at the same time. When I finally regained some composure, I realized the little she-devil didn't even stop.

"She almost hit me!"

"But she didn't," Piero pointed out.

Gritting my teeth, I held my tongue as I watched her taillights disappear. I spent more time than I cared to admit looking for her after she popped smoke and disappeared. Then, all of a sudden, she's right there in front of me, and there was nothing I could do to make her stay.

"Gentlemen, follow me," Luca instructed.

I signaled for Grant and Drew to follow me back inside. Fuck, I had no idea what kind of shit I'd inadvertently stepped in. If I could get a handle on my anger before we reached Luca's office, I was going to do my best to get out of it without involving the club.

Luca closed the door and took a seat behind his desk. "Explain."

"I met her a few months ago in Devil Springs and walked over to say hello," I shrugged. "I didn't know she was O'Shea's sister."

Luca silently stared at me while waiting for more, but I didn't have to tell him my personal business, and I wasn't going to.

When he realized I wasn't going to say more, he sat back in his chair and clasped his hands in his lap. "I can't have external animosity between my contenders. You of all people know what happens when fighters have problems outside of the ring. If you want to keep fighting here, don't approach her. Having said that, I can't do anything about it if she approaches you. If that happens, keep your personal shit out of and away from my club."

"Understood."

"Very well," he said and extended his hand. "We'll see you back here in two weeks."

Pissed off didn't even begin to cover how I was feeling. I'd tried to find her, on more than one occasion, after she left town without a word. Every avenue I tried was a dead end. But it suddenly all made sense. She was Lorcan O'Shea's daughter.

I fucked an Irish mob boss's daughter.

And I kicked her brother's ass.

I wanted to laugh at the thought but knew it wasn't the time. I'd have to double fist pump later.

Fuck. Her dad had the power to make his baby girl untraceable, which explained why I couldn't find her by her phone number or license plate. And it also explained why she was checked in under an alias. I'd suspected she was lying about why she was in Devil Springs early on, but finding out her real identity confirmed it.

Sloane may have thought she got away from me again, but it would only be until my next fight. Because regardless of what Luca said, I was going to see her again. I just had to make her come to me first.

WHEN WE ARRIVED AT THE CLUB, I TOLD THE DOORMAN I was expecting a guest and gave him her name. Then, I leaned closer and slipped some cash into his palm. "You need to escort her to my locker room and lock the door once she's inside. Otherwise, she'll sneak into the fights and get herself into trouble. She may try to check in as her brother's guest, Declan O'Shea. She pulled that shit two weeks ago, and Luca found her in one of the rooms," I said and gave him a pointed look.

"Got it."

After giving it some thought, I realized that I didn't need to do anything to get Sloane to come to me. Her tenacity and curiosity would bring her back without me having to lift a finger.

I smiled as I made my way to my designated locker room, wondering if she would come willingly or if she would be dragged in kicking and screaming. I snorted to myself and wondered if I should've slipped the guy some more cash.

When I reached the small locker room designated as mine for the foreseeable future, I put my earbuds in and started my prefight routine. Not that I needed to. According to Luca, this fight was going to be another knockout in less than a minute. But, I never wanted to be caught off guard.

Halfway through my routine, the locker room door flew open, and one of the bouncers shoved a pissed off Sloane inside.

"What in the hell do you think you're doing?" she demanded.

"Aw, baby, don't be like that," I said, knowing it would piss her off even more.

"Oh, baby's gonna be like that," she snapped.

"Damn, you're hot when you're pissy."

She huffed. "What the fuck do you want?"

"We've got some shit to talk about," I said, and then the coordinator knocked on the door. "Fuck," I cursed. "Gotta go. Stay put," I demanded and locked the door on my way out. "Ignore her if she starts screaming," I called out over my shoulder as I headed to the ring. With any luck, I wouldn't be gone long.

Grant and Drew were waiting for me in my corner. I preferred to warm up for a match alone, which worked out well since I didn't want them to know I sort of kidnapped Lorcan O'Shea's daughter and was holding her against her will in my locker room.

Just like the last fight, my opponent was laid out in less than a minute, and it was starting to make me feel like the playground bully. I wasn't there for easy wins or to manipulate my statistics. I wanted a good fight as much as I needed it. However, Luca assured me that everyone started out at the bottom of the roster and worked their way up. In other words, I had to earn my spot and fight to keep it. Even if I lost, I could still fight every other weekend, but I wouldn't advance or make any money if I was bested.

After the ref raised my hand in the air and declared me

the winner, I left as soon as I received the okay from the coordinator.

"You two can go ahead without me. I've got something to take care of," I told Grant and Drew. I never hung around after a fight, but I needed to get back to Sloane as soon as possible.

When I returned to the locker room, Sloane was nowhere in sight. I knew she couldn't have escaped, which meant she was hiding. After changing, I began to look for her. She was a feisty little thing, and I was enjoying every second of it.

"Sloane. Oh, Sweet Sloane," I called. "Come out, come out, wherever you are."

The locker room itself was relatively small, so there were only a handful of places she could be. After several minutes of searching, I found her tucked into one of the tall lockers with her head bent at an awkward angle.

"That was fun," I said, not bothering to hide the sarcasm in my voice. "What in the hell did you think hiding was going to accomplish?"

"I was hoping you'd think I'd gotten out and wouldn't look for me. That way, I could leave without having to see, hear, or speak to you."

"I wasn't expecting such hostility from you. I think I'm hurt," I said flatly. "My turn. Let's go," I said and reached for her arm.

"I'm not going anywhere with you."

I smirked. "Yes, you are, darlin'. It's just a matter of if you're walking or if I'm carrying you."

She dropped her chin to her chest and admitted, "I'm stuck."

"You're what?" I chuckled.

She huffed. "I'm stuck. Part of my dress is caught on one of the hooks or something."

"Well, I'm waiting," I taunted.

"Waiting for what?"

"For you to ask for my help."

She scoffed and rolled her eyes before she relented. "Will you help me get unstuck?"

"Say please."

"Fuck right off. Please," she snarked.

"You want help or not?"

She huffed and rolled her eyes to the sky. I could tell it was the absolute last thing she wanted to do and didn't bother to hide how much I was enjoying her predicament. "Can you help me get unstuck?"

"I can, but will I?"

She sucked in a sharp breath at the indignance. Or so I thought until she opened her mouth and screamed at the top of her lungs. "Declan! Help me!"

I slapped my hand over her mouth. "For fuck's sake. I'll get you out if you don't scream again. Luca's likely to come down here and kill us both," I said seriously. Luca was cool with me and the MC, but I knew he couldn't and wouldn't tolerate personal bullshit in his club. And I also knew he was quick to pull the trigger because I'd seen him end a life without even looking in the poor fuck's direction. "I'm serious as shit, Sloane. You gonna be quiet?"

With comically wide eyes, she quickly nodded her head. I cautiously removed my hand and took a step back to take a better look at her situation. "What do you need me to do?"

"I don't know. Try reaching around and see if you can find where it's stuck," she suggested.

I slid my hand along her tight waist and around her back, just above her hips. I wanted to feel my hands sliding over her bare skin again, remembering how it felt as silky as the material she was wearing.

My hand came to a stop when my fingers found the problem. At this point, my face was next to hers, our mouths mere centimeters apart. "Pretty sure the only way you're getting out of that locker is by unzipping your dress." She opened her mouth to argue, but I placed one finger over her lips and continued. "I think the fabric is caught on one of the screws holding the row of lockers to the wall. You can either unzip it to loosen the material or rip it. Your choice."

"So help me, if you're fucking with me," she growled.

I stepped back and met her eyes. "I'm not. What's it going to be?"

She inhaled deeply and dropped her head. "Go ahead. Unzip it."

My hand left her hip and smoothed its way up to the zipper. I knew what was going to happen, and so did she. Her dress was strapless. The moment I started to unzip it, her generous tits were going to spill right out, and there wasn't much she could do about it with how her arms were positioned. But, being the fucking gentleman that my mother raised me to be, I held the dress against her chest while I slid the zipper down until the slack in the material allowed me to slip it over the screw. "You're free. Step out, and I'll zip you up."

When she was back to rights, she looked up at me with a mix of confusion and anger in her eyes. "Thank you. Now, what in the hell do you want?"

I laughed. "You don't miss a beat, do you? I already told you. We need to talk."

"We have nothing to talk about," she snapped.

That was bullshit, and we both knew it. Cutting right to the chase, I crossed my arms over my chest and asked, "Then why'd you come back?"

"To watch my brother fight."

"What time's his fight?" I asked.

She opened her mouth and closed it several times before she settled on, "He told me to be here by ten o'clock and meet him in his locker room."

I snorted. "Your brother's fight was over an hour ago. Care to try again?"

"It doesn't matter why—"

Her words were interrupted by someone knocking on the door. "Black, you still in there?"

I met Sloane's eyes and held my finger over my lips. "Yeah, man, I'm about to head out."

"You good?"

"Yeah, just finishing up a phone call. I'm heading out now," I told him.

"All right. See you in a few weeks," he replied and rapped his knuckles on the door twice before his footsteps could be heard echoing down the hallway.

Turning back to Sloane, I didn't pull any punches. "You're going to keep that mouth shut and walk out of here," I said quietly and held up my hand to stop the protest I saw coming. "I don't care what you do when we get outside, but you're getting the fuck out of this club right now."

"Fine," she huffed and raised her hand with her thumb holding her ring finger down while extending the others. "Scout's Honor."

I damn near choked as I doubled over laughing. "That's The Shocker, not the Scout's Honor sign!"

"Oh, my bad. But this is the Ball Buster, right?" she asked and threw a punch aimed right at my junk.

I caught her closed fist before she made contact and smirked in her face as I leaned down and hoisted her over my shoulder. Then, I slapped my palm over her ass cheek, because

I wanted to and because she fucking deserved it. I should've known her lack of outrage was a red flag, but I didn't. So, she caught me completely off guard when she shoved her hands down the back of my jeans and dug her fingernails into my bare ass cheeks while I was carrying her up the stairs.

"Don't start something you can't finish," I warned.

She scoffed. "Then let me go, you big boxing biker brute!"

Originally, I planned to place her on her feet the moment we were outside of the club, but her hands down my pants had me carrying her down the alley to the parking garage. I spotted the same car she'd driven to the club two weeks ago and stomped toward it.

Unceremoniously dropping her onto the hood, she landed with a plop. Her nails dragged across my skin as her hands were pulled from my pants. Grabbing her wrists when they crested my shoulders, I followed her down and pinned her to the hood. "You're pissing me off and making my dick hard."

"I only like ragey muscles in the bedroom."

"Never have and never will put my hands on a woman in anger," I told her honestly.

"Says the man holding me down," she retorted and tried to move her arms and twist her body to get out of my grip. All she succeeded in doing was flipping herself onto her stomach.

Giving her some of my weight, I wanted to groan when my dick pressed against her firm ass, but she was pissing me off. "Enough!" I roared and released her. "What the fuck is your problem?"

She was on her feet in a flash, and she was livid. "You! You're my problem! You fucked me, made me think you were going to help me, and then you sent your brother to scare me off!" she yelled and inhaled deeply as if preparing to go again.

"The fuck are you talking about?" I shouted back. "I sent my brother to the hotel, and he said you were gone."

She scoffed. "He threatened me! Of course, I left."

"Bullshit!" I started but immediately changed course. "No, you know what? Fuck this shit. I'm out." I didn't have the interest or energy to argue with a woman who was clearly batshit crazy.

"You can't leave!"

"Yeah, I can, and I am," I said and turned to leave. The Sloane I met months ago and tried to find was not the Sloane standing in front of me. A year ago, I might have played her game a little longer, might have even tried to end the night buried between her legs, but everything changed after Blue was born. Since then, everything I did was for her. And having a screaming match with Lorcan O'Shea's daughter in a public parking garage—after I'd been warned not to do so again—was not in my daughter's best interest.

I whirled around when something hit me right smack in the middle of my back. Sloane was standing there barefoot—one shoe in her hand and the other on the ground near me. "Why'd you do it? Why'd you lie to me? You stole the only chance I had of meeting my sister!" With tears steadily streaming down her face, she dropped the other shoe and walked back to her car with her head down, and her shoulders slumped in defeat.

I wasn't like most men when it came to a crying woman. Nine out of ten times, the first sign of a tear pissed me off. Because based on my experiences, most women used tears as a means of manipulation. But hers were real. No one could fake the defeat and despair emanating from her. And I was a sucker for real tears.

Then, her words finally penetrated, and I was moving toward her before I could think better of it. "Sloane, wait. What're you talking about?"

"I lied to you!" she cried. "I wasn't there for an interview. I was looking for the sister I didn't know I had. And now she's gone!"

The sound of someone approaching reminded me of where we were. I wasn't afraid of Luca by any means, but I had a healthy respect for the man he was and saw no reason to piss him off unnecessarily. "This is the last time I'm saying this. You and I need to talk. Nothing you've said tonight makes any sense to me. If you wanna go somewhere public and have a conversation, I'll meet you there. If not, I'm walking away," I told her and held my hands up in surrender.

She wordlessly turned around and walked to the passenger side of her car. "Fine, we can talk. But you'll have to drive because I'm exhausted, and I've been drinking."

"Where to?" I asked and slipped behind the wheel of her car.

She answered by holding up her phone and snapping a picture. "I'm sending your name and picture to my best friend so she can pass it along to my father if anything happens to me."

I reached into my wallet, pulled out my driver's license, and tossed it onto her lap. "Make it easier and send a picture of that."

"It's probably fake," she muttered as she snapped the picture.

"It's not, but it wouldn't matter if it was. Luca knows where to find me. Hell, everyone knows where to find me. I'm the Vice President of the Blackwings MC. That's not a hidden fact, sugar. Now, where are we going?"

After giving me directions to a twenty-four-hour waffle and pancake diner, we rode the rest of the way in silence. I thought she was taking time to compose herself, but she continued giving me the silent treatment while we took our seats and placed our order. We almost went on to eat our food in silence, but she had to ask me for something.

"Will you please pass the ketchup?"

"Maybe. Are you going to put it on your eggs?"

Her nose wrinkled in disgust. "Eww, that's gross."

"It is," I agreed and handed her the bottle. Then, I watched as the little she-devil squirted ketchup all over her scrambled eggs and took a huge bite. I wanted to vomit. Instead, I focused on my food and tried to ignore her.

"I thought you wanted to talk," she said.

"I do, but not until you're finished with your bloody eggs."

"Mmm," she moaned obnoxiously and started making smacking noises with her mouth. "So good."

I reminded myself I'd been covered in piss, barium shit, and formula vomit many times over the past few months; I could handle the grossest combination in the history of food for a few minutes.

I looked up to see Sloane scraping the eggs off of her plate and into a napkin with a look of utter disgust on her face. "Okay, fine. You're right. That's gross. Moving on."

I shook my head. She was something else. And I needed her to start talking because I honestly didn't know what to make of her at that point.

She must have felt me studying her while she picked at her food because she looked up suddenly and locked eyes with me. "What?"

I sat back and gave it to her straight. "Two things you said stood out to me, and I was trying to decide which one I wanted to ask about first."

She was good. She kept her face a mask of steel, but I could see the hurt in her eyes when she asked, "Why didn't you tell me they were dead?"

"Why did you disappear when you found out they were?" I countered.

"Because your brother told me to!" she said loudly and then lowered her voice. "He came to the hotel the day after you ghosted me and told me in no uncertain terms to leave."

"Who was it?"

"He said he was your brother."

"It couldn't have been Copper, so who the hell was it?"

"I don't know! He didn't tell me his name when he told me he would make sure I left Devil Springs that day if I didn't go willingly."

If she was lying to me, she deserved an award for her performance. I found a picture of Copper on my phone and held it up to show her. "This him?"

Her eyes narrowed when she looked at the screen. "Yeah, that's him."

"That's Copper," I said and looked at the picture on my phone. "What exactly did he say to you?"

She held up one finger and reached for her own phone. "It's hard to hear, so put the speaker next to your ear and listen."

I did as she said and listened to the encounter between Sloane and my asshole brother. I replayed it two more times before I passed her phone back to her. "That motherfucker," I grumbled. He'd never meddled in my business before, and I was going to make damn sure he never did again.

I took a moment to rein in my anger, but I was still irate when I spoke. "I did *not* ask him to do that. And I'm going to kick his ass when I get back home."

"Glad we got that settled," she said dryly.

"We haven't gotten shit settled," I countered.

"Please, continue telling me how your brother took things into his own hands without your consent. I can't wait to hear the bullshit you've come up with to fill—"

"Sloane," I interrupted.

"You had my fucking phone number!" she yelled.

"I had a fucking baby!" I yelled back.

Her mouth dropped open in shock. Seconds later, her shock morphed into an anger so sharp it bordered on rage. "You motherfucker! You cheated on someone with me!"

A different waitress candidly interrupted our beautiful moment. "Pay up. And leave now or I'm calling the cops." Then she narrowed her eyes at Sloane. "O'Sheas aren't welcome here."

"Fucking hell," I muttered and reached for my wallet. Tossing enough cash on the table to cover the food and a generous tip, I got to my feet and walked outside with Sloane following closely behind me. I came to a stop beside her car and turned to face her. "Shall we continue this elsewhere?"

"I'm not sure what else there is to continue," she retorted.

"There's plenty to continue, and you know it."

16

SLOANE

I placed my balled hands on my hips and demanded, "Did you cheat on someone when you slept with me?"

"Not a cheater, Sloane. Never have been, never will be," he said with such conviction I believed him.

Exhaling slowly, he looked to the sky for a few seconds. "I'm not having it out with you in another parking lot. We can finish this in my hotel room unless you have another suggestion."

I laughed derisively. "I'm not going back to your hotel room with you. Been there, done that."

"No, Sweet Sloane, I'm the one who's been there and done that," he said in a tone that had tingles shooting through me.

I rolled my eyes. "Semantics," I quipped. "Where're you staying?"

"The Cherry Tree."

Frustrated, I ran my hands over my face and sighed. My curiosity was going to win out, and there was nothing I could do about it. I knew going back to his hotel wasn't the smartest decision, but he was right in front of me. And I desperately wanted to know what else he could tell me about Paige. "I know where that is. Let's go get your bike, and I'll meet you there."

With that, he got into the driver's seat and drove us back to the parking garage. "Are you okay to drive now?" he asked.

"Stone cold sober," I admitted. When he continued to scrutinize me, I huffed and recited the alphabet backward. "Happy now?"

"Um, did you just have a stroke? Should I call one of your brothers?"

"It's a field sobriety test. Or it used to be," I laughed. "When I was four years old, my grandmother told me I needed to know how to say the alphabet backward, just in case. It wasn't until I was much older that I realized the reason behind it."

"It's impressive. I don't think I know anyone who could do that sober, let alone drunk."

"Which is exactly why it's no longer used as a field sobriety test. At least, I don't think it is," I said and gestured for him to get out of my car.

He shook his head and opened the door. "I'll meet you in the lobby."

"Okey dokey," I acknowledged as I carefully climbed over the console and into the driver's seat, magically managing to keep from showing my good girl to the world.

On the short drive to the swanky hotel downtown, I tried to gather my thoughts. So much had already been said, and I knew there was more to come. I just couldn't fathom what else there could possibly be.

He didn't send his brother to threaten me.

He didn't ghost me.

He had a baby.

My phone ringing through my car's stereo scared the living shit out of me, yet again.

"Frankie!" I shouted.

"What's wrong?"

"Oh, nothing. The phone ringing scared me."

"Really? What're you doing?"

I scrunched my nose. I wasn't going to lie to her, but I decidedly did not want to tell her what I was doing. Because she was going to tell me how stupid I was being, and I was in a place where I didn't want to listen to reason.

"Going to The Cherry Tree to finish talking to Bronze," I admitted.

"What?! Have you lost your mind?"

"We went to a diner downtown to talk, but a waitress recognized me when we started arguing. 'O'Sheas aren't welcome here,'" I mocked. "So, we're going somewhere else. But let me tell you this real quick before we get there. I played the recording you sent of me and his brother—thank you again for doing that—and Frankie, I wish you could've seen his face. I wholeheartedly believe he didn't know anything about what his brother did."

"Okay, then why did he ghost you?"

"I don't know the whole story. That's when the waitress kicked us out."

"Tell me the half-story, Demon!"

"He had a baby!" I blurted.

"Men can't have babies, Sloane. Try again."

"That's all he said. 'I had a fucking baby!' Then Cunty McCunterson showed up. I'm going to find out which one of my brothers fucked her over and kick his ass. Why can't they fuck women from other towns?" I grumbled.

"Focus!" Frankie snapped. "We'll figure out how to punish your whore brothers later. In the meantime, what you're doing is unsafe and a bad idea. There, I said it.

Since I know you're going to do what you want anyway, be safe, and call me as soon as you can."

"I will," I promised and pulled into the hotel parking lot. "I'm here. I'll talk to you later."

Taking a deep breath, I got out and found him waiting for me outside the main entrance. "We can talk in the courtyard if you'd feel more comfortable there than in my room."

"Interesting choice. This place is a little froufrou even for my taste," I said to buy myself some time to consider his offer. He'd done plenty to piss me off, but I had never felt threatened by him—not really—and I still didn't.

"They have the best cookies out of all the hotels in the area."

"You have got to be kidding me. You're seriously staying here because of the cookies?"

"Hell yes, I am! They have kick-ass shower gel and shit too, but it's the cookies that keep me coming back," he shared. "So, what's it going to be?"

"Since things tend to get heated rather quickly, maybe we should talk in your room for the sake of privacy." Truthfully, I'd already shared the news of my sister while shouting in public once that night. I didn't want to increase the chances of someone overhearing by doing it again, especially before my dad and brothers knew. Plus, I slipped my thigh holster on and concealed my handgun under my dress before I got out.

"Right this way," he said and led me to his room on the third floor.

Inside was a standard hotel room with a king-size bed dominating the space. I chose to sit in the chair in the corner of the room. However, it was time for the shoes to go. Kicking off my heels, I propped my feet on the edge of the bed, crossed my legs at the ankles, and clasped my hands in my lap. "Ready for bullshit. Let's hear it."

Even if I got nothing out of our discussion, I figured at least some of it could be used in one of my future books. As much as I hated to admit it, Bronze bantered like a champ.

Kicking off his boots, he dropped onto the bed and mimicked my position. "You first."

I laughed sardonically. "I'm not the one who has a baby to explain."

He sat straight up and pivoted, then leaned in so he was almost looming over me. "I don't have to explain my daughter to you or anyone else," he seethed.

"Woah, back it up a bit, biker brute. That's not what I meant," I said, and bit down on the inside of my cheek to keep from asking what his daughter's name was.

Still staring at me with narrowed eyes, he stepped away and returned to his spot on the bed. "What did you mean?"

I huffed. Saying it again was going to make me sound like I was jealous when I had no right to be. Truthfully, I needed to know he didn't cheat on someone with me. I don't know if it had something to do with the way my dad always ran around on my mom, but I just couldn't live with the thought that I had been the other woman. Choosing my words more carefully, I tried to explain without telling him my life story. "I meant explain about her mother. You said you didn't cheat on anyone when you were with me. Is her mother not in the picture? And why didn't you just tell me you were expecting a baby?"

"Because I didn't know anything about her until she was placed in my arms the morning after I left your hotel room. She'd just been born a few hours before. And then I found out her mother died shortly after giving birth. So yeah, the night I was supposed to come back to your hotel room, I was at the hospital trying to figure out what in the hell was going on."

"You had my phone number, Bronze," I said flatly.

"Yeah, I did. In my phone that got fried from being soaked in piss. That's why I asked Copper to stop by the hotel and leave the number to the burner phone I was using until I got a replacement. The next few days were crazy, and by the time I got my bearings back, you were long gone." He paused and waited for me to meet his eyes before he said, "I left your room with every intention of seeing you again."

My mouth dropped open in shock, and my heart hurt for the little girl who would grow up without her mother. Regardless of how I felt about her father—and her uncle—that was a pain no child should have to experience. "I'm so sorry to hear about her mother."

"Serious as shit, Sloane. I'm tired, and I'm fucking pissed. We're not going to get anywhere if we're not honest. It's beyond clear to me that there's been a massive misunderstanding between us. So, stop pretending to be surprised and spare me the fake condolences."

Dropping my feet to the floor, it was my turn to lean in close. "How dare you? That wasn't fake! I know what it's like to not have a mom!"

"Enough!" he roared and got to his feet with his hands balled into fists by his side. "Tell me why the fuck you're doing this or get the hell out!"

"I'm not doing anything!" I yelled back.

"Really? Remind me again. Why were you in Devil Springs?"

"I was looking for Heidi and Paige Coleman," I swallowed thickly. "Because I had reason to believe one of them was my biological half sister."

"Then you know what happened!"

"No, I don't! I only know what happened to Paige. All of Heidi's information was blacked out or removed from the police reports." I dropped back into the chair, feeling deflated and defeated. "I just want to know what happened to make my sister commit suicide!"

His face paled while he took a stumbling step back. Catching himself on the bed, he sat down and dropped his head into his hands. "You think Paige is your sister?"

"I know she is," I countered.

I braced for the argument I knew was coming. However, he surprised me with words I never expected to hear. "That's not possible."

"What do you mean? 'That's not possible.' Why not?"

"Because Paige's parents are Walter Coleman and Phyllis Banner."

"You said Phyllis was dead," I pointed out.

"I thought she was," he said simply.

"Bullshit."

He shrugged. "Paige said her mother was dead. I had no reason to think otherwise until recently but believe whatever you want."

"Whatever. That part doesn't matter. Paige Coleman is my half sister, and I have a DNA test that proves she is. Phyllis could've had an affair and secretly gotten pregnant by my father. Alternatively, Walter could've known he wasn't the biological father and adopted Paige. I'm sure there are plenty of other possible explanations," I countered.

"Touché. Walter did adopt Heidi, so I guess it's possible he adopted Paige as well," he explained, effectively deflating my moment of pride by agreeing with me.

"What?" I asked in surprise.

"Walter married Adelaide after he and Phyllis

divorced. Paige moved in with him, Adelaide, and Adelaide's daughter, Heidi. I don't know when or why, but Heidi herself told me Walter officially adopted her after he married her mom, which is why she changed her last name to Coleman."

"What was her last name before?" I asked out of sheer curiosity.

"I don't know. She never told me, and I never asked."

I was in it to win it, and no matter how much it hurt to do it, I asked the question I desperately wanted answered. "Why did she do it?"

Bronze's shoulders dropped, and he looked to the floor as he inhaled deeply. "I haven't had to retell this story since the first few days of my daughter's life," he said and cleared his throat. "Pay attention, because I'm only telling it one time, and for fuck's sake, let me get through it before you hit me with fifty questions."

I sat up attentively and mimed zipping my lips. I could keep my mouth shut long enough to hear what he had to say—I hoped.

"Some of this I knew beforehand, and some of it I learned after their deaths; but, I'm going to tell it to you how it happened so it makes more sense," he explained. "Paige and Heidi were stepsisters first, then sisters by adoption, and ultimately a couple. Everyone assumed they were married because they had the same last name, which is what they'd hoped would happen. I knew a little more than others because of the relationship I had with them. Paige had a long history of mental health issues. Occasionally, she would stop taking her medications, and Heidi would get her back on track. That's how this all started. Paige quit taking her medicine. Then, Heidi found out she was pregnant. When she told Paige about the pregnancy, Paige left a note on the coffee table breaking up with her and moved out of their house while Heidi was at work. Several weeks later, Heidi was on her way to Precious Metals for a shift when Paige invited her to her new house to talk. Heidi went running at the chance to work things out with her. Unfortunately, Paige locked her in the basement, refused to let her out, and held her there for months. She was off her medications, and Heidi knew it. She tried to wait it out until she could talk some sense into Paige or until someone found out—whichever came first. Then, the baby came, and Heidi started bleeding. Paige shot herself after Heidi bled to death from giving birth to my daughter."

I bolted to the bathroom and crashed to my knees seconds before vomit spewed from my mouth. I heaved and heaved until my stomach couldn't heave anymore. Then, I fell back onto my ass and cried. I cried for the loss of my sister, the loss of what could have been my sister-in-law, and for the little girl who would never know her mother.

I don't know when he joined me, but when I realized strong arms were comforting me, I crawled into them. Because I needed someone to hold me together after a massive proverbial hole was blown through my heart.

17

SLOANE

"Heidi is the mother of your baby?" I sobbed.

I felt him nod against the top of my head. "Yes, she was. Is. Fuck!"

"I'm so sorry," I cried and hoped I conveyed the sheer sincerity I felt.

"It's the hand I was dealt," he said simply.

"It's a shitty hand."

"Preaching to the choir, Sweet Sloane," he agreed.

Suddenly, I pushed away and looked up to meet his eyes. "Can I meet her? Your daughter. I mean, I'm kind of her aunt."

He arched an eyebrow. "I don't know," he said slowly. "She's not keen on meeting people who're openly violent towards her father."

"I thought you were a con artist or something," I defended. "I didn't know!"

He got to his feet and helped me to mine. "I'll step out so you can freshen up. You want me to call downstairs and have them send up a new toothbrush."

Remembering my vomit breath, I slapped a hand over

my mouth and moved as far away from him as possible. "Yes, please."

After taking a few minutes to compose myself, I returned to the chair, but I wasn't quite ready to continue our conversation. Thankfully, I didn't have to.

"I need a shower," he announced and disappeared into the bathroom without giving me a chance to say anything. Glancing down at the dress I was wearing, I decided to do as he said, and made myself comfortable. Already barefoot, I unzipped my dress and stepped out of it, exhaling in relief when the constricting material released my body. Then, I reached into his duffel bag and pulled out a T-shirt to wear. When I slipped it over my head, I inhaled deeply and groaned as his scent filled my nose.

I glanced down at the gun strapped to my thigh. Deep down, I didn't think I needed it with me. I never would have followed him into his room if I did, but like my dad always said, "Your enemies will stab you in the back, but your 'friends' will stab you in the front while you're watching. Always be ready to defend yourself. Always." As a compromise, I took it off and laid it on the nightstand with my folded dress on top.

Crawling into the bed, I propped myself up on a mound of pillows and got comfortable. With my hands behind my head and my legs crossed at my ankles, I waited for him to exit the bathroom, knowing full well he'd only have a towel wrapped around his waist. Or I tried to wait for him, but he was taking forever. By the time he finally emerged from the bathroom, I had changed positions so many times I'd lost count and was in the middle of rearranging myself when I heard him turn off the water.

Scrambling to get myself back into my original pose, I bounced onto my back and crossed my legs moments before he opened the door and stepped into the room. And damn, he did not disappoint. I'd just seen him in only his boxing trunks, and I'd seen him naked several times, but there was something about a freshly showered man with only a towel wrapped around his waist that I found to be beyond sexy.

"Nice shirt. Is that a hint?" he smirked and dropped his towel.

I gasped and glanced between his gorgeous and deliciously hard cock and my shirt several times before deciding to focus on my shirt and figure out what in the hell he meant. *It's not going to suck itself* was printed across the front of the T-shirt with an arrow pointing down.

Realization dawned, and my eyes shot up just in time to see his boxer-briefs glide over his firm ass. "No, it's not a hint. It was the first shirt I found. I didn't want to rummage through your things!" I rushed to explain, my voice coming out fast and squeaky.

"*You* didn't want to rummage through my things?" he laughed. "I don't know you that well, and even I know you're too curious to believe that."

I rolled my eyes. "What? Were you expecting me to say something like, I didn't know how much time I'd have to find a sexy pose to display myself in before you finished with your shower?"

He grinned devilishly. "Oh, Sweet Sloane, as long as you're naked and it's accessible, I don't care how you display your pretty pussy for me."

"That's not what I was doing," I insisted.

He ignored my protest while his eyes continued to sweep over my body from head to toe. "But I think my favorites are going to be naked or wearing one of my T-shirts," he said huskily.

I watched his every move as my stomach began to tingle with nervous anticipation. He turned and quietly focused his attention on something for several moments. Curious as always, I sat up to get a better look.

"Woah!" I gasped in surprise. "What are you doing?"

With his nipple pinched between the fingers of one hand and something clasped in the other, he looked up and replied as if I should have known the answer. "Putting my jewelry back in."

"When did you get your nipple pierced?" I asked, sounding breathier than I intended.

"I got both done years ago," he said and chuckled. "I'm constantly changing them now. I can't wear them while I'm fighting or training, but I have to wear them when I'm not doing either one of those things to keep my daughter from mistaking my nipples as a food source when I'm holding her without a shirt on. She hasn't tried to do it since I started constantly wearing my jewelry when she was a week or two old, but I'm not taking any chances of it happening again. My newborn trying to nurse me was absolutely one of the most disturbing sensations I've ever felt, and I have absolutely no desire to repeat the experience." He turned back to the task at hand and pushed the bar through his nipple before screwing the ball on the end while I watched with rapt attention.

Before I could stop myself, I was on my knees scooting across the bed. "Can I do the other one?"

He arched an eyebrow. "You want to put my bar in?"

I nodded with wide, excited eyes.

"Here," he said and handed the bar to me. "Be gentle. My nipples are sensitive," he teased.

I was so focused on what I was about to do that I didn't even giggle. Instead, I carefully took his nipple between my fingers and slowly pushed the bar through. He handed me the little ball to screw on the end to keep it in place.

It happened before I could stop it. As soon as the ball

was tightened, I leaned forward and sucked his nipple into my mouth.

"Oh, you bad girl," he growled and fisted my hair, yanking me to my back while he crawled between my legs and hovered over me. "Is this what you wanted?" he asked and pressed himself against me.

"Yes," I breathed.

"Good," he rumbled and slammed his mouth over mine. "Because I've wanted back inside your tight cunt since I left it."

"You're so crass."

"And you like it," he said against my lips.

Yeah, I did like it. A lot.

When he slipped his hand between my legs, I moaned like a true harlot. "You are a bad girl," he said lowly and slipped a finger inside me. "Where are your panties?"

I don't know what came over me, but I felt compelled to give him the honest answer. "I took them off because they were wet."

He grinned wickedly and withdrew his finger, replacing it with two. "Oh, Bronze, please," I begged, unsure of what I was asking of him.

"Tell me what you want."

I ground down against his fingers. "I want to come."

"You do?" he asked seductively while his head moved down my body as he pushed the hem of my shirt up to bare my breasts. "I'm going to feast on your sweet pussy, and you're not going to come because I want to feel your cunt squeezing my cock when you do. Understand?"

"Yes," I panted. "B-b-but I—" My words were cut off by the guttural groan that erupted from within me when he buried his face between my legs and began relentlessly feasting on me. "Y-you have t-to stop. I'm gonna—"

In the blink of an eye, his face was in front of mine, and he was thrusting into me. Hard. "Come," he growled.

There were no words to accurately describe what happened to my body. It was an explosion of bliss, ecstasy, and unadulterated pleasure. It was almost too much. Almost. When I finally came down from my orgasmic high, Bronze was watching me closely while still moving slowly inside me. Then, he smirked and pulled out of me.

"Tits and knees to the bed," he ordered but proceeded to turn me over himself. With a slap to my ass, he entered me swiftly. "You better hold on to the mattress, sugar, because I'm about to make you come again," he declared.

With a firm grip on my hips, he thrust fast and hard as he yanked me back against him. "Play with yourself," he gritted out, punctuating each word with a thrust.

My body was at his command; my hand moved to my clit on its own volition. "Get your fingers nice and wet, so it feels like my tongue sliding over your clit."

My pussy clenched at the thought. A sharp slap to my ass had my muscles tightening again. "Now, Sloane."

My hand shot between my legs; my fingers went right to our connection. Reaching farther back, I wrapped my fingers around his shaft, covering them in my arousal. "Fuck, that feels good," he moaned and slapped my ass again. "But you're supposed to be playing with yourself, not me."

I moved my hand up and started circling my clit with two fingers. Within a few seconds, I knew I was going to have another orgasm, and I knew it was going to be as epic as the first one of the night.

"Faster, baby," he grunted and picked up his speed.

I opened my mouth to tell him I couldn't. That it was too much. Yet my hand continued to furiously circle my clit. Every muscle in my body tensed, and the only thing that came out of my mouth was a silent scream before the dam broke, and euphoria rushed through me. The following pulses and spasms that took over my body were so intense that they were almost painful.

"That pussy," Bronze hissed. "Fuck, it feels too good." He slammed into me even harder and faster than before. My arms and legs began to tremble when I felt my walls start to flutter. I wouldn't survive another orgasm so soon. Luckily, Bronze thrust hard and stilled a few moments later, groaning as he pulsed inside of me. "Fuck, I love that cunt." I was too relieved to avoid another orgasm and too blissed out from the previous ones to even care that I should have been pissed at what he said.

Apparently, I was so blissed out I fell asleep moments after the fucking of a lifetime. I woke up to the sun shining in my eyes and Bronze's face buried between my legs.

I felt him grin against my skin. "About time you woke up."

"I thought it was a really good dream," I confessed.

"Not a dream, baby," he rumbled and proceeded to make damn sure I was fully aware of my reality.

After devouring me until I climaxed, he pushed me over the edge two more times while fucking me like a well-oiled machine. Someone with incredibly poor timing knocked on the door while he was still inside of me, mere moments after he climaxed. He grinned, dropped a kiss on my lips, and got up to answer the door, discarding the condom and stepping into a pair of drawstring pants along the way. Meanwhile, I pulled the mess of blankets and sheets over my naked body and covered my head as well.

I had almost fallen asleep again when Bronze suddenly

yanked the covers away from me. "No!" I shrieked when the cool air hit my naked flesh. "Give it back!"

"Nope," he said firmly. "Now get up. I have to leave soon, and I want to have breakfast with you before I go."

I sat up with a pillow clutched to my chest, clinging to the tiny bit of warmth it provided, and looked at the clock on the bedside table before noticing the room service cart Bronze was standing beside. Not even a second later, the combined smell of freshly brewed coffee, warm maple syrup, and crispy bacon filled my nose, causing my stomach to growl—like the beast it was.

Bronze's eyes widened for a brief moment before he doubled over laughing. "Holy shit! I think that thing could take Audrey."

"Who the fuck is Audrey?" I asked and threw a pancake at him, hitting him in the center of his chest with an audible splat.

He looked down at his chest, and we both watched as the pancake slowly peeled away from his skin and dropped to the floor, leaving behind an area streaked with syrup. "If this syrup makes it to my dick, you'll be having my cock for breakfast while I finish your pancakes."

"And you'll have my fork in your balls if you don't tell me who Audrey is." I don't know why it got under my skin the way it did—maybe because he was laughing at something about my body while comparing it to another woman's—but I was ready to declare an all-out war over this Audrey bitch.

When he looked up, I couldn't decide if the smirk he gave me was insanely hot or extremely infuriating. "Batta's Old Lady, Tatum, named her stomach. Every time it growls or makes some other creature-like noise, she tells 'Audrey' to be quiet or says she needs to go eat because 'Audrey' is hungry."

"And you think my stomach can out-growl hers?" I asked once I'd regained some composure.

"Fuck, yes," he answered confidently. "Hell, I scanned the room for a wild animal before I realized the noise came from you."

"I'm weirdly flattered," I admitted and shoved a larger than ladylike bite of pancake into my mouth.

Picking up one of the other covered dishes from the cart, he joined me at the small table. "What if I ordered the pancakes for me?" he asked.

"Then you're shit out of luck unless you place another order for yourself. Because these are mine. And, I'm willing to fight for them," I declared while jabbing my fork in his direction to emphasize my point.

He snorted and shook his head. "You're a little ball of sunshine in the morning."

"Morning has nothing to do with it. I'm a demon when I'm hungry, no matter what time of day it is. Now, let me feed in peace," I said, lowering my voice to almost a growl on my last sentence, effectively making me sound somewhat demonic.

Surprisingly, he let me eat the rest of my pancakes in silence, which was a good thing because I wasn't kidding about turning into an evil monster when I was hungry. It was a character flaw, and I owned it. Finishing my coffee, I leaned back in my chair, feeling much more like the friendly human I usually was.

"Has Satan Sloane left the building?" Bronze asked cautiously.

I narrowed my eyes at him. "Why? She can easily return if she needs to."

"I don't doubt that one bit, but I need to speak to Sweet Sloane before I have to leave."

"Wish granted. Continue on."

"I want to see you again," he said without preamble.

Upon hearing his words, I accidentally took a large gulp of my coffee instead of a test sip and hissed when the hot liquid burned all the way to my stomach. Not that it would do any good, but I still scrambled for my glass of ice water and took several large swallows.

"You okay?"

"I'm fine," I said, even though I was completely flustered. Taking in a deep breath, I blew it out slowly. "Did you say you wanted to see me again?"

He grinned. "Yes. Now quit playing hard to get or whatever it is you're over there doing and say yes."

"Say yes to what? I don't recall you asking me a question."

"You're going to make me do this, aren't you?"

I blinked innocently. "I'm not making you do anything."

He tilted his head toward the ceiling and sighed before clearing his throat and facing me. "Do you want to do this again after my next fight?"

"What makes you think you'll be able to do this again next time? You might be the one to get knocked out."

He leaned back and smirked confidently. "Because, Sweet Sloane, I'm in the process of working my way up the ranks, and I'm not even close to getting matches with fighters that would be real competition for me."

"That's bullshit. You fought Declan, and he's good."

He crossed his arms over his delightfully sinful chest. "Yeah, and I'm fucking phenomenal."

I stared at him in return, unsure if his words pissed me off or turned me on. Either way, I wanted to know more. "How'd you get into fighting?"

He glanced at his phone. "I guess we've got enough time for the short version. I don't think I told you my grandfather started Blackwings. He was the original president, followed by my dad, and now my brother. So, roughhousing and fighting were always a part of my life growing up around the club. But I didn't get into organized, competitive fighting until I joined the Marines. I stopped fighting when I got out and didn't get the itch again until my club started running a gym." He paused and inhaled deeply, seeming to steady himself. "Then, I was injured and had a long recovery period. I'd just started training again when my little girl was born. After a short time off with her, I got back into training, and here I am."

"How'd you get hurt?" I bravely asked and masked my nerves by taking a sip of coffee.

"Sorry, sugar," he grinned and popped a piece of bacon into his mouth. "We don't have enough time for that story."

"So you've said," I grumbled and got up to start getting dressed.

Strong arms surrounded me from behind, and Bronze buried his face in my neck. "It's a long story, and I want to get home so I can spend some time with my baby girl before she goes down for her afternoon nap," he said against my skin, followed by a soft kiss.

And my ovaries exploded with a dire need to make more Bronze babies. Starting right that very second.

Grabbing my clothes, I hurried off to the bathroom to get dressed and compose myself. "I'll be out in a second!" I called out and quickly closed the door before he could follow me. Just being near that man got me all kinds of hot, but I was positively on fire the moment he touched me—every single time.

After I was dressed and presentable, I picked up my purse and phone and stopped by the breakfast cart to help myself to a few strawberries while Bronze got himself ready to go.

When I heard him exit the bathroom, I quickly finished the strawberry I was eating and dunked the last one into the dip as I stood. Popping the strawberry into my mouth as I turned, I suddenly bit down on it when I caught sight of Bronze. Creamy white dip spilled over my lips and ran down my chin, but I didn't care one bit. Bronze was dressed in head-to-toe black, and he was wearing leather pants. Leather. Fucking. Pants.

"Holy fuck," I breathed.

His eyes shot to me and fixed on the icing I'd yet to wipe from my face. "Holy fuck is right," he growled before his body slammed into mine. "It's going to be quick, but I gotta fuck you again before I go."

I didn't protest because I was beginning to learn that Bronze was capable of accomplishing amazing things in a very little amount of time.

18

BRONZE

I spent the ride back to Devil Springs thinking about Sloane and wondering if I made a mistake by asking to see her again. I wanted to. There was no question about that. But I wasn't sure if it was a good time for me to get involved in a relationship of any kind—be it casual fucking on the regular or a full-blown girlfriend.

On top of that, I had no idea how to handle having a daughter and dating women. If Sloane and I did end up dating, when would it be okay to introduce her to Blue? And would I want to bring Lorcan O'Shea's daughter around my family and possibly into my home? A year ago, I wouldn't have given it a second thought. But now that I was solely responsible for the life of my daughter, it was something I needed to seriously consider and possibly discuss with my brother.

I snorted at my thoughts. No, it was something I would have discussed with my brother before I found out he didn't have the same courtesy for me. Fuck, I'd tried not to think about it since there was nothing I could do until I was home, but my blood boiled every time I did.

Reminding myself that I needed to speak to him before jumping to conclusions, I focused my attention on the road and let my bike lead me home while the wind carried some of my worries away.

I called Layla when I was close to town, so she would be at my house with Blue when I got there. While I enjoyed having some time to myself—and I thoroughly enjoyed my night with Sloane—I couldn't wait to get back. I missed my little girl.

Blue tried to launch herself out of her swing when she saw me walk through the front door. "Daddy's home," I cooed and went right for her, not caring one bit that she was covering my face and half of my beard with her uncontrollable baby slobber.

"You must've had a nice evening," Layla prodded. She still didn't know where I went or what I did when I asked her and Copper to keep Blue for the night. From the first time I mentioned it to her, she assumed I was going out to get some pussy, and I let her think that because I didn't want to hear her or any of the other Old Ladies harping about my safety and the dangers of fighting.

"As a matter of fact, I did have a good evening. It ended with a bang," I teased.

"Stop!" she squealed and plugged her fingers with her ears.

"Why do you keep asking me questions you don't want to hear the answers to?"

"It's a bad habit I'm trying to break," she shouted because she still had her fingers in her ears. "We had a great night. Nothing out of the ordinary happened. Gotta go. Love you, Baby Blue."

"Your aunt can sometimes be a crazy lady," I whispered to Blue after the front door closed. Blue responded by chewing on my face.

After playing with Blue for a while, I made her a bottle and put her down for her afternoon nap. Since a nap sounded like a great idea, I decided to take one as well, though I planned for mine to be much shorter than hers.

Dropping into bed, I pulled the covers over me but surprisingly couldn't fall asleep. Because I couldn't stop thinking about Sloane. And not just her sexy as hell body. I was thinking about her gorgeous smile and the way she made me laugh with the funny shit she said and did.

Fuck! I was a goner.

After tossing and turning for at least fifteen minutes, I picked up my phone and sent her a text.

Bronze: Tell me about the story you're writing right now.

Sloane: That's creepy AF. How do you know I'm writing right now?

Bronze: Because you just told me. I meant currently.

Sloane: Um…did I ever tell you what kind of books I write?

Bronze: No, I don't think you did. What kind?

The dots on my screen bounced for several seconds before they disappeared for twice as long. She continued to repeat this pattern until I replied again.

Bronze: You must be embarrassed to tell me…Is it amphibian shifter romance? Or maybe snuff smut?

Sloane: Wait. How do you know about those genres?

Bronze: I volunteer/work in a bookstore. I know way more than I ever wanted to know about the different kinds of books.

Sloane: Are you genre shaming?

Bronze: I'm going to say no since I don't know what that is.

Sloane: Basically, it's judging someone for what they're reading.

Bronze: Uh, this seems like a hot topic. And no, I wasn't judging.

Sloane: It kinda is in the book world.

Bronze: The only hot topic I'm interested in is you.

Bronze: What do you write?

Sloane: Erotica

I damn near choked when I read her reply. Books weren't typically my thing, but erotica written by her was definitely something I wanted to read.

Bronze: Do you use a pen name?

Sloane: Yes.

Bronze: What is it?

Sloane: S.C. Lorcan.

Bronze: You used your dad's first name as your last name? Lol.

Sloane: I did it to piss him off.

Bronze: I'm guessing the S is for Sloane, but what's the C for?

Sloane: It's my mother's first name, Caitlyn.

Perfect. I searched her name and clicked on the first retailer link I found.

Sloane: Let me know which book you were going to buy. I'll send it to you instead.

Bronze: Now who's being creepy AF?

Sloane: I've had this conversation many, many times before.

Bronze: Not something I needed to know.

Sloane: I meant with friends and family, you giant alpha-hole.

Bronze: You say alpha-hole like it's a bad thing.

Bronze: What story are you working on? What's it about?

Sloane: It's about a live-in nanny who gets herself into a lot of debt and has to ask her boss for the money to keep from being arrested and sent to jail.

Bronze: How is that erotica?

Sloane: Because he agrees to loan her the money and let her repay her debt with her body.

Bronze: Sounds hot.

Sloane: Erotica kinda has to be.

Bronze: What happens to the nanny?

Sloane: I don't know. I haven't finished writing it yet.

Bronze: You have plenty of inspiration from last night.

Sloane: Oh, I don't write about my own experiences. I watch porn for that.

Bronze: You watch porn?

Sloane: Yes. Is that a problem?

Bronze: Fuck no! Every man dreams of finding a woman who likes porn.

Sloane: I watch it for work.

Bronze: Best excuse ever.

Sloane: So, uh, random…my brothers don't know Paige is our sibling. Neither does my dad. If you could not say anything about it, I'd appreciate it.

Bronze: My lips are sealed.

Sloane: Thanks.

Damn it. I was hard from just texting with her. I wanted nothing more than to rub one out and fall asleep, but one glance at my sleeping daughter was all it took to put a halt to my plans. Closing my eyes, I exhaled slowly, intending to get up and start a load of Blue's laundry before she woke up. But I fell asleep and didn't wake up until I heard Blue crying a couple of hours later.

THE NEXT MORNING, I WOKE UP AN HOUR BEFORE BLUE, which was unusual since I used her as an alarm clock. But I knew the reason behind it. I had some business to take care of, and I was apparently more excited about it than I thought.

Once we arrived at the gym, I got Blue settled and started my morning routine. It felt like the few hours before lunch lasted forever. But when the clock struck twelve, I dropped Blue off at the bookstore for her lunch date with Auntie Josie and Uncle Luke. Then, I went to the clubhouse for my own lunch date with Copper.

On most days, a handful of brothers and Old Ladies ate lunch at the clubhouse. When I pulled into the forecourt, I was pleased to see more than a few bikes and cars in the lot, but I grinned from ear to ear when I saw Layla's car.

I entered the common room and went straight for the food like I always did. But instead of joining Copper, I walked over to Leigh and Layla. Placing my plate on the table, I dropped a kiss on top of Layla's head and arched an eyebrow at my brother.

His eyes narrowed when they met mine, and he got to his feet. "The fuck are you—"

The words died on his lips when my fist made contact with his deceptive mouth.

Copper roared in anger and started to lunge for me, but froze in his tracks when Layla stepped between us—just like I knew she would. "Stop!" she cried. I hated to upset her, but I knew she could make Copper pay for his sins in ways that I couldn't.

"Move, Locks! Baby Brother's about to get his ass kicked."

Judge appeared out of nowhere and managed to take Layla's place, effectively moving her out of the way without her even realizing it. "What in the hell is going on?" he demanded.

I stepped back with my hands held up. "I'm good."

"Until I get my hands on you! What the fuck, Bronze?"

Crossing my arms over my chest, I held his stare. "You tell me what the fuck, Copper. Explain to me why you took it upon yourself to threaten Sloane and scare her away when I specifically asked you to tell her I'd be in touch with her in another day or two. Better yet, explain it to them because I don't want to fucking hear it right now!"

With that, I turned on my heels and drove back to the gym to finish out my day—knowing that Copper would spend the rest of his day dealing with his angry wife. I also knew a rift with us would eat at him until it was resolved, but I felt like he deserved to suffer for at least one night. Because he stole three months from me.

The next time I heard from Sloane, a few days had passed, and I didn't know what to think when I read her message.

Sloane: What kind of animal would be attracted to a rotting human body in the forest? Like to eat it.

Bronze: Should I be worried?

Sloane: Lol! It's for my book.

Bronze: Is this what happened to the nanny?

Sloane: Gasp! No! I finished the nanny and started working on my next story.

Bronze: And it involves animals eating dead bodies?

Sloane: Yes! A photographer witnessed something she shouldn't have and ends up in the witness protection program. Things get heated during the six months she spends at the safe house with the two agents.

Bronze: She gets with both of them?

Sloane: Eh...I haven't decided yet. She might, or maybe one will just watch.

Bronze: I'm glad that's not weird for you.

Sloane: What's not?

Bronze: Writing scenes like that.

Sloane: Why would it be weird?

Bronze: Because of my relationship with Heidi and Paige…

Sloane: Eek! Never mind. Yes, she'll get with both of them.

I found myself reacting to a situation in a different way than I would have before Blue was born. Maybe it was because the subject we were discussing was indirectly related to Blue. Whatever it was, I heard the hidden message in her words and felt the need to address her concerns without making her feel more uncomfortable.

Bronze: Too close to home?

Sloane: Yeah, I think so.

Bronze: Not something I would normally do, but given the circumstances, if you ever want to discuss them and me, just say the word.

Sloane: I think I'll pass on the details.

Bronze: Not what I meant and you know it.

Sloane: Thanks for the offer, but I'd rather drop it for now.

Bronze: Done.

While I was waiting for her to reply, Savior had arrived at the gym and was ready to start sparring. When I first got into the ring with him, well over a year—maybe two—ago, it was immediately obvious that he had an unrefined talent. Since then, we'd been sparring at least three times a week—when we weren't recovering from unrelated injuries. We went at it hard when we were in the ring, but neither one of us ever intended to hurt the other.

Savior was quick on his feet and kept his hands up to guard his body, which left me with very few opportunities to strike. He was a great sparring partner for me, but Coal and Grant were proving to be worthy opponents as well.

I chuckled to myself as the thought of putting together a team of fighters for the gym briefly entered my mind. Of course, no one in the club was interested in getting involved in any illegal moneymaking endeavors. We'd have to make it a legit team. Don't get me wrong, we weren't saints by any means, but crossing the line of the law for profit was where we drew the line.

From the time Copper and I were old enough to add and subtract, Grandpa repeatedly stressed the importance of keeping the club's money legal. "We have a good reputation in this town, and when the day comes for you boys to lead the club, it'll be on your shoulders to maintain what I've spent many years of my life building." We'd discussed it on numerous occasions, between ourselves as well as with the club officers, and we were all in agreement about upholding Grandpa Talon's legacy.

The next time I heard from Sloane, it was three days later—the same amount of time she waited between the first and second time she texted me.

Sloane: I have another book-related question.

Bronze: Shoot.

Sloane: Funny you should say that. Can a gun be fired after it has been submerged in water? Like dropped in a lake.

Bronze: The gun? Yes. The ammunition? Depends on how long it was submerged. A few minutes would probably be okay, but after a few hours, water will get inside the casing and make the bullets useless.

Sloane: Thanks!

Bronze: You know you can text me without using a question as an opening.

Sloane: Guess that means I'm busted for being socially awkward.

Bronze: You're not socially awkward. Maybe a little quirky. Definitely sexy. Hot as fuck, actually.

Sloane: What are we doing?

Bronze: Not charming you, apparently.

Sloane: You know what I meant.

Bronze: What do you want us to be doing?

Sloane: I just want to clarify whatever it is.

Bronze: Because of what happened last time.

Sloane: Maybe.

Bronze: I'm not seeing anyone else. And haven't since I met you. I wasn't planning on getting involved with anyone until my daughter is a little older.

Sloane: Understood.

Bronze: And then you were at my fight.

Sloane: I was there to see my brother.

Bronze: Doesn't matter. I saw you. And I wasn't going to let you get away again.

Sloane: I didn't get away last time.

Bronze: Stop fucking up my game, woman.

Sloane: Fine, woo me with your words.

Bronze: I can't now. The moment's over.

19

SLOANE

It was the day of Bronze's fight, and I was a nervous wreck. I'd spent the majority of the two weeks since the last time I saw him writing until my fingers were too sore to type anymore. I'd completed over half of the short stories I needed to write for the upcoming collection scheduled to be released next month. However, what I hadn't done during those two weeks was anything more than shower and brush my teeth.

One glance at my phone had my heart rate immediately increasing because I wasn't sure I had enough hours left in the day to do all of the grooming necessary to make me presentable by the time he arrived. On top of that, I was running out of time to ask him the one question I'd been working all week to build up the courage to ask.

I typed out the message, deleted it, retyped it, deleted it, and finally sent it after I typed it for the third time. With my eyes squeezed tightly shut, I tapped send, tossed my phone on the bed, and ducked under the covers to hide while I plugged my ears. I wouldn't know if he did or didn't respond if I couldn't see or hear my phone, right?

Sloane: Are you staying at the same hotel as last time?

Wrong. My plan would have worked if my ringer was turned on. Instead, I felt the vibration from his reply. With my eyes still closed, I blindly groped around for my phone and pulled it under the covers with me when I found it.

Bronze: They have the best cookies.

Sloane: Is that a yes?

Bronze: Have you been paying any attention to me?

Sloane: It's impossible not to.

Bronze: Good answer. Why'd you ask about the hotel?

Sloane: Well, I was thinking you could stay at my place if you wanted to.

Bronze: That works. Can you stop by the hotel and pick up my cookies before the fight? They're supposed to have two dozen boxed up for me.

Sloane: Are you serious?

Bronze: They have the best cookies.

Sloane: That's not an acceptable answer to every question.

Bronze: Blasphemy.

Sloane: So, I'll pick up your cookies and meet you at the club?

Several minutes passed with no response from him. I started to get nervous, thinking maybe he'd changed his mind about seeing me again when my phone dinged.

Bronze: No. Change of plans. There's no need for you to go to the club. I don't like the idea of you going by yourself anyway. Text me your address. I'll pick up my cookies and come to your place after the fight.

At one time, a request for my address would have sent me into a tizzy. My parents didn't allow me to have random friends over whenever I wanted. I had to clear it with them first and give them plenty of advanced notice so they could make sure none of my father's business dealings would be happening in or around our home. Apparently, I was still accustomed to living that way, even though I hadn't resided in the same house as my father for many years.

Inhaling a deep breath, I blew it out slowly and started typing my address while reassuring myself that it wouldn't be a problem. Bronze was well aware of who my family was. He could easily find out where I lived by doing a simple real estate record search.

Sloane: What time should I expect you?

Bronze: Probably around midnight.

His guess proved to be correct. The house phone rang a little after twelve, startling me from the catnap I was taking. "Ms. O'Shea, there's a Bronze Black at the gate to see you," the guard on duty said.

"Thank you, Dickerson. Please allow him through and give him directions to the front entry to my wing." After years of living in my own section of the house, I was still uncomfortable referring to it as my "wing," but I didn't know what else to call it. Basically, the mega-mansion consisted of three individual houses connected together, with the one in the middle being over twice the size of the other two. I lived on one side, and Tiernan occasionally lived on the other side.

"Yes, ma'am," Dickerson said slowly. I could only imagine what he was thinking about the biker arriving at the gate after midnight. Chuckling to myself, I shrugged it off and headed downstairs. I honestly didn't care what Dickerson or anyone else thought about anything I did.

Opening the door before he knocked, I was anxious to get my eyes on him and see how he was after the match. Even though the rational part of me knew he wouldn't have driven to my house if he was hurt, the emotional part of me needed to see that for myself. "How was your fight?"

He frowned. "Same as the last two times. Over in less than a minute. I didn't even break a sweat during this match."

I gestured for him to come inside. "You sound disappointed."

He exhaled slowly. "I for damn sure don't want to lose, but I'd like a challenge. I want to win, but I want to fight for it."

"That makes sense." I got the feeling he didn't want to talk about it, so I changed the subject. "I'm guessing you want to shower and change?" At his nod, I asked another pertinent question. "Would you prefer a bath or a shower?"

He grinned devilishly. “Tell me you’re asking because you’ve got some kind of badass hot tub somewhere in this ritzy place.”

I chuckled. “I wouldn’t have put it like that, but yes, I was asking if you’d like to use my bathroom with the rainfall showerhead and multiple body sprayers or the jetted whirlpool bathtub in the guest suite?”

“How big is the tub?”

My lips twisted to the side while I tried to formulate a guess. “It could probably fit four or five people. I really don’t know.”

“Enough said. Show me to the shower, Sweet Sloane.”

“Not the choice I expected,” I mumbled and led him upstairs to my personal bathroom. My mother had it redone for my birthday the previous year. I didn’t know then that it would be the last birthday gift I received from my mother. And I was thrilled with the opportunity to show it off.

“Oh, I’ll definitely be choosing the hot tub. But I want to get something to eat before I enjoy a nice hot soak with your naked body plastered against mine.”

With that, he walked past me and entered the bathroom, whistling slowly as he took in the posh surroundings. “Gotta say, I was expecting pink and fluffy.”

“I should turn off the hot water while you’re showering for that.”

“Go ahead. I’ll be finished before the tank runs out of the water that’s already heated,” he said on just that side of arrogant.

He reached out and gently gripped my lower lip between his thumb and index finger. “Don’t pout, Sweet Sloane. It was a nice try. Oww!”

“Ahh!” I yelled at the same time and dropped my ass to

the floor. With my foot cradled in my hands, I demanded, "What in the hell is wrong with your leg?"

He laughed and knelt down beside me, carefully replacing my hands with his. "This is what happens when a fairy kicks a giant with her tiny pixie feet. Little bones don't like it when they collide with bigger bones."

"Are you telling me my feet are too tiny to kick you?" I all but yelled as I struggled to control my anger and deal with the pain in my foot.

"Barefoot. I'm saying your feet are too tiny to kick things barefoot. You need shoes, preferably steel-toe boots or something similar, for protection," he clarified and glanced up from my foot to study my face.

"Don't even give me that look. It has nothing to do with you being a woman and me being a man and everything to do with physics. Now, quit trying to bicker with me, and let me see if it's okay."

"How are you going to know if it isn't?" I asked and immediately felt compelled to clarify myself. "I didn't mean for that to sound offensive. I really want to know how you're going to determine if it's okay." I shrugged. "I guess I'm asking you to teach me."

"I'm just going off of what I've learned through my experiences over the years. First, can you move it?"

I carefully rotated my ankle, which wasn't sore at all, and slowly worked my way down to try wiggling my toes. "It hurts a little more when I move these two," I said and pointed to the first two toes on my right foot.

"Guess we better call a *toe* truck," Bronze said casually.

It took me a few seconds longer than I cared to admit to catch the joke. When I finally did, I playfully slapped his chest, causing him to flinch. "I'm sorry! Did I hurt you?" I asked and reached out to pull him closer.

He laughed and shook his head. "No, you didn't hurt

me. Other than my pride." He paused for a moment and cast his eyes toward the ceiling. "I flinched because I thought you were going to hit one of my nipples. I just got the motherfuckers to stop bothering me, and I don't want anything to irritate them again."

I held it together for five, maybe six, seconds before I doubled over in laughter. The kind that makes you spray a mouthful of drink across the room.

"You just wait!" he said and pointed a finger at me. "When you have kids and start breastfeeding, you'll know exactly what it feels like."

"I think the important question here is how do you know exactly what it feels like?" I asked and chewed on the inside of my lip to keep from smiling as I waited for him to realize what he'd said.

"Oh, fucking hell!" he swore when it hit him. "One of the Old Ladies in the club had a baby not too long ago. Anyway, she said the pain and symptoms I was describing were the same ones she had when she was breastfeeding. That's all I meant," he said vehemently and held his hands in the air. "Now, is your foot okay?"

"Yeah, I think it's fine now. It hurt like hell at first, but it's eased off. I'll probably have a nasty bruise in the morning."

"Good. Then, I'm going to get in the shower. I'm starving, and clearly my brain needs sustenance to function properly."

I carefully got to my feet, testing my foot a few times before fully putting my weight on it. Once I was sure it was okay, I looked to Bronze. "Help yourself to whatever you need in here. I'll be in the kitchen working on something to eat. If you get lost on the way back, press the middle button on any of the intercom panels to talk to me. There's one in every room in the house," I said and pointed to the one strategically placed in the bathroom to be convenient yet hidden.

"Sounds good," he said and leaned down to kiss my cheek.

I waited until he turned and dropped his towel to head to the kitchen. But first, I darted forward and slapped my open palm on his bare ass as hard as I could before I hightailed it to the kitchen, hysterically laughing the entire way.

20

SLOANE

As I followed Bronze back to Devil Springs, I wondered what in the hell I was thinking when I agreed to attend a cookout at his clubhouse. His clubhouse. As in, the badass boxing biker invited the Irish princess to his clubhouse to meet his friends, his club brothers, and his blood brother—the one who told me to leave Devil Springs and not come back. Bronze thought I was nervous about seeing him again and repeatedly assured me that Layla was on Team Sloane; therefore, Copper was on Team Sloane.

To be perfectly honest, I was nervous, but it had nothing to do with Copper and everything to do with meeting Bronze's daughter. Were babies capable of judging people? Because I was certain his little girl was going to judge me and not in a good way.

My phone ringing through the car's stereo startled me, causing my heart to slam against my ribs for a few painful beats. "Hello!" I answered, sounding every bit as frazzled as I was.

"Why do you always sound like you're dying when I call you?" Frankie asked.

I let my mouth hang open and tried to quietly catch my breath. "I do not," I said and managed to sound somewhat normal.

"Well, prepare yourself, because you're about to."

"What?" I asked, scrunching my forehead in confusion.

"Hold on. What are you doing right now?"

I chewed on my lower lip for a few beats before deciding to tell her the truth. "I'm following Bronze back to his clubhouse in Devil Springs to meet his brothers and his daughter at a cookout," I blurted.

"Let me tell you something, girl. I already knew all that. Want to know how?" she asked, though she never paused for me to answer. "You texted me asking what someone would wear to a casual barbecue. Then, a few days later, you asked the same question about a biker bar. But the big clue was when you sent me the beta copy of your latest story—The Fighter and The Sports Journalist. Now, tell me, Sloane, what day is it today?" she asked calmly. Too calmly.

"It's Sunday?" I guessed, even though I thought I knew what day it was.

"Yes, it is. And when are you planning on returning home?" she asked.

I felt like I was being led into the wolf's den for dinner, and it was too late to cancel my reservation. "Um, I don't know exactly. I mean, it's a three-hour drive, so I was planning on staying the night. I'll probably get a room at the same hotel I did the last time I was in Devil Springs—"

"Don't even pretend like we all don't know you're staying in that man's bed tonight and probably tomorrow night, too," she interrupted.

I huffed as if I was frustrated. "Fine. You know me too well."

"Hold that thought. If I mathed right, you'll be

heading back to Cherryfield on Wednesday, probably getting home in the evening."

"Yeah, that sounds about right, assuming everything goes well."

"I'll give you your pep talk about that in a minute. I've already made a sticky note. Now, tell me, Sloane, Writer of Words, Rider of Bikers, and Forgetter of Flights, what is happening on Thursday?"

I gripped the steering wheel tightly and screamed at the top of my lungs. "Shit! What am I going to do now?"

"We both know you're not going to change your current plans, which means you'll end up scrambling to get your shit together and make it to your flight on time. You'll calm down on the plane. I'll pick you up at the airport, and we will kick ass at this signing like we always do."

"Have I told you how much I love you?"

"Not today, but you've had biker booty on the brain. Go play with his baby, eat his frank, and swallow his beans."

"Eww! You made it sound dirty in a dirty, gross way."

"I did, didn't I?" she giggled. "How far from his clubhouse are you?"

"I don't know. Let me look—twenty minutes!" I shrieked. "I'm not ready!"

"Stop it. You're fine. Touch up your makeup at the next stoplight and run a brush through your hair. There's no reason to be nervous. You've already met him, and some of the people he's associated with. You're going to go in there and make them fall in love with you like you do every time you meet new people. Now shush it, because I need the next ten minutes to go over our schedule for the event with you."

"Yes!" I excitedly agreed. "That'll be the perfect distraction. Let's hear it."

Precise as always, she finished reviewing the schedule of events for the weekend in just under ten minutes, followed by another quick pep talk that left me with one minute to myself before I pulled into a gated parking lot in front of a warehouse-type building.

I assumed we would park in the front lot, but Bronze continued around several buildings and parked behind the last one.

"I figured you'd want a minute to freshen up before meeting everyone. This is the back way to my room," he explained when I got out of my car.

"Thanks," I murmured. "Appreciate it."

He took my hand in his and gently squeezed. "Are you nervous?"

"A little," I admitted.

"Is it because of Copper? Or is it because you're meeting the rest of your man's family for the first time?"

My steps faltered, and I tripped, careening forward but never hitting the ground. Bronze's arm snapped out and grabbed a handful of my shirt, yanking back to stop my fall. Thankfully, it worked. Unfortunately, the move also ripped my top in several places.

"Shit! Are you okay?"

"Yeah, I think so." Pausing to catch my breath, I looked myself over as best I could. "But I don't think my shirt is," I said and pointed to one of the torn seams.

"Damn. It was the only way I could catch you."

"Don't apologize. I'd much rather have a torn shirt than a busted face or broken arm. Besides, I have a change of clothes in the car."

He hooked my belt loop and pulled me closer. "You better have more than one change of clothes with you."

My stomach fluttered in delight. "My brothers were

boy scouts. They taught me to always be prepared," I grinned.

He threw his head back and laughed. "*Your* brothers were boy scouts?" He shook his head. "Around here, you don't have to hide who your family is. We're bikers, babe. We're not saints."

Damn if that didn't make my pussy purr.

"Keys," he demanded and slapped my ass when I failed to respond.

"Hey! What was that for?" I asked and swatted him back, suddenly realizing he'd led me back to my car.

"You need your keys to unlock the door," he said slowly. "To get your change of clothes."

Opening my purse, I unhooked my keys and handed them to him.

He looked from the keys to me and back with a look of exaggerated confusion on his face. "What mystical sorcery is this? I've never seen a female find her keys that fast in real life. Wait a minute. Was that a magic trick? Oh, please tell me I'm on one of those reality shows right now."

A giant gust of wind blew right that very second, and slammed my large, heavy purse right into his abdomen, producing the most beautiful, "Oof!"

"It's called a carabiner hook, you big dufus. I don't know why other women, or at least the ones you've been around, don't use them, but I've kept my keys on one since I was eighteen years old. I clip them inside my purse or on the strap, and I hang them up in the same spot as soon as I get home. It's rare that I ever lose my keys. And let me take this moment to make it clear that if you hide my keys and try to claim I lost them, I'll superglue your balls to your taint while you're sleeping." With that, I pointed to my keys. "You gonna unlock it or keep palming my fob?"

He clicked unlock while staring at me with an odd look on his face. "I think I'm supposed to be putting you in the crazy pile and sending you on your way, but I'm strangely turned on by your threat. You got any more where that one came from?"

Ignoring his question, I shook my head and reached into the trunk to retrieve my bag when a tattooed forearm filled my vision. "Are you new here? I know you can do it, but when I'm around, you don't have to, and I don't want you to."

"Thank you," I said and stepped out of the way. "And for the record, I'm not offended by chivalry, but I appreciate your concern for my feelings."

He smiled shyly. "My mom was a very laid-back woman. She didn't have many rules for us growing up, but being respectful of others and minding our manners were two she was strict about."

"She sounds like an interesting woman. I'd love to hear more about her sometime." I genuinely did. It'd been almost a year since my mom died, and I cherished every chance I got to share my favorite memories of her with someone.

I followed him in through the back to his room a few doors down on the right. I'm not sure what I was envisioning his room to be, but it wasn't a bedroom just like any other bedroom you would walk into.

He noticed my expression and laughed. "What did you expect?"

I shrugged. "I don't know. Wood paneling on the walls, popcorn ceilings, a variation of orange or brown carpet, a lot of dust, and I was definitely anticipating some sort of musty smell."

He laughed so loud I just knew he'd have the entire club knocking on his door in a matter of minutes. "Shh!" I insisted and ran into the bathroom without grabbing my bag. "Damn it!" I whispered and whirled around to get it. However, Bronze had moved it to right outside the bathroom door. "Thank you," I called while snatching my bag and quickly closed the door.

After changing into a new shirt, I realized I needed to change into a different pair of jeans, which led to another pair of shoes, followed by a change of jewelry, and finally, another style of bra. When I emerged almost fifteen minutes later, Bronze was sitting on the edge of his bed, bouncing a beautiful baby girl in his arms. She turned her head toward me and grinned.

"Hi there," I cooed and wiggled my fingers in the air.

"Blue, this is Sloane. Sloane, this is my daughter, Blue Talon Black," he said proudly.

"She's beautiful," I whispered, mesmerized by her stunning blue irises. "Did you name her Blue because of her eyes?"

He laughed and shook his head. "No, I didn't. I always said that's what I'd tell people, but since you know the real story, it was because she was wrapped in a blue blanket when she was first given to me."

Realizing I had inadvertently brought up a sensitive subject, I changed the subject and put myself at the center of attention. "Let's do this before I chicken out and run for my car," I said and held up my keys.

He rose to his feet and ushered me toward the door. "There's no reason to be nervous. Yeah, a couple of the guys, and maybe one or two of the girls, might give you a little shit, but I promise they'll only be fucking with you. Everyone here's excited to meet you."

"Oh," I said, exaggerating my surprise. "And what have you told them about me?"

He snorted and gently bounced Blue in his arms. "I didn't say anything other than I was bringing a friend to the cookout. And now's probably a good time to mention that the girls don't know about me fighting. I told them we met at a club, which isn't a lie."

"No need to explain to me. I know how things work in worlds like this. Besides, you got a deal as long as you don't mention my sibling to my brothers or my father. Or anyone for that matter."

He stopped and held out his hand. "Deal," he said with a curt nod.

I laughed but shook his hand. "Deal."

Blue giggled and unexpectedly launched herself at me. Bronze clearly wasn't expecting the move and fumbled to catch her. Since I was still shaking his hand, I was close enough to reach up and grab her, pulling her safely into my arms.

Bronze's hands continued to try to catch Blue after she'd been caught by me, and we ended up in a tangled hug while Bronze and I caught our breath.

"She's never done that before," he said in disbelief. "Well, not when I've been holding her. She does it if I've been gone for a while and walk into the room when someone else is holding her."

"Oh, well, I'm a little flattered, even though it worries me. What if I'm too far away and can't catch her? I don't want her to get hurt."

I felt him place a kiss on the top of my head. "Sweet Sloane," he murmured and gently pressed his hand against the small of my back to cue me to start walking again, leaving Blue cradled in my arms.

I paused when it became clear we were headed for a set of doors instead of an outdoor area. "I thought you said this was a cookout."

He laughed. "It is. But for various reasons, many I can't recall, we set everything out and eat in the common room. One of the guys usually grills right beside the back door."

"You won't have any complaints from me. I'd much rather eat inside with air conditioning and without bugs."

"You don't like bugs," he repeated. "I'm guessing that means you don't like spiders either?"

"Nope, no, and nuh-uh."

"What about snakes?" he asked slowly.

I shrugged. "I don't have a problem with snakes as long as they stay in their approved zones."

"And what are those?" he chuckled.

"Anywhere that isn't in my house, my car, my swimming pool, or any of the patios, decks, or balconies."

He nodded. "Good. Then you shouldn't have a problem with the two snakes that live here."

"What?" I shrieked and protectively held his daughter against my chest as I scanned the area.

With his hand resting on the knob, he nodded to the door. "Inside. Copper and I each have a ball python. They share a habitat in another brother's room. You won't see them unless you open the door to his room and go inside. But, I thought you should know they were there," he explained, a little too much.

"What aren't you telling me?" I asked.

"I knew I heard voices!" a woman shouted as the door suddenly opened. "What're y'all doing out here?"

Blue started wiggling two seconds before she started crying. Bronze scooped her from my arms and tried to soothe her. "It's okay, Blue Bean. Aunt Leigh didn't mean to scare you. She was just being impatient. We'll forgive her for some cookies, won't we?"

"Bronze Black, hush your mouth and get in here so you can introduce us to your friend," the woman presumed to be Leigh said.

"And be quick about it. She won't let us eat until 'everyone has arrived and been properly introduced,'" a large man with strawberry blonde hair and light eyes that danced with a mischievous gleam said.

"Trey, if I learned one thing over my many years, it's don't piss off the woman that feeds you," an older version of Trey said. He stepped forward and smiled kindly. "I'm going to get this ball rolling. My name's Bear. That knucklehead behind me is my son. He goes by Batta around here. His Old Lady, Tatum, and her sister, Josie, should be here soon."

I reached out to shake his hand. "Nice to meet you and your son," I returned. Rinse and repeat as I met every member of the club, the Old Ladies, their children, several parents, and a few other various friends or family members. But I drew the line when they started trying to explain who was related to whom among the various chapters. "I'm doing good to keep up with the names of the people here. If you want me to know everyone else and all the caveats that go with them, I'm going to need a diagram of some kind."

Bear chuckled. "Nah, we can save that for when you meet them. Besides, you just need to learn the women's names," he shared and pointed to a patch displaying his name on the front of his cut. "All the men in the club have their road name patch right here."

"Thank you," I said sincerely. Remembering half of the names for the current crowd was doable for me. My stomach fluttered at the thought of meeting even more of his family. Was I ready for that? I didn't know, and I didn't care because I knew I'd regret it if I didn't give things with Bronze a chance.

With Blue in one arm, Bronze took my hand and led

me down a hallway. "There's one more person for you to meet."

"Oh, yippee," I said flatly. "I bet it's the asshole brother."

"See," Bronze said as he entered an office. "I'm not the only one who calls you that. Sloane, this is Copper, my asshole brother."

I moved to step forward and introduce myself, but Bronze's firm grip stopped me. "He doesn't get to shake your hand."

I stepped back beside Bronze and waited for his lead. "Go ahead, asshole brother."

Copper glared at his brother before he cleared his throat and softened his expression. "You're welcome here until Bronze, and only Bronze, says otherwise."

Without thinking, I pulled out my phone and started a voice recording. "Make a note in the character profiles that alphas don't apologize."

"Neither do assholes," Bronze muttered as we left the room. "He'll keep his distance, but let me know if you're uncomfortable at any time."

"The Irish princess isn't scared of the biker president," I teased. And I wasn't—well, not anymore. While I didn't see myself having warm and fuzzy feelings for Copper any time in the near future, I wasn't going to draw a line in the sand and make things awkward between us for the foreseeable future. Instead, I smiled and promised to kill him in a book the first chance I got. "So, who's hungry?"

To my surprise, Blue reached for me when we sat down to eat, our plates loaded with food. "No, no, baby girl. Let Sloane eat," Bronze said and shuffled Blue to his other side.

She grunted and stretched herself across his forearm with her little hands opening and closing. "I really don't mind," I said with a genuine smile on my face. "I love babies," I cooed and clapped my hands once before holding them out to her in invitation.

Bronze relented and handed her over. "Just say the word if you want me to take her back."

"Got it," I said with an exaggerated nod. "It'll be when she cries, poops, or vomits. Or does anything else involving body fluids. Never mind. I'm going to stop talking," I blabbered and took a huge bite of my hamburger, groaning when the juicy goodness filled my mouth. "Thh a ooo ooddd."

"What was that?" Batta asked.

"She said, 'This is so good,'" Bronze clarified.

"How the fuck did you understand her?" he asked.

Bronze stared at Batta pointedly, while my eyes stayed fixed on him. Did the man not realize what he was asking? I didn't know what to say or do, and I couldn't get Bronze to look at me.

Finally, I finished chewing the overly large bite of food in my mouth and swallowed. After wiping the crumbs away with a napkin, I inhaled deeply and said, "He knows what I said because I say it a lot when my mouth's full of his," I paused and cupped my hands over Blue's ears, "dick," I finished with a stage whisper. The room erupted in laughter while I brought my burger to my mouth for another bite.

After our meal, Blue had a bottle before Bronze put her down for a nap. He left me in the common room with the others after I assured him I would be fine. They'd been nothing but friendly, and I honestly felt comfortable around them, even Copper. He would still be on my shit list if it weren't for Layla.

She'd pulled me to the side and apologized for Copper's behavior. "I won't make excuses for what he did.

I know as well as anybody how much of an asshole he can be. After he got it from Bronze, he got it again from me. Like I said, I won't excuse what he did, and I won't tolerate it either, but I can promise you that his heart was in the right place. He just went about it all wrong."

"Thank you for that," I smiled. "Bronze basically said the same thing. I have three older brothers; I completely understand how irrational they can be, especially when they think someone has wronged their family."

She laughed. "Oh, you have cavemen in your family too? Perfect. You'll fit right in."

She also told me that Copper had been warned to keep his distance from me. "I wanted to make sure you knew that and didn't think it was because he doesn't want you to be here. Just think of him as a naughty kid who's spending the day in time-out."

Two new women entering the room pulled me from my thoughts. One went to the kitchen while the other joined us at the table. "Sorry, I'm late," she said, somewhat out of breath. "We had to stop by the bookstore and meet Luke to give him some paperwork."

"Why didn't you invite him to join us?" Layla asked.

"I did, but he was on his way out of town," she explained and dropped into an empty seat. Her eyes landed on me immediately. "Well, hello," she smiled knowingly.

I sighed. I knew that smile. Just when I thought it was smooth sailing, an Old Lady who was obviously some kind of law enforcement officer walked in the door and recognized me.

The other woman returned with her plate of food and took her seat. "Is Bronze's *friend* here yet?" she asked and bit into her burger before looking up to glance at the faces looking back at her.

"Look up, Josie," the first woman, who I presumed to be Tatum the law enforcement officer, said.

"Hi," I waved with a small smile.

Josie's mouth fell open, causing the bite of hamburger inside to fall out and land on the table with a loud plop. She looked at the wad of meat in horror before she disappeared underneath the table. "Why didn't anyone tell me S.C. Lorcan was here?" she shrieked.

Shit. She recognized me. I hoped it was in a good way since she called me by my pen name, but I couldn't tell for sure. Her reaction was completely unexpected, and I didn't know what to do. "Uh, I'm not sure if that was a good scream or a bad scream. Should I leave?" I asked no one in particular.

Josie's forehead and eyes appeared over the edge of the table. "No! Don't go! Just…oh, this is so embarrassing. Can we please forget the last five minutes and start again?"

"What in the world is going on?" Leigh asked, though it wasn't a question. "This is Sloane O'Shea."

Tatum, who'd been laughing since Josie dropped under the table, waved her hand to get everyone's attention. "S.C. Lorcan is a best-selling erotic romance author. Josie's just fangirling," she explained and turned her attention to her sister. "Stop acting like a ding-dong and come talk to her. Maybe you could invite her to the bookstore," she stage-whispered.

"Wait a minute! I think I know you!" I exclaimed as realization dawned. "Are you JC with Blogging from The Bookstore?"

Josie emerged from her hiding place and returned to her seat, clapping her hands together excitedly. "Yes! That's me!" She squealed. "Tatum! Look, it's S.C. Lorcan!"

"I know," she said and gave me an appraising look that left me feeling uncomfortable.

Cocking my head to the side, I studied her closely for a few moments, trying to decipher the hidden meaning.

Tatum turned toward me and gave me a pointed look. "My sister and I know who you are for two very different reasons."

I knew exactly what she was implying and wished Bronze had returned from putting Blue down because I was about to tell everyone in the room exactly who I was—and was not. "Let me guess. Your sister knows me because I'm a semi-popular erotic romance author. But, you smell like a fed, so I'm guessing you know me because of my father—Lorcan O'Shea."

Tatum's back went ramrod straight, and she made a show of sniffing her armpit. "I smell a fuck of a lot better than those sweaty assholes."

"You're wearing tactical pants and aviators indoors. Not to mention you've got a piece at your back and in your boot. The right one. If you were trying to hide it, you did a shitty job," I told her honestly.

Tatum clapped her hands together. "I like her! Are we gonna keep her?" she asked while focusing on something over my head. I turned to see Bronze casually leaning against the doorframe with the baby monitor in his hand.

"Glad to see you can hold your own with this bunch. Not that I was worried. Because they promised to behave," he said loud enough for the entire room to hear and made his way to my side. "You okay?" he murmured against my hair when he took his seat.

"I'm fine," I replied quietly and placed a kiss on his cheek.

"You didn't answer my question," Tatum called out teasingly.

"Batta!" Bronze shouted. "A little help here?"

Batta held his hands up in surrender. "She knows too many ways to kill me slowly and get away with it."

"Tatum," Bear said and winked at me as he approached the table. "Did you bring that rifle you wanted me to look at?"

"I did!" she said excitedly and got to her feet. "It's in Copper's office," she continued and walked away from the table. Pausing at the entrance to the hallway, she turned back to the room. "For the record, I'm with the Bureau, and that's how I knew you. It's my job to know those kinds of details. Having said that, your family isn't on my radar. Even if they were, I judge people individually, not based on their family. As long as you're good to him," she said and nodded to Bronze, "and our Baby Blue, you're welcome in my book." With that, she turned and disappeared down the hall before I had a chance to thank her.

"Are you going to be at the signing in Fairview this weekend?" Josie asked excitedly.

I shifted uncomfortably but smiled and answered. "Yes, I am. I was just going over the details with my assistant on the way here."

"When do you have to be there?" Bronze asked.

"My flight leaves on Thursday. For some reason, I thought it was next week, not this one," I shrugged and stopped myself from saying that at least I'd be in town for his fight—or after his fight.

"Did you know Avery's a graphic designer? She's really amazing and works with a lot of authors." Josie interrupted and pointed to the woman approaching the table.

Avery laughed nervously and wiggled her fingers when she waved. "Oh, thank you for the recommendation, Josie, but I'm sure *S.C. Lorcan* has her graphic needs taken care of."

"Hang on a sec," I said and propped my elbows on the table. "What kind of graphic design are we talking about here?"

"I can do pretty much anything book-related—teasers, covers, banners, bookmarks, logos, website design, branding, etc. Is there something particular you need?"

"Yes! Book covers. I hate designing covers. Do you have a card or a site where I can check out your work?"

Avery reached into her purse and handed me a business card. "Here's my website and contact info. If you like what you see, let me know. I'd love to work with you."

"Thanks. I appreciate it," I replied and pocketed the card.

"There!" Josie pointed to the woman named River. "She designed that logo for Jackson Security. River, stick your boob out so she can see it."

"That's not how I usually greet people for the first time, Josie," she laughed and walked around the table to show me the logo.

"Wow!" I exclaimed. "That's impressive. We need to talk soon," I said excitedly.

"Ladies, if you'll excuse us," Bronze said and gently placed his hand on my arm, helping me to my feet.

"No! You can't steal her away just yet," Josie whined.

"Sorry, Jose. I want to show her around the rest of the clubhouse before my little alarm clock goes off," he said and wiggled the baby monitor.

"Fine," she huffed. "Blame the baby."

With that, he took my hand and led me down a hallway and back to his room. "I thought you were going to show me around."

"I lied," he said and stepped closer, hooking his fingers

in my belt loops. "I didn't think you'd like it if I told them I was taking you back to my room to fuck you against the wall while my daughter is asleep."

"You can't fuck me while she's in here," I hissed and swatted at his chest.

He rolled his eyes. "She's not in here. She's next-door in her own room." He pointed to a door I hadn't noticed when I first entered. "We had the doors put in to connect the rooms after she was born. Now, get naked."

21

SLOANE

Frankie was right. After staying in Devil Springs until the absolute last minute, I made it home with barely enough time to pack before Dickerson called to tell me my ride to the airport had arrived.

Running through the airport like my ass was on fire, I made it to my gate just as they called for the first-class passengers to begin loading. I usually waited for everyone else to board before I did, but I was exhausted and hoped to sleep for as much of the hour-long flight as possible.

However, my hopes were crushed ten minutes into the flight when the pilot announced that we were being rerouted due to bad weather. That was how my one-hour flight turned into a daylong tour of various airports scattered throughout the mid-Atlantic area.

After we landed for the third time, I contemplated renting a car and driving to the event, but Bronze and Frankie both pointed out that I was in no shape to drive.

I stumbled off the plane and fumbled my way to the baggage claim area. Frankie was perched on top of one of the carousels while scanning the area with a pair of rhinestone-covered binoculars.

"Demon! You made it!" she shouted at the top of her lungs and jumped down from her makeshift watchtower.

"Save me!" I cried and used the last of my energy to propel myself in her direction.

"Your chariot is right this way."

"Hang on, I checked two bags I need to get."

She snorted. "There's no way in hell your luggage made it here. Let's get you to the hotel for a nap. No. A shower first because you stink. Then, I'll work on locating your luggage while you get some sleep."

It didn't occur to me that there might be another reason Frankie was in a rush to get back to the hotel until I walked into the room to find a cloven-hooved animal snoring on what was not the bed I would be sleeping on.

"Frankie," I grumbled.

"This way, Demon. You're hallucinating. I'll turn the shower on for you—" was the last thing I heard before I faceplanted into the pillows.

Frankie only let me sleep for two hours, claiming I wouldn't be able to go to sleep that night if she'd let me sleep any longer. "Oh, see those boxes over there?" she asked and pointed to the boxes stacked along the wall. "Those need to be sorted and signed. So, whenever you're ready."

I groaned. "Coffee or alcohol? Your choice."

A knock at the door interrupted our conversation. I cocked my head to the side and looked at Frankie. "Are you expecting anyone?"

"No," she said slowly and shooed me with her hand. "Go see who it is."

I was in no way, shape, or form prepared for what I saw when I looked through the peephole. Yanking the door open, I squealed in delight and launched myself into his arms. "Bronze! What are you doing here?"

"Coming to see my woman," he rumbled and stepped into the room. In a flash, he dropped his bag and had me pinned against the wall seconds before his lips devoured mine—until the sound of a throat clearing had him pulling away from me and scanning the room.

"Hello!" Frankie sang and wiggled her fingers in the air.

"I didn't know you'd have company," he mumbled near my ear.

"I don't have 'company.' We're sharing a room. This is my assistant and dear friend, Frankie."

Right on cue, there was a loud thump on the other side of the connecting door. I sighed in exasperation. "That's what you get for lying to the man," Frankie pointed out and got up to open the door.

"It's called a joke. Tell your pig to play along next time," I retorted.

"You know I don't have any control over him. He does what he wants. And judging by the sound of that headbutt just now, I'd say he wants your man." With that, she opened the door and unleashed the beast before I could give Bronze a fair warning.

"Brat! No!" I yelled and tried to block him while shoving Bronze into the bathroom. "Frankie! You're going to get us kicked out of here. I told you not to bring him."

"Well, it would've been fine if your man hadn't shown up. You know what a hussy he is when males are around,"

Frankie countered as she tried to corral Brat. I cringed with every thump, rattle, and bump I heard.

"I'm torn. I don't know if I should ask why there's a pig running around your hotel room or ask why you're calling it a brat first?" Bronze teased.

"Brat, short for bratwurst, is Frankie's pet pig. Brat loves men. *Loves* them. So, until she gets that sassy little ham back into the other room, you're better off in here."

"Okay, it's safe to come out," Frankie called.

"Why did you let him into the room in the first place?" I asked curiously.

"You think I did that on purpose? Bitch, please. I was going in there to put him in his crate for the night. Then, he almost sent me ass over teakettle when he got a whiff of your man and barreled into the room."

"How did you manage to sneak him into the hotel without getting caught?" he asked and made himself comfortable on the bed.

"Frankie put his crate on the luggage cart and covered it with a blanket. She rolled him in through the back door when no one was around."

Bronze burst into laughter, surprising both of us. "You smuggled a pig in a blanket!"

I joined in with him while Frankie rolled her eyes and tried not to crack a smile. I wasn't having that. All it took was one well-timed snort from me and soda shot from her nose when she laughed while swallowing. "Damn it, Demon! Why must you always do that to me?"

"At least you weren't near your desk this time," I pointed out.

"This is my cue to return to my room. Please keep the fucking to a manageable noise level. And if you could wait, eh, say thirty minutes for my sleeping pill to kick in, that would be stellar." She turned and pointed a finger at

Bronze. "She has places to be and things to do tomorrow. Do not keep her up all night. She gets these bags under her eyes, and they show up in the pictures, and then—"

"Good night, Frankie," I said sharply and started escorting her to her room. "I've got my alarm set for eight o'clock. I'll be ready to head out by nine."

"Did you hear that, mister man? We have to leave by nine in the morning to have time to set up. We cannot be late. The queen has spoken. Good night," she said theatrically and closed the door behind her.

"And that's Frankie," I said and joined him on the bed. "So, what're you doing here?"

He shrugged. "Josie told Layla about your book signing this weekend, and Layla insisted on keeping Blue so that I could surprise you."

"That was so thoughtful of her. Please thank her for me."

"You can thank her yourself the next time you see her," he countered.

"But I don't know when that's going to be, and I don't want to be rude."

He slipped his arm around my waist and pulled me against his warm body. "Thought maybe you'd want to come back to Devil Springs with me after my fight next weekend. I have to work Monday through Friday, but you could use one of the extra rooms at my house or my office at the gym to write," he offered.

A smile from deep within my soul slowly appeared on my face. "Could I sit at one of the tables in the bookstore and write?"

"Yeah, but can you work with Josie staring at you the whole time?" he joked.

"Oh, stop. She was totally relaxed around me after five minutes. Actually, I would like to spend some time with her. She has a genuine love for books, and I'd like to get her thoughts on a couple of ideas I have," I explained.

"Sloane," he rumbled and rolled me to my back. "I need an answer."

I arched an eyebrow. "To what? You haven't asked me a question."

He buried his face in my neck and rubbed his beard all over my sensitive skin. "Stop it, you big bearded brat!"

We both heard an unidentifiable sound and froze. "Thanks for yelling his name, Demon!" Frankie shouted through the door.

"Sorry!" I yelled and slapped my hand over my mouth to stifle my giggles.

"Oops," I whispered. "I didn't mean to."

"It's okay. I know how to make sure it doesn't happen again," he said and proceeded to keep my mouth occupied for the next several hours.

22

BRONZE

I'd just pulled my jeans over my ass when Frankie burst into our room without warning. "Okay, Sloane, this shit's getting freaky! A breakfast tray was delivered to my room, and there was a tray of fruit with Brat's name on it! And I bet there's a tray for you and one for Bronze sitting outside of your door right now."

Sloane started to move toward the door. "No fucking way," I insisted and quickly moved in front of her to open the door myself. Sure enough, two breakfast trays were waiting for us right outside the door.

"One of you needs to start talking and tell me what the fuck's going on."

Sloane kept her mouth shut, but Frankie spoke up loud and clear. "I'm sorry, Sloane, but I'm telling him. He's more than capable of protecting you if he knows," Frankie said and turned to me. "She's being bullied online, and we think she has a stalker."

"We don't know either one of those for sure, particularly the online stuff," she argued.

I turned to Sloane, shocked that she hadn't mentioned

anything to me. Instead of focusing on that, I went into work mode and started grilling her for answers.

From what I could get out of both girls, a few of Sloane's social media accounts had been shut down for various reasons that weren't explained by the administrators. Shortly after that began, she started receiving unexpected gifts. Most of the gifts arrived at events, but at least two had been delivered to her mother's estate. Fortunately, none of the surprises were anything other than what they outwardly appeared to be—a nice gift.

I rubbed my chin, just like all the other men in my family, and grinned as I carefully chose my words. "I know someone who can help you with the online issue if you're interested. Actually, I know a few people who can help with this one," I said and paused. "You should've said something about your stalker to someone way before now. I'm not necessarily saying me, because we didn't know each other that well then, but you could've and should've told your father or your brothers. In the meantime, I'll act as your security detail for this event, and then we'll make sure you'll have personal security at all of your future events."

"Um, not that I disagree with your plan, but I'd appreciate it if you'd include me on decisions that affect, well, me," she said firmly.

"It's not in my nature to pose things as a question. Doesn't mean what I say is the law. You can say no, or disagree, like you just did," I explained.

"Are you hearing this shit?" she asked Frankie. "Is that not the most alpha thing you've ever heard? 'It's not in my nature to pose things as a question.'"

Frankie giggled. "It's definitely up there in the top ten."

"Ladies," I said and redirected the conversation. "We

need to focus on Sloane's security. Since we don't have time to arrange shit, the best plan I've got is to keep you by my side at all times."

"I don't have a problem with that," Sloane practically purred.

"Okay, here's what we're going to do. Do not eat the breakfast from the unknown trays and finish getting ready. We'll get food on the way. I'll call the organizer and tell her we need another spot at your table. I can explain why and have her sign an NDA when we get there. And I just sent a text to see if the pig sitter can come early. There. We have a plan. Move it or lose it," she said and snapped her fingers before disappearing into her room.

"I really don't think it's anything to worry about," Sloane explained as she continued to get ready for the day. "We don't have any proof that the gifts were from the same person. The only thing they've all had in common is that there's never a note." She paused before adding, "Correction. Two things in common—no note and no return address."

"It *is* something to worry about. There's a reason people don't sign their names to gifts, and more often than not, it's not for a good reason."

"But none of the gifts were harmful or anything bad," she argued.

"Yet," I said and turned to face her. "Are you checked in under your name?"

"No, the rooms are in an alias my family frequently uses. Why?"

"Is that something that's widely known?"

She shook her head. "It shouldn't be."

"Then, how did your stalker know which rooms you were in, and specifically which one was yours and which one was Frankie's?" I asked and waited for it to click.

"You think someone's watching me?" she gasped.

"That's what it looks like to me," I told her honestly.

After that, Sloane remained unusually quiet until we arrived at the event venue.

"How many signings have you been to?" I asked, hoping to get her talking while I helped her set up her table.

"I don't know the exact number. Maybe ten," she shrugged. "I usually go to three events a year, but I have a few more this year because several new events popped up that looked like fun."

"Are they all like this?"

She laughed. "No, they're not. This is one of the smaller events I attend. Most of the time, there's a meet and greet the night before, the actual signing, a dinner or gathering after, and occasionally there's an activity scheduled two days before the event for those who come in early."

I didn't miss the way her voice slightly shook when she spoke. Placing my hands on her cheeks, I met her eyes, "Are you worried about your stalker?"

She shook her head. "No, it doesn't have anything to do with that. I always get nervous right before an event. I don't think that will ever change—no matter how many I attend."

I didn't think that was what was really bothering her, but I let it drop since they were about to allow the first set of readers into the event. When we first came down to set up her table, a long line of people waiting to get in had already formed at the entrance, so I was expecting a decent-size crowd once the doors finally opened. Clearly, Sloane and I had different definitions of a "small" event.

I was right. Before long, a line had formed at Sloane's table. Frankie spoke to the readers in line while she gathered orders and handled payments. I, on the other hand, sat back and never took my eyes off of Sloane.

She was in her element. The genuine smile she wore on her face was broad and beautiful. It was obvious to anyone in the vicinity how much Sloane loved her job and cared about her readers. She spoke to everyone who came to her table, took pictures with those that asked, signed whatever was handed to her, and even rounded the table to hug several readers.

Two particular women caught my attention when they arrived at Sloane's table again. "This is the third time they've been by here," I said low enough for only Frankie to hear.

"There's a reason for that," Frankie replied cryptically.

"Bronze, will you carry their books out to their car for them?" Sloane asked and pointed to the large box behind her chair.

What was she thinking? There was no way in hell I was leaving her side, but I didn't want to look like a jackass, especially in front of her fans, so I…misled them. "I would if I could," I started and rubbed my hand over my scar. "I almost lost my life to a stab wound, and I was given very strict limits on the amount of weight I could lift when they released me from the hospital."

All four women gasped at my words. "Oh, no, no, no! We can't have that," Ginger insisted. "If you have smaller boxes, we can divide them up and make two trips to get them to the car."

Once they were gone and there was a lull in traffic, Sloane turned to me with narrowed eyes. "Why did you lie about not being able to carry their books?"

I sat forward and held up one finger. "One—I'm not leaving you for any reason whatsoever while I'm in charge of your security. I don't know them, and neither do you."

Pausing, I raised a second finger. "Two—I didn't lie. I did almost lose my life from a stab wound, and the doctor did put strict limitations on the amount of weight I could lift. What I didn't specify was *when* that happened."

It wasn't long before she once again had a line at her table and returned her attention to her readers. Thankfully, there was no unusual activity, and I didn't notice anyone that seemed suspicious to me. And I would have noticed because I was scanning for enemies like I was in an active war zone until Sloane turned to me with panic in her eyes. "I maybe, kinda, sorta forgot to tell you about the photo shoot I have scheduled this evening."

"Say what now?" I asked. Already on alert, her odd behavior did nothing but increase the tension.

"Um, well, I-I," she stammered.

"She scheduled a boudoir-type photo shoot after the event, and she's embarrassed to tell you," Frankie blurted. I liked her, and the way she said what needed to be said, even if Sloane didn't want to say it.

I grinned devilishly. "Oh, this is going to be fun."

"No! You can't come!" Sloane all but shrieked.

Moving closer, I pulled her to me. "That's what you'll be saying if you try to stop me."

"Fine, you can come," she muttered and placed a kiss on my cheek. "But, I really do need to get packed up, so I have time to shower and redo my hair before my session."

"You're still not going by yourself. Not after everything you told me this morning."

"I wasn't going to go by myself. Frankie's coming with me."

Frankie smiled. "He can come with me and Brat."

"How's that going to work?" Sloane asked and arched a brow. "You won't be able to keep that hog from humping his leg."

"Ah, shit! You're right. I'll be right back," Frankie said and darted across the aisle to another table.

"What's she doing?"

Sloane shrugged. "Probably going to see if Suzanne will watch Brat so you can come to the shoot with us."

"Does she need to go if I'm going?"

Sloane laughed. "Yes, she does. She has her own session booked after mine." I stared at her blankly and waited for more. "Oh," she said, finally realizing the issue. "Frankie's having some shots taken for her website and updating her headshots. She won't care if you're there."

"Suzanne and her husbutt are going to watch the ham!" Frankie announced in delight.

I cleared my throat. "Why didn't you leave the pig at home?"

"Oh, one second, please," she said and reached for her phone. "Let me show you what happens when an angry pig has a temper tantrum."

I scrolled through pictures of various degrees of destruction—including chewed up carpet, a destroyed laundry basket, and something that looked like an explosion of glitter. Shaking my head, I handed the phone back to her. "Enough said."

WE ARRIVED A FEW MINUTES EARLY FOR SLOANE'S appointment, which turned out to be a good thing because my presence changed the entire session.

"Sloane! It's so good to see you!" a woman greeted when we entered the room. When her eyes landed on me, she froze. "I didn't know you were bringing a model."

"Oh, he's not a model. Amy, this is Bronze, my friend,

and he's my security detail today. Bronze, this is Amy, the photographer," she introduced.

"Ain't your fucking friend," I rumbled against the top of her head while I pinched her ass cheek—hard—since I knew she wouldn't appreciate me slapping it in front of her colleagues.

Amy studied me for several long beats before she turned to Sloane and mumbled something I couldn't clearly hear. Sloane's reply was even harder to make out, but I felt the need to intervene when she started shaking her head, clearly disagreeing with Amy. "What's going on, Sloane?"

She turned to me with a smile on her face. "Everything's fine. We were just discussing the plans before we begin." Directing her attention to Amy, she added, "I'll go ahead and get changed so we can get started."

With that, Sloane took my hand and led me to the bathroom. Or so I thought. "What kind of bathroom is this?"

Sloane giggled. "We're in the dressing room where the bride and bridesmaids get ready for the wedding. Amy likes to reserve bridal suites for these kinds of sessions," she explained.

"What kind of sessions?"

"Boudoir," she mumbled and focused on digging through her bag of outfits. "I'll be right back," she announced, holding up a wad of clothing.

Boudoir. It didn't register to me what she meant. Not when she emerged from the bathroom with a robe wrapped around her. Not when she walked into the other room and stopped beside the bed.

No, it was when she turned to the camera and dropped her robe to the floor, revealing her lingerie-clad body. She was standing there looking like the ultimate sex goddess in a black bra and matching G-string framed by a garter belt and thigh-high stockings.

Pressing the palm of my hand against my dick, I stifled a groan when my eyes landed on the strappy stilettos adorning her feet. But that was the last semblance of control I had.

Ripping my shirt over my head, I tossed it across the room and stomped toward Sloane from behind. I slid one hand around her neck and the other around her stomach, roughly pulling her back against my bare chest. With my face buried in the crook of her neck, I asked low enough for only her to hear, "The fuck you doing? I thought this was for a book cover."

"It is," she breathed. "For one of mine."

I didn't attempt to muffle the groan that erupted from me. For one of hers. Erotica. My grip on her tightened briefly as I fought to rein in the urge to bend Sloane over the bed and fuck her in front of everyone in the room. Knowing she wouldn't like it helped me get a handle on the moment. That and the photographer catching my attention.

"Yes! Holy shit! That's hot," she praised, followed by hundreds of clicks.

"You're in so much trouble," I whispered.

She fucking quivered again. "Motherfucker. You're killing me, baby," I told her and moved both hands to her hips, pulling her back so I could grind my hard cock against her ass.

"Fuck, yes! Keep going. Turn her around," Amy instructed excitedly.

And so it went from there. We went through a cycle of poses, Sloane changed outfits, and we did it again and again. However, when Amy finished with Sloane in her last outfit, I had my own request, if I could get Sloane to agree to it.

"I want her to take some of us naked. Just for you and me," I started.

"No way. Not happening. Nope," she said before I finished the last sentence.

Stepping closer, I ran my hands over her shoulders and down her arms. "I'm not talking about dirty pics that show everything. I mean sort of like the ones she just took," I explained and thought a demonstration might help my cause. Covering her breasts with one arm, I slid the other down her torso and covered her pussy with my splayed palm. "Like this," I said against the shell of her ear and nipped her earlobe for good measure.

"Okay," she breathed. "I'll ask Amy if she has time for a few more shots."

When she returned a few minutes later with pink-stained cheeks, I knew Amy had agreed.

"You sure you're okay with this?" I asked. I was notoriously shameless and had no qualms about being naked in front of other people.

Sloane nodded. "Yeah. She's going to finish with Frankie and send her assistants home so we won't have an audience."

"Frankie's going to be pissed," I teased, hoping to help ease her nerves.

Sloane cracked up laughing. "Yeah, she will be, but not for the reason you think."

"And what's that?"

"Uh, let me put it this way—don't be surprised if she asks you for a dick pic in the very near future."

We continued talking, and Sloane seemed adequately relaxed when Amy said she was ready for us. "I'm going to get the cameras set up and adjust the lights. You two let me know when you're ready," she shared and turned away from us, providing a little bit of privacy that I knew Sloane appreciated.

Kicking off my boots and unzipping my jeans, I proudly dropped them to the floor and bared my naked ass. Sloane, on the other hand, stripped as fast as she could and plastered her front to mine, causing the sound of a light smack to echo off the bare walls.

"Nervous?" I chuckled.

"A little," she admitted. "I trust Amy, but I'm not used to being naked in front of more than one person, and it's a little odd."

"You'll get used to it," I started and wanted to smack my forehead the moment it came out of my mouth. Thinking quickly, I added, "But I'm sure we can turn up the heat to keep you comfortable."

"What?" she asked in confusion.

"Didn't you say it was a little cold?"

"No, I said it's a little *odd*," she reiterated.

"Are you two ready?" Amy asked, thankfully interrupting my shitty attempt at not sticking my foot in my mouth.

I deferred to Sloane. With more confidence than I expected, she declared, "Yes, we are."

"All right," she said gleefully and clapped her hands. "Let's get to it."

23

SLOANE

Since Bronze drove his truck to Cherryfield, I rode with him to Devil Springs, instead of following him back the Sunday after his fight. Which meant I would be staying with him for almost two weeks before we left for my next book signing.

On the other hand, I was beyond excited for the opportunity to write my stories in a bookstore. Bronze had mentioned it again when he invited me to stay with him, almost as if he was trying to ensure I would say yes. Little did he know, I would've said yes no matter where he asked me to go, but listening to him confirm it with Tatum and Josie was the icing on the cake.

When Monday morning rolled around, I pulled Bronze's truck into the lot and grabbed my bag, nervous as hell. In fact, I was so much on edge that I jumped and almost screamed when the entry bell sounded. "Morning!" I called out with a bit too much enthusiasm in an attempt to cover my trepidation.

"She's here!" I heard Josie squeal from somewhere I couldn't see. She appeared moments later and motioned for me to follow her. "This way. We have a surprise for you!"

"Oh, you didn't have to do that," I managed to say. Graciously accepting compliments or gifts was not a strong point for me.

"We wanted to," she replied and came to a stop in the far corner of the bookstore. Positioned in front of a black backdrop hanging in front of the far wall of bookshelves was a small table, topped with a black tablecloth and adorned with twinkle lights. A comfy-looking leather office chair sat behind it.

"Voilà!" Josie beamed.

"I love it!" And I honestly did. "Especially how the twinkle lights set the mood. I'm going to have to do this in my home office."

"Yay! I'm so glad you like it," she said, sounding relieved.

"Wait!" Tatum shouted with an overwhelming amount of excitement. "I also have a surprise." She moved behind the table and pulled the black backdrop to the side, revealing several different life-sized cardboard cutouts of Bronze wearing a hot pink evening gown.

I started laughing so hard that no sound came out for several seconds before I inhaled deeply and laughed until my stomach started cramping.

"Oh, this is the best surprise ever!" I cheered and studied the replicas. "Is his hair pink in that one?"

Tatum frowned while Josie explained with a grin. "Obviously, Bronze lost a bet. The loser had to dye their hair pink and wear a pink dress to work every day for a month. Tatum forgot to specify the type of hair dye or the length of time, so Bronze picked the kind that washes out in one day."

"I bet Avery has software that will easily change his hair to whatever shade of pink you'd like," I suggested.

"In case you didn't know, I'm a permanent member of Team Sloane," Tatum said seriously.

"Make yourself comfortable, and we'll try to stay out of your hair. Customers shouldn't be a problem because we don't have a lot of traffic. And, please, let one of us know if you need anything. We'll both be here all day."

"Thank you so much, Josie. I can't tell you how much I appreciate the opportunity." Leaning closer, I lowered my voice, "A little secret—I'm going to try to write an entire story from start to finish while I'm here."

Josie used her fingers to simulate zipping her lips. "That's so exciting! And your secret's safe with me," she promised.

"I really hope I can pull it off because it's sort of poetic—a book's full circle."

Josie wiped under her eyes. "I think I'm going to cry."

"I think I'm going to vomit," Tatum said flatly, causing me to chuckle. She cleared her throat, and her tone completely changed. "Josie, once Sloane's settled, I need to talk to you about the delivery we have scheduled for later this week."

With that, Tatum returned to the office, and Josie spent another few minutes fussing over me before she joined her sister. After setting up my laptop, I put in my earbuds, selected ocean waves as my white noise, and started writing a new story.

I was having a great time and writing more words per day than usual. I don't know what it was, but something about the bookstore profoundly spoke to my soul. At the rate I was going, I could possibly complete two short stories during my stay in Devil Springs.

Like Tatum said, they didn't have many customers, but

the ones who did come in didn't seem to notice me. I was anticipating numerous interruptions, but Tatum and Josie stayed busy and left me alone to work.

The first part of the week flew by. Since Bronze spent his days at the gym next door, I met him there when the bookstore closed for the day and spent the evenings with him and Blue. Copper was still keeping his distance, but the rest of the club seemed to enjoy having me around—if the number of times someone stopped by unexpectedly was any indication. By the time Thursday rolled around, I was beginning to wonder if the three of us would have any evenings to ourselves. Unfortunately, I didn't get the chance to find out as all hell broke loose the next day.

AFTER ANOTHER PRODUCTIVE MORNING OF WRITING, I removed my earbuds and was headed for a bathroom break when the store's phone rang. "Hello, Books, Books, and Books. Can I help you?"

Josie's eyes landed on me as her face paled. She held one finger over her lips, telling me to be quiet, and then she pointed to the office and mouthed, "Tatum."

I darted behind the checkout counter and into the office. "Josie needs you," I blurted. "Seems urgent."

She got up and went to see what was going on faster than I expected, which left me with a growing sense of unease. Before I could process what was happening, Tatum herded Josie and me into a room in the back of the store and locked the door.

"That phone call was someone threatening to 'send the store up in a ball of flames,'" Tatum said matter-of-factly. "Sloane, we'll have to explain along the way, but we're leaving now."

"Oh, okay, um, I'll just grab my laptop and bag, and I'm ready to go."

Tatum grimaced. "I'll have to bring it to you a little later. We have to leave now," she explained, though she didn't seem as panicked as I felt. I hadn't realized I'd been following her as she was talking until she came to a stop in front of a bookshelf in the back room. She removed a book from the third shelf and revealed a hidden keypad.

Once she entered the code, a secret door opened, and she ushered us inside, the sound of the locks sliding into place echoing around the dark, bare room. I wasn't scared of the dark by any means, but I also wasn't crazy about standing in a secret room with zero visibility.

"What's going on?"

"I'll explain everything once we get to safety."

At that, I shut my mouth and followed instructions. It only happened once—as far as I could recall—when I was younger, but I remembered that time vividly. Part of what stuck with me was my mother's voice. I never found out what happened, but she conveyed her fear and the seriousness of the situation solely by the tone of her voice. And Tatum's tone was damn near an exact replication of my mother's.

Moments later, more locks clicked, and light illuminated the small space before another door opened. "Sorry," Tatum apologized. "It's hard to find the hand scanner in the dark," she explained and pointed to a device mounted on the wall.

After my eyes adjusted from the sudden brightness, I realized we were in what looked like another type of safe room, and thankfully it was one with lights. "Almost there," Tatum shared and set about opening yet another door, which opened into the bookstore's office. "Where are we?" I asked.

"Not where you think," Josie murmured and took my hand to pull me along behind her. She quickly moved through the store and, to my shock, out the front door.

"Wait! I can't leave without telling Bronze!" I insisted as I increasingly became alarmed.

"He already knows," Tatum told me while practically shoving me into the backseat of the weirdest looking four-door Jeep.

"Is this Jeep pink?" I asked, unable to stop myself.

Tatum huffed while Josie laughed. "Barely. I made one offhanded comment about preferring a pink Jeep over a minivan, and my boss thought it'd be hilarious to make my dreams come true by having this bitch painted the palest shade of pink he could find before delivering it to me."

"So, this is your work vehicle? As in, belongs to the Bureau?"

She shrugged, failing to notice how I was gearing up to have an epic freak-out. "I wouldn't call it my work vehicle, but it does belong to the government."

"And it's bulletproof," Josie supplied.

"Why am I in a government-owned, bulletproof vehicle?" I asked through clenched teeth while my voice became increasingly louder.

Tatum cleared her throat and fulfilled her promise to explain. Sort of. "I can't tell you the reasons why, but we have plans in place for a variety of possible situations—one being the need to escape quickly and quietly with minimal risk of detection. In order to do that, we created safe rooms on each end of an existing underground tunnel that connects the bookstore to the party supply store on the other side of the shopping center. Right now, we're taking you to a safe location. We'll figure out the rest when we get there."

I turned in my seat to look out the rear window. "But what about Bronze and Blue?"

"They're already on their way."

"What? How?"

"They were able to leave before we were since they could just walk right out to his truck, but they'll arrive after us to not draw extra attention."

"Where are they going to go until they get there?"

Josie reached over and clasped my hand, giving it a gentle squeeze. "They're completely safe. He usually drives around for fifteen or twenty minutes this time of day because Blue has trouble falling asleep for her midday nap if it's a busy day at the gym. Them leaving around this time would be expected for anyone watching."

Her words silenced me for a large portion of the drive. I couldn't help wondering if the threat was related to me, not them. The thought played on repeat in my mind until I figured out a way to ask without asking. "Has anything like this ever happened before?"

"No," Tatum answered, "but we haven't been open that long either."

"Oh," I replied and chewed on my lower lip. I wanted to ask, but there was no way the threat had anything to do with me. It couldn't have. The only person who knew I was working in the bookstore was Frankie, and I trusted her implicitly.

"Are you wondering if this is about you?" Tatum asked.

"Maybe a little," I confessed.

"We don't know. My colleagues are working on a trace now. The caller didn't give away any clues that I picked up, but I haven't had a chance to listen to the replay." She shrugged. "This is amateur shit. They'll probably know who it is before we arrive anyway."

With every breath of my being, I hoped she was right.

"Wait until the garage door is completely closed. Then, we'll get out and go inside. You'll go with Josie while I find out what's going on. I'll update you as soon as I know something," Tatum explained.

Josie led me through the kitchen to a set of stairs that led to a wine cellar. She removed a bottle of wine from the shelf and pushed against the wall. Once again, a secret room was revealed—thankfully with working lights.

"I'm not sure how long we'll be in here, but please make yourself comfortable," Josie said as she closed the door and secured it.

I glanced around at the cozy sitting area that looked like it should be featured in a home décor magazine instead of hidden in the middle of a mansion behind a secret wall. "What is this place?" I wondered aloud, letting my imagination take over to keep my fear from reaching uncontrollable levels.

Josie took a seat on the small sofa across from me and cleared her throat. "As Tatum said, we can't give you the details, but I can tell you that the room you're in was created for the sole purpose of safety."

I nodded absently, a story already beginning to develop in my head. "Um, you wouldn't happen to have a pen and some paper, would you?"

Josie grinned knowingly and disappeared into what I assumed was another area of the safe room. Returning with a pen and notepad, she handed them to me with a bright smile. "Got a new idea?"

"I do," I replied excitedly. "I always try to jot them down somewhere as soon as they hit me, but this time, I think it'll be a nice distraction from whatever's going on."

"I wish I could tell you that it's nothing to worry

about," she trailed off, leaving me to silently fill in the rest —*but it probably is*.

"I wish you could too, but we have to face whatever challenges life presents us with, and right now," I gestured to the small room, "this is one of mine."

"I'll be quiet and let you do your thing, but do you want something to eat or drink first?"

"Water would be great," I said with too much enthusiasm. "Sorry, I didn't realize I was so thirsty until you mentioned it."

With my thirst quenched, I wrote down my new idea for a story—The Federal Agent and the Protected Witness. As usual, the ideas kept coming, faster than I could write, and I longed for my laptop. Or any of my electronic devices since all of my files were saved in cloud storage.

Feeling somewhat secure in my current location, I let myself get lost in my new story until a familiar coo interrupted my thoughts. Carelessly tossing the notebook to the side, I jumped to my feet and ran toward Bronze and Blue with my arms wide open. "You made it! Thank goodness!"

Bronze caught me with the arm not holding Blue and pulled me against his chest. "You okay?"

I wasn't prepared for the relief I felt when he held me to his body. It was that moment that I knew with one hundred percent certainty that he would do anything to protect me or die trying. It was a sense of security I hadn't known I was missing.

Exhaling slowly, I rested my cheek against his chest while I reached up and ran my fingers over Blue's cheek. She immediately reached for me, and I secretly wanted to beam with pride every time she did it. "I am now," I breathed.

"Everything's going to be okay," he assured.

"What's going to happen now?"

"I can answer that," Tatum announced as she entered the room with a file folder in her hand. She cleared her throat and seemed unsure of herself, and in the short time I'd known her, even I knew that was out of character for her. "We're still working on identifying the caller and pinpointing their location. I've since listened to the phone call numerous times and heard nothing that would help us in the search. What that means is we're shutting down all operations for this office and diverting any incoming traffic to other areas until this has been resolved. Since we can't rule out that this is related to Sloane, we need to move her to a different location as well."

"Where're you thinking? Badger's cabin?" Bronze asked.

"Say what now?" I interrupted. "I can't just up and disappear to a safe house in an undisclosed location. I'm leaving for my next event a week from today."

Tatum cut her eyes to Bronze. I watched in awe as they seemed to have an entire conversation silently, though I almost cracked up laughing at the weird faces they were making with widened eyes and twisted lips.

"I can't decide if what you two are doing is fascinating or extremely rude," I observed. "Either way, whatever you were discussing is a moot point if it pertains to me."

"How so?" Bronze asked with a hint of challenge in his voice.

Blue wrinkled her nose and made an unhappy face at her father. She had no idea what was going on, but her timing was perfect. "See, even she agrees with me."

"You haven't said anything."

"Neither did you or Tatum," I countered.

"Sloane," Bronze said slowly.

"Fine," I huffed. "There's no need to arrange anything

for me. My mother's estate is gated and guarded. Over the years, there were times when we needed to temporarily increase security for one reason or another. I'll call the company and have them add more guards to our plan until further notice."

"And what about the event? It's not safe for you to attend. Not unless this threat wasn't related to you."

I rubbed my hands over my face in frustration. He was right, and I knew it, but I couldn't back out of the event. It was the biggest one of the year for my genre, and I knew of several readers who were making the trip specifically to see me. I was as much for safety as the next person, but I couldn't rationalize allowing an unknown entity that possibly didn't even exist to have any impact on my career decisions.

"Listen, I see where you're coming from, and I agree with you. It's not safe. But I have to go," I said and held up my hands. "Let me finish before you start arguing with me. I have to at least attend the signing, but I'm willing to skip all of the pre-event activities on Thursday and Friday. I would really like to attend the party after the signing for at least the first hour, but I'm willing to skip that too if you think it's too risky."

He studied my face for a few seconds, seeming to realize I wasn't going to budge on my stance and agreed, but with his own stipulations. "That should work, but you and Frankie need to make all new travel plans. And I mean everything from the time you leave to the place you stay. All of it needs to be different. Also, you need to ditch your usual aliases and use one you've never used before. Better yet, we'll make the reservations under my name."

Tatum cleared her throat and wiggled her fingers in the air. "Hello," she said slowly. "I'm sure your local FBI agent can make those secure travel arrangements for you. What city is the signing in?"

"Cedar Valley."

"Okay, and what about Frankie? What're her plans?"

"She's going to drive there and meet me at the hotel Thursday afternoon," I explained.

"Does she live in Cherryfield?"

"Oh, no, she lives in Tuckersville. It's about two hours from me."

"Let's have Frankie drive to your mother's place instead of going to Cedar Valley. The sooner she can arrive, the better. I'll arrange transportation to an undisclosed location on Friday, where you'll stay until the time you leave to set up for the event. I'll take care of transportation to and from the venue, additional security, and…" she drew out and paused for a few moments, "whatever else needs to be taken care of so that you and Frankie can do your jobs as safely as possible."

"Should she come now? Or wait until closer to Thursday?"

"The sooner the better. Now being the best."

"When can I call and tell her?" I asked anxiously. On more than one occasion, Frankie had driven to Cherryfield and spent the week working from my house, so I knew it wouldn't be a problem for her—particularly because I allowed her to bring Brat.

"You can't," Tatum said pointedly. "But I can."

"She won't believe you unless you give her our secret password. Well, it's actually a phrase, or technically, it's a sentence. I really should know this."

"I don't care if it's a comma splice with tautology that ends in a preposition. I've already paid my debt to grammar. Just give me the secret password/phrase/sentence."

I leaned forward and lowered my voice. "I like anal," I mumbled.

"I'm sorry. I didn't catch that." I knew damn good and well that she heard me. "What did you say?"

"I like anal," I said a bit louder with a touch of frustration.

"I," she said slowly as she made a show of writing it down. "Like." She paused before drawing out each sound in the last word. "Anal. Correct?"

I sighed in exasperation and slapped my hand over my face. "Yes, that's correct. I mean, the phrase is correct. Wait, no. I mean, that is the correct passphrase." I pretended to wipe sweat from my forehead. "It was funny when we never thought we'd have to use it," I tried but cracked a smile. "Okay, it's still funny."

Tatum clapped me on the shoulder. "You totally fit in around here."

After discussing the details and finalizing the plans, all of my belongings, along with everything Bronze and Blue would need for their stay, magically appeared at the safe house. Then, the three of us and all of our luggage were loaded into a behemoth of a vehicle provided by Tatum and sent on our way.

I waited until we were on the highway before I turned to Bronze and said, "Well, this was an unexpected turn of events."

He snorted. "Yeah, it was. You okay?"

I shrugged. "Yeah, I think so. The whole thing shook me up for sure. But, based on what Tatum said and the things I saw, the chances of the threat having anything to do with me are slim to none."

I glanced at Blue's sleeping face in the mirror mounted in front of her car seat. "You're sure we're not putting her in harm's way?"

He reached over and squeezed my hand. "She wouldn't be here if I thought otherwise. The safest place for her is with me at your mom's place. Speaking of, how is it still your mother's place?"

"Technically, it's not. My brothers and I inherited it. Kian and Declan wanted to sell, but Tiernan and I didn't. So, we bought them out and split the property between ourselves, though he acts like it's my home. Shit!" I cursed when I realized I couldn't use my phone. "Tiernan's home until the end of next week; he doesn't know Frankie's on her way. She'll probably get there before we will."

"Is that a problem?"

"No, not a problem, per se. It's just that Tiernan has been so good about letting me know when he's coming and going and, well," I paused and finally admitted something I'd refused to acknowledge for years. "Frankie and Tiernan don't get along. At all."

Bronze chuckled. "What about the pig?"

"Shit," I groaned and covered my face with my hands. "That's why he and Frankie don't get along. He's never even met Brat, and he already hates him. And you know how Brat loves men. Oh, this is going to be a disaster."

"Why does he already hate him?"

"Frankie came to visit me when Brat was a piglet. She'd only had him for a few weeks. Anyway, she set up this portable contraption for him in the guest room they were using. She put a litter box in there and promised me the pig would use it. Well, while we were asleep, Brat used his nose to tip the enclosure over and set himself free. And then he went straight to Tiernan's room where he tugged the blankets off the bed and made himself a love nest. But when his love didn't come home, he shit on the blankets and turned over every potted plant on Tiernan's side of the house."

He laughed. "What's with the potted plants?"

I shrugged. "He wallowed in each pile of dirt, but no one knows why he did. Frankie thinks it was nothing more than a pig wanting to wallow in dirt, but I think he did it because it ground that dark, rich soil into his plush white carpet, ruining it forever."

"I'm surprised he didn't roast that pig for dinner."

"He tried. And he probably will if they get there before we do," I said, not at all joking.

As luck would have it, Tiernan wasn't home when we arrived, and Frankie was still over an hour away, which gave me plenty of time to prevent a disastrous meeting between the two. In other words, it gave me plenty of time to hide Brat and threaten Frankie with revealing the secret we never spoke of.

However, I still needed to find out when Tiernan would be back so we could plan accordingly. I also wanted to give him a heads-up about my guests, and I wasn't sure which one I was more concerned about—Bronze or Brat. But after calling his cell phone and texting him with no response, I called the front gate and asked Dickerson if he knew where Tiernan was.

"He left the day before yesterday on an unexpected business trip. He did mention he had a mess to clean up and didn't know how long he'd be gone. I'll be sure to let you know if I hear from him," he explained.

"Thanks, Dickerson. I'll do the same for you."

Knowing I would have plenty of warning before Tiernan came home allowed me to relax. With that potential disaster avoided, I returned to the kitchen to find Bronze making a bottle for Blue.

"Can I feed her?" I asked.

He glanced at me over his shoulder with his little girl cradled in his arms and grinned. I damn near died right there in the middle of the kitchen. "You can do anything you want, Sweet Sloane."

"Behave, dirty biker man, and give me the baby," I teased.

He easily passed her to me, and I giggled at the confused look on her face. She was still in the process of waking up from her long nap in the car, which Bronze explained was the equivalent of a much-needed, deep, hard sleep for an adult.

"Peek-a-boo, Blue. It's Aunt Sloane," I sang cheerfully, and promptly froze, wishing my hands were free so I could slap my hand over my mouth. "I'm sorry. Some of my friends' kids call me Aunt Sloane, and I guess it just came out."

He looked up from where he was testing the temperature of the bottle. "Doesn't bother me as long as you know I'm not your friend."

"You're not?" I asked in mock surprise.

Leaning close, he placed his lips against the shell of my ear. "We'll talk about this later. When I've got your naked body underneath me, and I'm balls deep in your tight cunt." He punctuated his words with a pinch to my ass before he held out Blue's bottle for me.

When I reached for it, he pulled it back slightly, in a way that made me think he wasn't comfortable letting me feed her. "If you're not okay with this, just tell me."

He shook his head and handed me the bottle. "It has nothing to do with you and everything to do with me. She choked when she was a few days old, and it scared the ever-loving shit out of me. It hasn't happened again, but I still hesitate every time someone new feeds her for the first time."

I paused with the bottle in my hand, unsure of what to

do. Blue made the decision for me when she reached for it and pulled the nipple to her mouth.

"If it makes you feel any better, I know CPR and the Heimlich maneuver, or whatever it's called now, though I've never had to actually perform either one," I told him, keeping my eyes on Blue as she drank her bottle with fervor.

"I hope you never do," he murmured, and by his tone, I knew he was speaking from experience. Though, I couldn't help but wonder if he was the one on the giving or receiving end.

Before I could ask, Blue finished her bottle and looked at me expectantly. "Here's the deal, little missy. I'll burp you if you promise not to spray milk down my back. Or maybe we should let Daddy do it."

As if she understood my words and was playing along, Blue reached for me and pulled herself impossibly closer. "Okey dokey, I'm trusting you here, so don't let me down." After a few pats on her back, Blue let out the cutest little burb followed by a contented sigh. "That's my girl!" I cheered, careful not to jostle her too much.

"Yoo-hoo!" Frankie called from the other side of the kitchen window. I flinched, Blue started crying, and suddenly there were only two panes of glass separating Bronze's gun from Frankie's forehead.

To her credit, Frankie didn't so much as bat an eyelash. Instead, her eyes crossed as she tried to study the weapon without moving. "That's a pretty one. Can I touch it when it's not pointed at me?"

"For fuck's sake, Frankie! I could've killed you in front of Sloane and my daughter. How in the hell did you get past the gate without us knowing?"

She completely ignored everything he said after she heard the word baby. "There's a baby in there. Let me in!

Let me in! Let me in!" Her outburst startled Brat and caused him to start squealing. And let me tell you, when a pig starts squealing in fear, there's no stopping it.

Even with the baby crying and the pig practically screaming, I couldn't help but smile at Frankie's arrival because it meant we were all safe.

THE WEEK PASSED MUCH FASTER THAN I EXPECTED. Frankie and I were even more productive than usual, which was quite a surprise to me since I had my boyfriend and his baby in my house.

I'm not sure what I was expecting, but he never once asked me to watch Blue. Not even for a few minutes while he took a shower or used the bathroom. During the day, she stayed with him while he worked out in the gym located in the main house. Meanwhile, Frankie and I made use of my home office, the kitchen, and the upstairs balcony. But, we spent the most time working by the pool.

Frankie knew the water had always been a source of inspiration for me, and since I was having trouble finding the right words for my work in progress, she suggested working by the pool, which turned into working *in* the pool after I tossed her a waterproof case for her tablet.

I don't know how much time had passed when a deep laugh pulled me from my fictional world. Raising my sunglasses, I blinked up to find Bronze snapping photos with his phone. "What are you doing?" I shrieked and started frantically paddling to turn my pool float away from him.

He continued to laugh hysterically. "You and Frankie have your noses glued to tablets while floating around on a giant inflatable cloud, complete with a rainbow arching over it, and you expect me not to take pictures?"

That's when Brat made his presence known and started swimming for the sausage. "Oh, fuck, I didn't see the little ham hock," he groaned and took a few steps back. "Is he supposed to be in there?"

"Pigs love to swim, and it's safe for him because it's a saltwater pool," Frankie explained.

Bronze watched warily as Brat busted his chops to get to him. "Can he get out on his own?"

Frankie clutched her stomach and fell over laughing, almost capsizing our cloud. "He hasn't been in your pool before, has he?"

"No, I haven't," Bronze huffed. "Why?"

Frankie pointed and managed to get the words out right before Brat made his exit. "It's a walk-in. As soon as his hooves touch the bottom, you better run."

"If that pig so much as gets one drop of water on me, you better run," Bronze returned and crossed his arms over his chest.

"Fuck," I groaned and covered my mouth with my hands while Frankie launched herself off the float and went after her pig, causing the float to tip over and plunge me into the water.

I thought I was only under for a few seconds, but when I surfaced, Frankie had a pissed-off Brat wrapped in a towel, and Bronze was holding Blue while she fixated on the pig and giggled.

"Come on, you big ham, let's get you inside for a treat."

I gasped. Frankie only bribed him with treats when it was an absolute necessity. And I guess she thought my biker was serious when he threatened to burn her bacon.

"Would you two like to go for a swim?" I asked. I

wasn't ready to go inside. It was such a nice day, and I wanted to enjoy it a little longer. "We could have something for dinner delivered and eat by the pool," I suggested.

He shook his head. "We'll have to pass. We haven't had a chance to go swimming before now, so I haven't gotten her a swim diaper yet."

"Does she need one? I mean, a little bit of baby pee in this giant pool isn't going to bother me," I told him and lowered my voice. "Do you think she's gonna poop anytime soon?"

He chuckled. "If I knew when that was going to happen, I would've saved myself a shitload of trouble, literally."

"Seriously, get in. The water feels great. I'll be right back," I said and hoisted myself out of the pool on the side near the pool house. A few minutes later, I returned with a float my mother bought for one of my baby cousins a few years ago. "Do you think she would like this?"

"There's only one way to find out." With that, he stripped down to his boxer-briefs and proceeded to undress Blue. "I just put a clean diaper on her, so she should be good for a little while."

He carried her into the pool slowly, dipping her feet in first to see how she responded. "She loves bath time, so I doubt this will be any different."

He was right. Blue loved the water. Once he got her situated in the float, she flashed us a big, gummy grin. Every once in a while, she would randomly smack both hands on top of the water and laugh when she made it splash.

At some point, while I was pushing her float around the pool and watching her enjoy herself, Bronze moved behind me and slipped his arm around my waist. "You're good with babies," he rumbled.

"Thanks," I squeaked and cleared my throat. "I love kids. I want to have a houseful someday," I told him, not realizing I was nonchalantly sharing my future hopes and dreams with him.

"I knew I wanted to have kids one day, but never gave it much thought until Blue was born." He snorted. "I still haven't given it much thought, but right now, I'm focusing on the one I've got."

"You've got a good one," I said wistfully.

"That I do," he agreed and kissed my cheek.

24

BRONZE

Since Sloane previously agreed to skip the events for the first two days of the convention, we planned to load up and drive to the "undisclosed" location where Tatum made arrangements for us to stay. Even though Tatum forbade it, I debated on telling Sloane we were headed to Croftridge anyway. Because I knew she would be pissed if she didn't have time to adequately make herself a nervous wreck and change clothes fifteen times before she met the rest of my family. I understood it was how she dealt with her nerves because my mom was the same way anytime she was meeting a group of new people.

While I trusted Sloane, and I knew Sloane trusted Frankie, I didn't know Frankie well enough to trust her; therefore, I couldn't risk putting us all in danger if it turned out Frankie wasn't trustworthy or sucked at keeping secrets. However, in the best interest of my own ass, I found a way to skirt the rules.

"When you're packing and getting ready to leave, pretend like it's the first time I brought you to the clubhouse for the cookout."

She whirled around with a look of confusion on her face. "What? Why would I do that?"

"Trust me, Sweet Sloane," I said cryptically and covered her lips with mine before she could argue. "I'll be back in a few hours to pick up you and Frankie."

"And Brat," she helpfully reminded me.

I rolled my eyes. "How could I forget?"

"Please be careful," she said, ignoring my disdain for the swine. And then she stole my heart when she smoothed her hand over Blue's hair and placed a soft kiss on her forehead. "I'll miss you, but I'll see you soon, Baby Blue."

With a soft smile, she closed the door and returned to my window, trying and failing to stealthily blink away the tears in her eyes. Like the smart man I was, I dutifully ignored them and kissed her goodbye.

While I drove to meet Copper and Layla halfway between Cherryfield and Devil Springs with Blue, Sloane and Frankie finished packing for the trip. When I returned a few hours later, we loaded up and headed to Croftridge.

"Why won't you tell us where we're going?" she asked. Again. "You obviously know."

Frankie sighed. "It's because he doesn't trust me. He doesn't want to upset you by telling you that, so he's been hemming and hawing trying to keep the peace. Am I right?"

"So right it almost hurts," I acknowledged.

Sloane gasped and playfully slapped my arm. "Are you serious? If Frankie wasn't trustworthy, we'd know by now. Because we all know that Tatum ran a background check on her that's more invasive than a colonoscopy."

I pinched the bridge of my nose. "I never thought Frankie was a bad person. If I did, I wouldn't have had my kid around her. But," I paused and cringed, hoping she would understand, "Some people aren't very good at keeping secrets, and I didn't know if Frankie was one of them. It would only take a small slip of the tongue to put both of you in danger," I explained.

"For the record," Frankie interjected, "I agree with him. He doesn't know me and shouldn't trust me just because you do."

"Fine," she huffed. "I get that, but why can't you tell me now? There's no way for her to tell anyone."

"You're kind of a bra—"

"Don't say it!" Frankie shouted, cutting me off. "You have got to pick a new word. Any word, but that word. Or any word that includes that word."

"What word?" I teased.

"Br—" Sloane started.

"Damn it," Frankie cursed.

"This wouldn't happen if you would've named him Nacho," Sloane teased.

"You didn't win the bet, so you didn't get to choose the name," Frankie snapped.

"Ladies," I shouted to get their attention. "We're here. Finish your argument before you get out, would ya?" I said and didn't bother to hide my sarcasm as I got out and closed the door.

"They ain't gonna do that shit the whole time they're here, are they?" Ranger asked from his perch on his front porch.

"No, they usually behave in front of company," I joked and moved to shake his hand. "Thanks for letting us crash here."

He clasped my hand in his and pulled me in for a hug. "No need to thank me. Aside from the club, you pissed on me the day you were born. That makes us family in my book."

The sound of two car doors opening and closing had

me glancing over my shoulder with a grin. Sloane was making her way toward us while Frankie was rounding the back. I cleared my throat and asked, "Tatum did mention Frankie was bringing her pet, right?"

"She said two pretty ladies and a fat pig," he said and paused as it sank in. "Motherfucker! I knew something was off. She never talks about people like that. Damn it! Well, that thing ain't staying in my house."

"Loooook at the cute little piggy!" Gabby squealed as she darted across the yard to the pig leashed and harnessed by Frankie's side. "Can I touch it?" she giggled and excitedly bounced on her feet.

"Does it bite?" Ranger asked.

"No," Frankie replied confidently. "He never has, and it would be a shock to me if he ever did."

"Can I touch his nose? Pleeeeaaasssse," she begged. "It looks so cute and squishy."

"How about we let Frankie get him inside and settled into his new home away from home? Then, after he's had some time to rest and something to eat, we can introduce you properly," Ranger replied.

"Come with me. I'll show you where your room is, and then I'll make a special bed for the prince piggy for his royal slumber. I'll bring my princess blanket too. Can I sleep with, um, what's his name?"

"Bratwurst, but we call him Brat."

"Oh, I'm not supposed to say that word. Can I just call him Prince Piggy?"

"You can say that word if you're saying the pig's name," Ranger told her.

"Okay, Papa, I promise to only call the pig a brat."

Ranger slapped his hand over his face. "Fuck," he grumbled. "Keegan just got her to stop asking for a pet pig a month or two ago. I'm sending her to you when she's looking for someone to yell at."

"Trust me," Frankie said and lowered her voice. "She won't want a pet pig after spending a little time with this one. Go ahead and let her have a sleepover with the prince. Just make sure whatever she uses to make the bed is something you don't care about getting back."

Ranger opened his mouth like he was going to tell Frankie and her pig to take a hike, but he paused and cocked his head to the side. "I think I see where you're going with this. I'll allow it. But I draw the line at shitting in the house."

"He's litter box trained. Does that count?"

"That pig is litter box trained? You serious?" he asked and started to laugh.

"He is. And if you want to hang around his crate after he eats, you'll get a free demonstration."

Ranger wrinkled his nose in disgust. "I'll take your word for it."

With that, Gabby led Frankie and Brat to their guest room, while Ranger showed Sloane and I to ours. "You gonna introduce me to your woman, or were you trying to be an asshole on purpose?"

"Fuck," I cursed. "Ranger, this is Sloane O'Shea. Sloane, this is Ranger. He was the youngest of the original club members when my grandfather started the club."

"And still the best looking one in the whole bunch," he said with a wide, charming smile. "It's a pleasure to meet you, Sloane. Let me show you where you'll be staying for the next two nights," he said and started down the hallway.

"Make yourselves comfortable," he said as he opened the door to our room. "The bathroom's through that door over there," he pointed out and turned to leave. "Oh, I ordered a couple of pizzas for you. They should be here in about fifteen minutes. Holler if you need something. I'm going to go make sure Gabby isn't trying to put a tutu on your friend's litter-box-using pig."

"You gonna be able to keep her from telling everyone that we're here?" I asked, only half kidding.

"According to Tatum, I only have to keep her quiet until Sunday morning, which won't be a problem because we're leaving to go fishing first thing in the morning. We'll be back long before you're finished with the event, but she always falls asleep early after a day on the water. Come Sunday morning, she's going to want to call her sister and tell her all about the fish she caught, and all about the new pig she made friends with. This is your only warning." With that, he closed the door and went to check on Gabby.

"If she puts a tutu on Brat, I want a picture first," Sloane joked and headed for the bathroom. "I'm going to change and wash my face before dinner gets here."

I called to check on Blue while she was changing, not at all surprised when Layla said she had gone down for the night. She usually did after a long ride in the car. And I couldn't blame her. After all the driving I'd done, I was exhausted.

Sloane emerged from the bathroom around the time Gabby ran down the hall announcing that the pizzas had arrived. Everyone else must've been as tired as I was because we practically ate in silence before we said goodnight and went our separate ways.

Once in our room, Sloane flopped onto the bed and yawned. "I don't know why I'm so tired. Would it be rude if I went to sleep now?"

"Fuck no," I said and shed my clothes. "Because I'm about to do the same." With my arm wrapped around her waist, I pulled her against me and did just that.

25

BRONZE

When we arrived at the event venue, I was taken aback by the size of the convention center as well as the amount of people waiting in line to enter. "How many people do you think are going to be here today?" I asked.

She shrugged. "A couple hundred, I'd guess."

"You don't go anywhere without me. Not even to the bathroom," I reiterated the main point of our safety plan.

"Yes, caveman biker. Your grunted order has been received."

"Sloane," I warned.

"Yeah, yeah. I won't run off or try to lose you, but you're responsible for keeping up with me."

"Not a problem," I replied confidently.

Frankie laughed. "Oh, you have no idea."

Ten minutes later, I was ready to pull my hair out. "Sloane!" I bellowed at the top of my lungs, garnering the entire room's attention.

"Over here!" she replied cheerfully and waved her fingers in the air to help me find her, which was surprisingly at the table to the left of the one she was assigned to.

"Bronze, this is Sophia," she introduced and pointed to something on the floor I couldn't see until I was closer. "And this is her dog, Freya."

I peeked over the table to see a beautiful boxer with watchful eyes at Sophia's side. "Nice to meet you," I said and started to extend my hand to her when I looked up to see the biker approaching us. Suddenly, I remembered the text I got from Phoenix mentioning a patched member of the Northern Grizzlies MC would be in attendance.

"Excuse me one sec," I said and turned to the man.

Sloane and Sophia laughed. "That's my Old Man," Sophia pointed out.

"Chains," he said and extended his hand.

"Bronze," I shared and returned his shake. "Nice to meet you."

"You too," he started but was interrupted by a series of overhead announcements.

"Come on," Sloane said excitedly. "It's about to begin."

With that, we returned to our table moments before the ticketholders were allowed to enter.

WE WERE THREE HOURS INTO THE SIGNING WHEN I NOTICED the same two women from the previous signing, Jennifer and Ginger, hovering at the end of Sloane's aisle. I thought maybe they were nervous, but after ten minutes, I became suspicious. Rising to my feet, I started to walk toward them when they disappeared around the corner. Unwilling to leave Sloane, I continuously scanned the area but didn't spot them anywhere.

I was just about to mention it to Frankie when I saw Jennifer practically running toward the table. She skidded to a halt and barely avoided crashing into me. She did, however, grab my shirt with both hands and pulled me toward her. "I have to talk to you. Right now!"

"What is it?" I demanded, instantly on alert.

We took a few steps away from the table, and she motioned for me to lean down. When I did, she whispered, "I overheard a woman in the bathroom saying she was going through with her plan to put an end to Sloane! I ran out of there as fast as I could when I heard something that sounded like a gun being chambered. You have to get Sloane out of here!"

"Do you know who it was?" I demanded.

She shook her head. "No. She was in the bathroom stall so I couldn't see her. Please do something!"

Even though I wasn't sure I believed Jennifer, I thought it would be best to move Sloane out of public view and discuss our next move. "Sloane," I called out and returned to her side.

The tone of my voice had her immediately turning to me with concern in her eyes. "What's wrong?"

"We need to—fuck!" I shouted when my eyes landed on a woman walking in our direction with purpose. She noticed me at the same time I noticed her.

The next few seconds were a blur of activity. I pulled Sloane against my chest as the woman raised a gun far too large for her petite frame and pointed it at us.

I responded instinctively, my gun appearing in my hands seconds before I aimed and fired. Sloane screamed in pain and her body flinched in my arms, while a sharp pain tore through my shoulder. I briefly thought the shot sounded much louder than it should have as Sloane and I fell backward to the floor.

"Fuck!" I cursed when my body hit the hard concrete. With my arms wrapped around Sloane, there was nothing I could do to brace our fall.

People were screaming, and I could see dozens of feet running by us just on the other side of the table.

Suddenly, I felt someone trying to pull Sloane away from me. Tightening my hold, I shifted her so I could use my other arm to push myself up.

Sloane's author friend, Sophia, from the table beside us appeared in my line of sight. "I was a medic in the Army. I can help her."

Reluctantly, I relinquished my hold on Sloane. As soon as I did, Chains extended his hand to help me up. "Shooter's down," he said and nodded to my shoulder. "Looks like she got both of you with one shot."

"Sloane," I breathed and moved to her side. I faltered for a brief second when I saw the amount of blood on and around her upper body. "How can I help?" I asked, desperate for something to do with my hands.

"Keep her talking and keep your hands out of my way. I'll let you know if I need any help," Sophia said reassuringly.

Cupping Sloane's cheeks, I met her eyes and told her what I'd wanted to say for some time. "I love you, Sloane O'Shea."

"I love you, Bronze Black, and your little Blue, too," she said as her eyes started to close. They suddenly popped back open, and she gasped when her eyes landed on my shoulder. "You're hurt!"

"I'm fine," I reassured her. "Trust me. I've been blown up, stabbed, and almost hit by a car. This little flesh wound is nothing."

"Sloane," Sophia interrupted. "You're bleeding. A lot. Are you taking any kind of blood-thinning medication?"

"No, but I've always been a bleeder, and I bruise easily," she explained.

"I'm afraid this is more than that," Sophia said worriedly.

"Why do you say that?" I asked right as the paramedics arrived.

A familiar voice caught my attention before she could answer. "No one touch anything while I'm with my family. You've fucked up enough as it is!" Tatum fumed as she stormed to me and Sloane.

She dropped damn near all of her weight on me when she bent her knees to hug me. "I knew you were okay, but I had to see for myself!"

"You're killing me, Tatum," I groaned and let go of Sloane to hold my aching shoulder.

"Oh shit! You got hit?" Tatum said and let go of me. "The shooter's in custody. I have to get back over there since I'll be taking her in and leading the interrogation because these bozos couldn't even execute a simple apprehension correctly. But I'll meet you at the hospital as soon as I'm finished." She got to her feet and held out her hand. "Sorry, Pinky, I'm going to need your weapon."

I grumbled under my breath when I gave it to her, knowing it would be weeks—if not months—before I saw it again. She took it and started to walk away before she turned back and said, "I haven't had a chance to call the club yet."

"I took care of that," Chains interjected. "I'd spoken to Phoenix earlier this week to get his permission to wear my colors through Blackwings territory. He said to tell you that he'll meet you at the hospital."

"Thanks, man," I said and extended my hand to him. "Your Old Lady saved my Old Lady's life, so as the VP of the Devil Springs chapter, I'm extending a marker to you and yours."

He shook my hand. "Anytime, man. I'm glad we were able to help."

"We're ready to go," one of the paramedics announced. "Is someone riding with her?"

"I am," I declared and stepped forward.

"But you're hurt," Sloane argued.

"I'll get it checked out at the hospital," I promised and gestured for them to start moving.

Once we were in the ambulance and moving down the road, one of the paramedics said, "Ms. O'Shea, are you on any blood thinners?"

"No, I'm not taking any medications other than birth control," she replied. "Why does everyone keep asking me that?"

"Let me start by saying it's nothing to be overly alarmed about just yet, but you're bleeding a bit more than usual for this type of injury, and I'm having a hard time getting it to slow down."

"Sloane," I said slowly as a thought I wasn't ready to process occurred to me. "The tooth you used for the DNA test. How did you know it was Paige's tooth?"

"I saw a picture of her with gauze in her mouth and an ice bag held against her cheek," she explained. "Why?"

I sighed and pinched the bridge of my nose. "I know what picture you're talking about. That was taken when Paige had gum surgery a few years ago. Where did you find the tooth?"

"In a small jewelry box that was in the stuff from the rental house."

I cleared my throat and reached for her hand, unsure of how she was going to react when she heard what I had to say. "I remember when she had to have the tooth removed. Since she wasn't one to frequently call in sick to work, I clearly remember when she asked for a few days off to take care of her tooth a few years ago. She joked about keeping it as a reminder of how much unnecessary pain she was in because she was too stubborn to go to the dentist before it got bad. However, I didn't realize she'd actually kept it," I paused and gently squeezed her hand. "It was Heidi's tooth, not Paige's."

"Why are you telling me this?" she shrieked. I blinked, taken aback by her reaction. "Answer me, damn it!"

"Because Heidi had an undiagnosed clotting disorder that caused her to hemorrhage and die after giving birth. If she's really your biological half sister, then there's a chance you could have the clotting disorder too."

"Wouldn't I know that by now?" she asked, seemingly slightly dazed.

"Not necessarily," the paramedic chimed in. "Many times, less severe forms go undiagnosed until the individual undergoes a massive trauma to the body, like a gunshot wound or giving birth."

"You're absolutely certain that tooth belonged to Heidi?" she asked.

"Positive. Paige got a flat on the way home. She called the club for help, and I was the one who went and changed her tire. Then, I helped her get Heidi home and into bed. But Heidi kept going on and on about her tooth. She told me to put it in the green bag in her jewelry box. I did it to appease her, but I had no idea she actually kept it," I prattled on.

"Then that means Blue is my niece," she mumbled before her eyes closed and her head lolled to the side.

"Sir, I need you to sit back so I can work. Her BP's dropping, and she's lost consciousness."

It took everything I had to let go of her hand and move

out of the way as best I could. All the while, I kept my eyes focused on her pale face and prayed she'd wake up. I couldn't go through losing another person I loved.

It was a blur of activity when we arrived at the hospital. Sloane still hadn't woken up, but I managed to kiss her and tell her I loved her once more before a team of people clad in masks and scrubs whisked her away.

A smaller team approached me. "Sir, let's get you to a room and have a look at your wound," one of them said, eyeing me cautiously and obviously terrified to come any closer.

My woman was fighting for her life, and once again, I'd almost had my life taken from me. I was on the verge of a breakdown and needed a distraction before I lost my shit without my brothers around. I turned to the frightened medical student, took one step forward, and shouted, "Boo!"

He jumped and let out a high-pitched scream while I threw my head back and laughed. "Let that be a lesson to you about judging a book by its cover. Now, if you'll point me in the direction of my room, I might even be willing to comply and put on the gown."

"Right this way," a middle-aged woman said and escorted me to my room. "I just need to get a little information from you, and we'll get you fixed up shortly."

"Can I give you the information on the woman they just brought in first? I know her name and most of her details. But the important thing is we believe she has a clotting disorder. The same one that her sister died from a few months ago. They need to know that before they do anything to her," I insisted and blurted Sloane's basic information while she wrote it on a scratch piece of paper.

"Thank you. I'll be right back," she said and quickly left my room, hopefully relaying the information I shared.

When she returned, I asked before she had a chance to speak. "How is she?"

"I can't tell you much because of the privacy laws, but I will tell you that they're taking her to surgery to get the bleeding under control. From the looks of it, we should be able to get you stitched up and out of here around the time she'll be in recovery."

"Works for me. Let's do it," I said and settled back onto the thin plastic pad they called a mattress.

A short while later, the doctor came in, removed the bullet from my shoulder, and stitched the wound in less than ten minutes. "All right, we need you to hang around for a little longer to make sure you don't have a reaction to any of the medications we gave you. Your nurse will let you know when it's okay for you to leave."

"Thanks, doctor," I said and shook his hand.

Shortly after he left, the door opened again. Expecting it to be my nurse, I kept my eyes closed and waited for her to start going over my instructions. "The fuck you doing getting shot at a book signing convention?" Phoenix rumbled from the door.

I flinched, followed by a grimace. "Fuck if I know. Trouble follows me everywhere."

"You got that right. You doing okay?"

"Yeah, I'm good. It's just a flesh wound. I'm worried about Sloane, though. She's in surgery now."

"Knock, knock," my nurse said before she entered the room. "I have your discharge papers to go over with you, and then we can get you out of here."

"Let me save us all some time," I interrupted. "I've had stitches more than once before. I know how to take care of them. If I have any questions, I have a very good friend who's a nurse and one who's a paramedic that I can ask."

"Okay, I need you to sign here, and here, and then you're free to go."

"Thanks," I said and got to my feet. Turning my attention to Phoenix, I asked, "Is Copper on his way?"

"Yeah," he nodded. "Should be here soon. Shaker left to go get him as soon as I got off the phone with Chains."

I stopped by the front desk and asked the receptionist where I could find Sloane. My eyes flicked to hers when she made a choking sound. She sat ramrod straight in her chair and kept her eyes focused on the screen. "I need you to verify the password before I can provide any information."

I pinched the bridge of my nose and shook my head. No, she didn't. She wouldn't. But I knew she fucking did. Sighing, I tilted my head to the sky and uttered the words I was going to spank her ass for making me say, "I like anal."

The secretary was trying to contain her laughter and looked like she was about to have a seizure. I rolled my eyes and huffed. "Just fucking laugh and tell me where my woman is."

We followed the directions to the surgical waiting area and made ourselves comfortable. It seemed like only seconds passed before Copper, Judge, and Batta arrived. And Batta looked pissed.

"Oh, fuck. She didn't?" I asked, already knowing the answer—she left without telling him she was attending the book signing with the intent of taking down a criminal.

"She fucking did," he grumbled, "but I'll take that up with her. Right now, I'm just glad you and your woman weren't hurt worse than you were."

"Family of O'Shea," a female voice called from behind me. I stood and made my way over to her. "She's in room three. It's the third door on the left once I buzz you through."

With that, she pressed the button that opened the door giving me access to Sloane's room. Without hesitation, I made a beeline for the third door on the left and almost tripped over my feet trying to enter the door too quickly.

I sagged in relief when I saw Sloane awake and looking somewhat healthy. Rushing to the side of the bed, I reached for her hand and leaned over to place a kiss on the top of her head. "How are you feeling? Have you spoken to the surgeon? What did he say?" I rattled off.

My relief vanished when Sloane began to speak. "I fleel grapes. A bully went zippy zoom through me flesh, and Dr. Groan plucked it out with his mighty plucker. But they took me titsling, and now me boobies is a wee bit nippily," she slurred and erupted into a fit of giggles when she finished.

I whirled around to look for a nurse and found one sitting in a chair at the nurse's station. "What the fuck is wrong with her?" I demanded.

"She's recently had some pain medicine and is still coming off the anesthesia. The combination made her pretty loopy. She was singing songs from *Disney* movies at the top of her lungs until she dozed off a few minutes before you came back," she shared.

Exhaling in relief, I smiled, "That sounds like something she'd do. Did everything go okay?"

"Yes, it did. The doctor was able to stop the bleeding and close the wounds. He'll be by to go over things in more detail with Sloane when she's awake and alert."

"Thank you," I said and extended my hand to her.

Suddenly, Sloane started loudly blurting random words, one at a time. "Big."

"Badass."

"Biker."

"Bronze."

"You calling for me, Sweet Sloane?"

"Mmm," she moaned. "I thought I smelled you."

I laughed. "You don't handle narcotics well, do you?"

"I'd say yes since I'm as motherfucking cheerful as a cheetah cooking clam chowder."

Slapping my hand over my mouth, I tried to at least muffle my laughter because there was no other way to control it. Then, an idea hit me, and it was too good to pass up. Clearing my throat, I deepened my voice and said, "Today's letter is P."

"Penis. Peen. Pecker. Pipe. Python. Package. Pole. Prick. Pussy pounder. Pu—"

"Stop," I wheezed, laughing so hard I could barely breathe. "Shit, Sloane, you have to stop."

"S. Slap. Smack. Spank. Strike. Swat."

"Fuck," I cursed and realized my mistake immediately. "Wait! Let's count!" I suggested before she could start listing F words.

"One, two, three," she started and dozed off somewhere around two thousand six hundred and thirty-two, which coincidentally was around the same time they came to move her to her hospital room.

Refusing to leave her side, I sent a text to Phoenix telling him and the guys to meet us upstairs in her room on the post-surgical floor.

"On that note, now that Sloane's awake, I have some business to take care of," Tatum announced with Batta following her out of the room.

"What did she mean? Does she need to ask me some questions?" Sloane asked, her forehead wrinkled in confusion.

"She meant she was going to go interrogate the shooter now that she's seen for herself that you're okay," I explained.

"Aw, that's so sweet."

"It is, but don't tell her that if you want her to keep liking you."

When Tatum returned to the hospital several hours later, she didn't come alone. "Ginger and Jennifer would like to stop by for a visit," she said and held up her hand. "I ran backgrounds on both girls and didn't find anything to be concerned about."

"I don't have a problem with it, but it's up to Sloane," I said and returned to my seat by her side. "Do you feel up to having them stop by?"

"Yes, I want to see them," Sloane mumbled. "Will someone tell them to come up?"

"You got it," I said and nodded to Tatum.

"I'll be right back," she said and disappeared into the hall.

"Who exactly are Jennifer and Ginger?" my brother asked for clarification.

"Patience, old man. I'll introduce them when they get here." I said, grinning when he grumbled in irritation.

Tatum returned to the room with Jennifer and Ginger in tow several minutes later. Surprisingly, neither one seemed to have any qualms with entering a room full of bikers.

"This is Jennifer and her friend, Ginger," I said to the room. "They're both huge fans of Sloane's, and they helped save her life today."

The guys went around the room introducing themselves before ending with Tatum. "We've already been acquainted, but I'd like to add one thing. I specialize in disappearances. As in orchestrating them. Both living and dead bodies. Carry on," she said, her tone changing to cheerful on her last sentence as she gestured for Jennifer to start talking.

Jennifer choked on something and went into a fit of coughs for several awkward moments before she recovered enough to speak and introduce herself to the room. "I'm Jennifer, as you already know. I-I'm an avid reader, proud book nerd, and professional librarian," she said, her voice growing stronger toward the end.

Tatum grinned. "Josie, and our friend, Adrianna, are both avid readers. They're always trying to get me to read their romance books, but I only like to read the dirty parts."

Jennifer didn't miss the opportunity to do what she did best. "Then you would love Sloane's short stories. She sets the scene and introduces the characters within a few paragraphs, maybe a chapter at most. Then, she uses a few chapters to build the tension or set up a dilemma before she goes right into the good stuff." Jennifer paused to fan herself. "I'm telling you; they're short, to the point, and hot as hell. Make sure you have some fresh batteries handy after you read one."

"She's trying to go green, so she uses me instead of batteries," Batta interjected, causing everyone except me to laugh.

I was exhausted, and my shoulder was starting to throb. I just wanted to know what happened so I could make myself comfortable in the recliner and go to sleep. "Can we get on with it? What did you find out?" I snapped.

Tatum sighed. "I have a lot of information to share with you regarding the shooter, but I've just come from listening to the biggest load of absolute bullshit that's ever been spewed at me, and I do not have the ability to repeat it to you in a professional capacity. In other words, if you want to know what happened, I'm going to speak freely."

"I've been hanging around with a bunch of bikers; I think I'll be okay," Sloane joked.

Tatum shook her head and dropped into a chair. "Let me start by apologizing in advance. This is a long and fucked up story. Side note: I'll refer to the shooter as Dill from this point forward since we're still in the process of verifying her legal name."

She paused and inhaled deeply before beginning. "Dill was one of your fans—a superfan is the term that was used, I believe. Of course, she had all of your books. When she got engaged and moved in with her fiancé, she hid her collection of your books in her closet. At some point, the fiancé found the books, read them, and became obsessed with you."

"What?" Sloane gasped.

Tatum nodded and continued. "Yep. He was obsessed with you to the point that he started asking Dill to dye her hair the same color as yours, and he even made requests for her to dress like you did in some of your pictures on social media. She didn't figure it out until he made a few requests in the bedroom that were very similar to scenes from some of your books."

Tatum paused and looked down at the phone in her hand before she continued. "By this time, Dill was on your ARC team. This is when she started suggesting that you write things for her and her fiancé to try in the bedroom. She wanted him to think it was based on scenes from your stories when it was really her idea. According to her, that worked for almost a year. Everything went to shit when you repeatedly rejected one of her ideas. She said you eventually refused to speak to her about it anymore and kicked her off of your review team. This part was somewhat unclear, but she said your stories had changed, and she wasn't willing to go along with it anymore. Which ultimately led to him breaking up with her. She blamed you for ruining their relationship."

"She did all of this just to get back at me for something I didn't even do?" Sloane asked.

"Actually no," Tatum said and leaned forward on her elbows. "She did all of this to prevent you and your books from ruining other relationships."

"You have got to be shitting me?" I shouted and got to my feet, cringing at the slight burn in my shoulder.

"Don't get upset and hurt yourself because of me," Sloane said. The concern in her voice had me closing my mouth and settling back into my seat. "I'm not upset," I clarified. "I'm pissed."

"Shut it, Pink Diva, I'm not finished."

I glared at Tatum. She knew how much I hated those fucking nicknames. "One day, you'll lose, and it's going to be glorious."

She rolled her eyes and completely ignored my threat. "Seriously, I have to know. What was the idea you rejected?"

Sloane's cheeks flushed while her eyes darted wildly around the room. "Uh, I'll have to fill you in on that one later."

Frankie, who'd been surprisingly silent, answered for her. "No, you won't. It's because her suggestions started with things like incorporating ice cubes or strawberries in foreplay, but her suggestion to start using vegetables for penetration was where Sloane drew the line."

Sloane slapped her palm over her face and groaned while Tatum threw her head back and laughed hysterically. "Oh, shit," she said and wiped the tears from her eyes. "I just got it. Dill Doe," she barely managed to say before cracking up again. "A cucumber dildo," she wheezed.

Frankie gasped and grabbed her phone. "Has anyone in here read Dill's books?"

Almost in unison, everyone answered with, "No."

Moments later, Frankie held her phone out to show us the screen. "This is one of her books. *Corn Porn*, featuring a married couple living on a farm and spicing up their marriage with their new harvest of corn."

Sloane groaned in a way that had me instantly by her side. "You have to stop! It hurts when I laugh."

"If that happens again, I'm making everyone leave," I announced and made eye contact with each person in the room.

"Yeah, yeah, we got it. What did she say about the stalking part?"

Tatum glanced to Jennifer and Ginger, and I could tell by the look on her face that something was up.

"What's going on, Tatum?" I asked suspiciously.

A sudden movement from the side caught my attention right as Jennifer leaned over and cradled her side with a loud, "Oomph!"

"She has something she needs to tell you," Ginger announced and crossed her arms over her chest.

Jennifer rubbed her side, presumably where Ginger had elbowed her, and faced Sloane, looking very much like a child about to confess to a parent. "I'm responsible for your birthday present, the publishing anniversary present, the surprise breakfast at the event, a few other small surprises, and I'm the one who sent the bottle of wine to you in Devil Springs," Jennifer confessed.

"What? How?" Sloane asked.

"Tatum!" I shouted. "You let her fucking stalker in here?"

Tatum glared at me. "No, I didn't. Shut up and listen.

"You okay with this?" I asked Sloane. Because if she wasn't, I was ushering them the fuck out of there.

"I want to hear what she has to say," Sloane said quietly.

"Well, your birthday and your hometown are listed on social media. So, I searched for your name and hometown to find your address to send you a present. Since I already had your address when you mentioned your publishing anniversary on social media, I thought it would be nice to send you another present. As for the bottle of wine, you took a picture of your workspace and posted it in your reader group. When I zoomed in to see what you were working on, I saw the name of the hotel on a notepad beside your computer."

"What about the breakfast trays? How did you know about Brat?" Frankie demanded.

Jennifer laughed. "Look at the picture you posted of you two sorting the orders the night before the signing. The key card with your room number on it is in the left corner, and a very visible pig hoof is in the right corner. I just got lucky on the tray placement."

"What about Bronze?"

"That was also a coincidence. I passed him in the hallway when he surprised you. I was only walking by to see where the rooms were so I would know where they were when I delivered the breakfast trays."

Her laughter died down, and her eyes filled with tears. "I'm so sorry, Sloane. I didn't mean to scare you, but I was too shy to sign my name on the gifts. And, I guess I got too excited and didn't realize I was overstepping boundaries. I understand if you want to remove me from your groups and block me from your social media."

"Uh, Jennifer, you saved my life today. Pretty sure that

negates any possible misunderstanding we may have previously had," Sloane said vehemently. "And for future reference, please sign your name to any gifts you send. A lot of people like to reciprocate, or at the very least send a thank you note."

"Really?" Jennifer gasped in disbelief.

"Really. I know how hard it is to put yourself out there. So what if you did it and came out looking like a stalker? It ended well, and it'll make a great line for a story," Sloane assured her and yawned, followed by a small grimace of pain.

"All right, time for everyone to clear out," I said and turned to start herding people out the door.

"Step aside, Alpha-hole. I'm not leaving until I hug her," Frankie declared and barged her way past me.

"And I'm not leaving until I've had a great big hug from you." Tatum stood and gave me the quickest hug in history before she jumped back with mock disgust. "I was wrong! Ew! Feelings!"

26

SLOANE

After the room cleared out, I closed my eyes and relished in the quiet. Unfortunately, when I woke the next morning, my peace and quiet vanished before I'd even had coffee.

"Sloaney Bologna!" Tiernan called out as he barreled through the door to my hospital room followed by Declan and Kian.

"Crap," I grumbled. "I thought I'd have more time before having to introduce you. Declan, I believe you've already met Bronze Black. Tiernan, you probably know him as well. Kian, I'm in love with Bronze Black. He's a biker, and I don't care what any of you think. Now, keep your shenanigans outside of my room, because it's time for my nap."

"Dad will be here soon," Tiernan said.

"What?" I asked in surprise.

"He was in the air within minutes of me telling him about the shooting."

"Well, that's certainly not what I expected."

Right on cue, Lorcan O'Shea and his two personal

bodyguards entered the room. "Sloane! I've been worried sick. Are you okay? How bad is it?" he blurted.

"Dad!" I groaned. "You didn't have to come," I said and did nothing to hide the fact that I did *not* want him there.

"You were shot by a crazed fan, nearly bled to death, and had to have surgery. Where else would I be?"

Bronze rose to his feet. "Let's step out and give them some privacy." I glared at him and each of my traitorous brothers as they left me alone with my father—who I decidedly did not want to speak to.

Once the room was cleared, my dad pulled a chair next to my bed and took a seat. "What's going on? I get the feeling you're upset with me."

I crossed my arms over my chest and tried my hardest to keep myself from bursting into tears. Because they were going to be angry tears, and I hated it when I cried angry tears.

"Come on, Sloane. Nothing ever gets resolved without proper communication. Now, out with it, lass. Tell me what's wrong so I can take care of whoever was stupid enough to attempt to take the life of a member of my family."

"That shit right there!" I exploded and jabbed my finger in his direction, surprising myself by my outburst. "You can't just kill everyone who crosses you or your family."

He brushed non-existent lint from his suit and used the lapels to readjust his jacket. "I can if I don't get caught."

"Dad!" I groaned and flopped back against the scratchy, crinkly pillows.

"If you would start talking to me, you wouldn't be forced to listen to my dad jokes."

"Fine!" I huffed and exhaled slowly. "Damn it," I whispered when I felt tears fill my eyes.

My dad moved closer as his face morphed into one of grave concern. "Whatever it is, honey, tell me so I can fix it," he insisted.

"You can't fix it!" I screamed. "You cheated on Mom and had a child with another woman, and now she's dead! Not even you can fix that!"

"What on earth are you talking about?" he demanded and got to his feet.

Exhaling in resignation, I said, "Sit down, Dad, and I'll tell you everything." After taking in a deep breath, I did just that, as quickly and robotically as I could, but my emotions eventually got the best of me.

"Don't tell me you didn't know about her! I remember when her mother came to the house and asked you for money when she was pregnant. You told her to leave and never come back, or you would kill her and the child."

"Sloane, you're mistaken," he started.

"No I'm not! I remember her!"

"Stop and think about it for just a minute. You said you didn't recognize Adelaide when you saw pictures of her. That's because the woman who came to the door wasn't Adelaide."

"Then who was it?"

"Phyllis Banner."

"What?" I asked, thoroughly confused. "But I thought Paige wasn't my sister. Are you telling me she is?"

"No, Paige isn't your sister. There's absolutely no way for that to be possible because I never slept with Phyllis."

"But, you admit to sleeping with Adelaide?"

He sighed. "Sloane, now isn't the time, but you and I need to sit down and have a discussion about your mother and I. For now, I'm going to stick to the facts, and we can discuss the details later." He paused and cleared his throat. "Adelaide and Phyllis were best friends who were hired as summer interns at my company. Within a few weeks, I began having an affair with Adelaide. Phyllis was also interested in carrying on with me, but I declined her offer. Apparently, that started, or continued, an ongoing rivalry between the two."

"If you never slept with Phyllis, why did she come to the house and say she was pregnant with your child?"

"I don't know. I always assumed she was trying to cause trouble between your mother and me because she never got what she wanted from me," he said, trailing off at the end.

"Are you thinking it might be something else?"

"Now, I'm wondering if Phyllis knew Adelaide was pregnant."

"That doesn't make any sense."

"Neither do crazy bitches, and that's what they both were. Honestly, I wish you would've asked me about all this. I could've told you Paige wasn't your sister."

"But what about Heidi? You really didn't know about her?"

His eyes softened, and he cupped my cheeks like he used to do when I got hurt as a child. "No, Sloane. I didn't know a thing about her. It brings me great pain to know I fathered a child I'll never meet in person," he confessed, and I could tell his words were sincere.

I tilted my head toward the ceiling and closed my eyes, knowing he would eventually find out but thinking it could wait a bit longer. There was no need to rush things.

"I know that look. What is it?"

I pulled the blanket over my head to hide my face. "Nothing."

"Have you not learned anything from the last fifteen minutes? Talk to me, child of mine!"

"Heidi had a baby. Congratulations, Grandpa, it's a girl. And I'm in love with the baby's father," I blabbed as great big tears streamed down my face. "And I don't care what you or anybody else thinks about it."

"That's my girl," he said as a proud smile took over his face. He leaned forward and kissed my forehead. "For the record, I know you're in love with Bronze Black, and while little Blue's relation to our family is news to me, I still don't have a problem with it as long as he makes you happy."

"Who are you? Where's my father? No, wait. I know. It's got to be the pain meds."

He chuckled. "You shouldn't be surprised by my approval. He understands this lifestyle. Though, I'm sure you know, we have to come to an agreement about his boxing."

I held my hands up to stop him from saying any more. "That involves him, not me."

"Yes, that's why I plan to discuss it with him. Telling you was a courtesy."

I rolled my eyes dramatically. "There's the dad I know."

"Are you hungry? I can send one of my guards to get something to eat."

"I'm allowed to be cranky or mad without being hungry!" I shouted.

"Yes, I know, but I was simply asking if you'd like something to eat. I haven't had breakfast yet, and I'm starving."

"Oh," I said sheepishly. "In that case, I want a biscuit and gravy with an extra biscuit. No, wait, make it two orders of biscuits and gravy, an order of their version of hash browns, and a coffee. I want them to put a medium-sized coffee in a large cup and fill the rest with cream and sugar."

After typing something into his phone, he glanced up at me with a smile. "Sean's leaving now to pick up our breakfast."

"Dad! I didn't ask Bronze if he wanted anything! And what about the boys?"

He chuckled. "Sloane, they're all out in the hall. I told Sean to get their orders before he left. I'm going to have to work on my image. I didn't realize everyone thought I was such an asshole," he teased.

"I'm sorry, Dad. I've been given a lot to process in the last twenty-four hours," I explained.

"It's all right, lass. You're okay, and that's all that matters," he said and gently squeezed my hand. "Now, shall we invite your man in by himself before Sean gets back with our food?"

"Why?" I asked suspiciously.

"Have a little faith, child," he said and tapped out another text on his phone.

Moments later, Bronze returned and resumed his seat in the recliner. "You wanted to see me?"

"I don't believe we've been formally introduced," my father said and rose to his feet, extending his hand to Bronze. "I'm Sloane's father, Lorcan O'Shea."

"Bronze Black, but you already know that," he returned and shook my dad's hand.

"You fought one of my sons, and you're dating my daughter. Of course, I already knew that. You'll do the same when Blue starts dating."

Bronze's entire body stiffened while a look of horror, mixed with surprise, washed over his face. Confused by his reaction, I leaned toward him and whispered, "You okay?"

"Yep," he replied, keeping his eyes on my dad.

"Bronze," I said, trying to get him to look at me.

"What does he know about Blue?" he asked, and I knew exactly what he meant by the tone of his voice.

My father answered before I could. "I know she's my granddaughter. I give you my word that I have no intention of trying to disrupt your life. However, I would like the chance to get to know her."

"I don't have a problem with that as long as we don't have any trouble," Bronze said like the protective father he was.

"We won't," he assured. "Well, there is one thing we need to discuss, but I'm certain we can come to an agreement that suits us both."

"What is it?" Bronze asked. When my dad's eyes flicked to me, Bronze snorted. "I don't keep shit from her, so go ahead."

My dad smiled at his words before his face returned to business mode. "Now that your relationship with my daughter is known to the public, it's a conflict of interest for you to continue boxing in my club."

"Your club?"

"You thought it was Luca's?" I wasn't sure who he was asking, but Bronze and I both nodded. "Good, that's what you're supposed to think."

"So, you want me to quit?" Bronze summarized.

"What? Dad! You can't do that!" I yelled, pissed at his high-handedness.

"What?" he asked incredulously. "I can't let him knock out my son in thirty-eight seconds and allow him to continue to fight in my club. That's bad for business, Sloane."

"Dad," I groaned.

"It's also for the safety and well-being of my daughter and granddaughter," he added and held up one finger.

"Yes, I do want you to stop fighting at the club, but I'd like to talk to you and your brother about having some of my fighters train at your gym, particularly with you and your trainers."

Bronze nodded. "I'll let Copper know, and we'll be in touch if he wants to discuss it further."

"His brother's an asshole, Dad," I whispered loudly.

"What're you telling me for, lass? He's a fighter with an undefeated record," he joked and pointed to Bronze.

Two sharp knocks sounded, followed by, "Food's here!"

"Come in!" I shouted much louder than I meant to. "Sorry," I shrugged. "I guess I'm hungrier than I thought."

It was close to dinner time before I had an opportunity to speak to my father alone. Thankfully, my annoying brothers had "business to attend to" and left not long after they arrived.

Before I could open my mouth to begin, my dad turned to me and asked, "What is it?"

"I want to talk to you about Adelaide and Phyllis."

"Sloane, it's better for you if we don't discuss either one of them," he countered.

"That's not what I meant." I swallowed thickly and repositioned myself in the bed so that I could see his face while I spoke—or rather, so he could see mine. "Dad, please let the police handle Adelaide and Phyllis."

"Is that really what you want, Sloane? The police haven't been able to locate them in over three months. Do you want them to get away without any consequences for their actions?"

"It's not up to us to decide what the consequences should be. And frankly, each one of the lost their only child. That's more than enough."

Dad cupped my cheek and smiled proudly. "It'd kill me if anything happened to you, or any of my children," he said and turned away from me to get his emotions under control.

"I'm sorry for assuming the worst instead of talking to you about it when I found Mom's folder about you possibly fathering a child with another woman."

He sighed. "It's all right, lass. I'm well aware of what people say about me, and I've never done much to disprove their speculations, but right here and now, I want to make sure that you know without a doubt that I am first and foremost your father."

The door opened and Bronze entered the room. "So, is this a good time to ask for permission to marry your daughter?"

"What?" I blurted while my dad laughed.

"Your fiancé just helped me win some cash off of your brothers."

"How?"

"By asking for permission to marry you. I said he'd ask within the week. They disagreed," he shared with a genuine smile I rarely got to see on his face. He turned his attention from me to Bronze. "You have my blessing to marry my girl," he said and paused for effect. "I'm not going to threaten your life if you mistreat her or do anything untoward to her. Because honestly, if you didn't already know that, then you're sufficiently fucked."

EPILOGUE

SLOANE

I wasn't as nervous as I thought I would be when I pulled into the driveway of my new home for the first time. I don't know why I thought it would be different than any of the other times I'd been there, but something about it being the first official time coming home to the place as *my* home had me filled with excitement.

Bronze and Blue were waiting on the front porch to greet me when I arrived. As expected, Blue launched herself at me, and I caught her with a practiced ease. "Honey, I'm home," I joked and turned in a circle to amuse her.

"Do you need anything out of the car right now?" he asked.

"I don't think so. Why?"

"Because I was going to get whatever you needed right now. The rest can wait until the prospects get here to unload everything."

"I'm still not comfortable with them unpacking my belongings," I admitted.

"I think you're confusing unloading with unpacking."

"Oh," I said, somewhat disappointed. "Does unloading include carrying everything upstairs?" I asked hopefully.

He grinned, "It does if you want it to."

I didn't even try to be modest about it. "Yes, please," I said and headed for the stairs. "Do I still have time to take a decent nap before the party tonight?"

I breathed a sigh of relief when the answer I wanted to hear left his mouth. "Yes."

"Great!" I exclaimed. "Do you want me to give Blue her bottle and put her down for her nap before I take mine?"

"Maybe. What's the catch?"

"You're responsible for answering the baby monitor."

He laughed. "Not a problem. Go get some rest because Satan Sloane wasn't invited to the party."

In the short amount of time I had been around the Blackwings MC, I learned that they would use any excuse to throw a party—including the day I officially left my home in Cherryfield and moved in with Bronze and Blue. I had a feeling there was more to the party, but I didn't want to ruin any surprises by asking questions. I also didn't want to set myself up for disappointment by getting my hopes up. So, after my nap, we headed to the clubhouse to see what was in store as soon as the three of us were ready to go.

When we arrived, I was shocked by the number of vehicles in the parking lot. "Seems like there're more cars here than usual," I observed.

"Looks like the same crowd to me," he said casually. Too casually.

"Bronze," I drawled. "What aren't you telling me?"

"What was that? I couldn't hear you," he said and didn't bother to try to hide the fact that he was lying.

That's when I decided to leave him in the parking lot and go on inside to find out what was going on. My fingers had just wrapped around the doorknob when Bronze called out, "Wait!"

"What was that? I couldn't hear you," I repeated and opened the door to go inside.

Bronze and Blue caught up to me right as I stepped over the threshold. The onslaught of multiple voices shouting "Surprise!" at the same time caused me to startle, and Blue to start crying.

"You should have known better than to walk into a surprise party while carrying her," Layla teased and offered to take Blue. But when Bronze shook his head, Layla stepped back and gave him a knowing look.

"What's going on?" I asked.

Instead of answering me, Bronze dropped to one knee in the middle of the clubhouse with his beautiful baby girl cradled in his arms. "Sloane O'Shea, will you marry us?"

"Fucking hell!" Bear shouted. "What is it with you boys? First, you fall for the daughter of the member of a rival club," he said, pointing to Copper. "Then, you fall in love with an FBI agent, and now here you are with an Irish mob princess. Do y'all have an end goal in mind, or are you just trying to keep things lively around here?" Bear teased.

"There's no cause for alarm. They have my blessing," my father said from somewhere within the crowd.

"Dad!" I squealed. "I didn't know you were going to be here."

"Well then, I guess that means you didn't expect us to be here either," Tiernan said from his perch at the corner of the bar with my other two brothers.

"Did you guys really come all the way to Devil Springs just to watch me get engaged?"

"No, they came to see me," Frankie announced making a grand entrance in a way that only she could. Seconds later, she was immediately upstaged when her rogue pig barreled through the common room and immediately collapsed.

"Brat!" Frankie cried.

"Is he okay?" I asked and rushed to Frankie's side.

"What's wrong?" Bronze asked as he cautiously stepped closer and stared at the twitching pig.

"Frankie! Is he doing what I think he's doing?"

Frankie gasped in horror. "Oh no! No, no, no," she yelled and frantically looked around the room.

"What's he doing?" Batta asked while Bear turned toward the wall to stifle his laughter.

Brat made a noise that could only be described as obscene, while Frankie glanced at the door longingly.

"Don't even think about it! You're not leaving your pig in the middle of the common room to have an unsupervised orgasm for thirty minutes!"

I heard a commotion behind me and tried to pretend like I didn't know it was Copper fuming in the distance. But then I heard Layla say, "We're on Team Sloane, remember?" And I didn't need to turn around to know that she was likely pleading with him to hold in his anger. But, really, who could blame him? I didn't know anyone who would enjoy the free entertainment he was being provided at what would surely be a cost to him.

"That's not what he's doing," Frankie insisted.

"Well, what is he—?"

Bronze cleared his throat and interrupted me. "We're not so patiently waiting for your answer."

"What?" I asked distractedly.

Bronze reached for my hand and gently helped me to my feet. "What's it going to be?"

"I guess I'll marry you, but it'll cost you some cookies."

"I'll always share my cookies with you, and our little Blue, too."

SPECIAL APPEARANCES

Nikolai Volkov and Maxim from *Nikolai* by Sandy Alvarez and Crystal Daniels

www.authors-cdaniels-salvarez.com

Gabriel DeLuca and Pietro from *Snare My Heart* by Kristine Allen

www.kristineallenauthor.com

Chains and Sophia from *Chains* by M Merin

www.mmerin.com

ACKNOWLEDGMENTS

Cover Designer: CT Cover Creations
Cover Model: Dylan Horsch
Cover Photographer: Golden Czermak/Furious Fotog
Proofreader/Copyeditor: Kathleen Martin
Chaos Coordinator: Brittany Franks

Special thanks to Brittany Franks, Kathleen Martin, Melissa Rivera, Jennifer Ritch, Jenna Sage, Tina Workman, and Ginger Powell.

Super special thanks to my Beard, who was by my side through the hell that was my first deadline. He powered through with me until the end, and I wouldn't have made it on time and in one piece without him. Love you, Mean it.

ABOUT THE AUTHOR

WWW.TEAGANBROOKS.COM

Follow Me

ALSO BY TEAGAN BROOKS

Blackwings MC - Croftridge

Dash

Duke

Phoenix

Carbon

Shaker

Badger

Blackwings MC Box Set

Christmas in Tinsel Town

Blackwings MC - Devil Springs

Copper

Judge

Savior

Batta

Bronze

Coal

King Mountain Shifters

Slade

Standalones

Beached

Printed in Great Britain
by Amazon

46381134R00175